LOST
COVENANT

ALSO BY ARI MARMELL

LOST COVENANT

A Widdershins Adventure

ARI MARMELL

an imprint of Prometheus Books
Amherst, NY

Published 2013 by Pyr®, an imprint of Prometheus Books

Cover illustration © Jason Chan
Cover design by Nicole Sommer-Lecht

Inquiries should be addressed to

Pyr
59 John Glenn Drive
Amherst, New York 14228–2119
VOICE: 716–691–0133
FAX: 716–691–0137
WWW.PYRSF.COM

17 16 15 14 13   5 4 3 2 1

Library of Congress Cataloging-in-Publication Data

Marmell, Ari.
    Lost covenant : a Widdershins adventure / by Ari Marmell.
        pages cm
    ISBN 978-1-61614-811-9 (hardback)
    ISBN 978-1-61614-812-6 (ebook)
    [1. Fantasy. 2. Gods—Fiction.] I. Title.

PZ7.M3456Lo 2013
[Fic]—dc23

                                                      2013028123

Printed in the United States of America

To Jessie C.,
for helping Shins grow up just a little;
and to Jess H.,
for her probably futile attempt to do the same for me.

PROLOGUE: DAVILLON

"Name?

"Business?

"Thank you. Welcome to Davillon. *Next!*

"Name?

"Business?

"Thank you. Welcome to . . ."

And on. And on. Irritating as a poorly tuned violin, played by a poorly tuned cat, just to listen to; she couldn't begin to imagine how utterly mind-numbing it must be to say, person after person, day after day.

Still, she found herself smirking ever so slightly to hear it. After so long, after such struggle to figure out who she was—*what* she was—what she *wanted*—she was coming home.

The line shuffled. She shuffled with it, hard-packed and harder-frozen dust scraping beneath her feet. It wasn't *much* of a line, this. Fewer than a dozen people ahead of her, and only a few of those even had carts or pack animals with trade goods. Not a hard winter, this one, at least not here, but still enough to postpone all but the most desperate travels or the most vital of imports.

It was one of the reasons she and her . . . ally . . . had chosen to return now.

Shuffle. Step.

"Name?"

Step. Shuffle.

"Business."

Step. Shuffle. Step.

7

"Name?"

The guardsman's eyes were glazed as a pastry, his expression so bored that even his mustache clearly wanted to be somewhere else. The silver profile of Demas—patron deity of Davillon's City Guard, worn by every member as amulet or icon—was clearly more alert than he.

"Colette d'Arnville." Her name was, of course, nothing of the sort. None of the ones she'd used recently were. It was just the first that came to mind.

The sentry's dull gaze focused just a bit at the sound of her voice. For the first time he looked at her, truly looked. The threadbare cloak and hood she wore against the voracious nibbling of the winter breeze only barely blocked the chill; it did nothing at all to block the roaming imagination of the man beside her.

"Business?"

Did he actually just make his voice deeper? How precious.

"Coming home," she said, deliberately curt. (Not that "curt" was any real stretch for her.)

"Been away long?"

You don't need to attract the attention. You don't need to attract the attention. You don't need . . .

Mantra repeating in her head—often and loud enough to drown out the nigh-overwhelming urge to hit him, if only just—she managed a good two minutes of inane small talk until the grumbling of the folks behind her in line grew audible enough to penetrate the soldier's fascination.

"Umm, right. Thank you. Welcome to Davillon. *Next!*"

The hitch in her step, the limp she normally made such effort to conceal, was on full display as she pushed past the guard and beneath the arched stone of the barbican. Anything to appear less desirable; he was *probably* just your average lecher, visually groping whoever caught his fancy before utterly forgetting them, but she wasn't about to take the risk.

She couldn't help but chuckle, however, at the thought of all her planning—all *their* planning—interrupted by a smitten guardsman so young he probably still thought his job actually *meant* anything to this cesspool disguised as a city.

It was a mirth that faded swiftly, however, as her memory insisted once more on replaying the suffering her impediment had caused her, all the circumstances behind it. She drew herself up, prideful, scowling. The bustling crowds of Davillon's gateside square, through which she swam like a desperate salmon, already blocked her from the sight of anyone standing at the gate. No reason any longer to humiliate herself, or allow *too* many people to see her weakness.

Her potentially memorable, describable, identifying weakness.

A bit of muttering—so soft it would have proved inaudible in an empty privy, let alone the flesh-crammed, roughly cobbled road-ways of the city—and she was off. All trace of a limp was absent, now; in fact, she seemed to almost glide through the throng, slipping through even the most densely packed logjams without slowing, without effort. Between that and her hood, which she'd pulled over her head once more to shield her distinctive face and hair from casual discovery, she might just as well have been a ghost.

Apropos, that—since she'd come not to honor or reacquaint herself with the city, but to haunt it.

Her mind wheeling with anticipation for all that was to come, Davillon's prodigal daughter—well, one of them—slipped through the milling sheep that were the city's oblivious citizens, and was gone.

CHAPTER ONE

The young woman watched, irritated, as the world turned white beneath her.

She ought to have been happy with the drifts and flurries that danced in the air like butterflies in white fur stoles. Between the snow and the gray overcast of a sky clearly grieving for a sun it hadn't seen in weeks, if not months, nobody was likely to spot her as she went about her business.

Of course, nobody was likely to spot her anyway, given the skills and abilities at her disposal. But even less likely was better.

It's just, she was *so* tired of snow!

"You came from a land like this, yes?" She cocked her head, listening even though the answer she awaited had nothing whatsoever to do with voice or sound.

"Colder?!"

A surge of emotion, within her and yet from something outside her. It conveyed confirmation, for the most part—but she couldn't help but detect a slight trace of patronizing smugness, too.

"This is *too* cold! Just because *you* don't feel it, all nice and snug in your coat of—of—*me*, that doesn't mean that the rest of us aren't *gleep!*"

Widdershins—former thief, former tavern keep, former citizen of Davillon—dropped to her belly atop the wall of heavy gray bricks. Her unseen companion's warning had come only a split second before it was too late. Two armed soldiers, clad in the ludicrous baggy pantaloons and gleaming cuirasses of the Church guards, but carrying their brutal halberds with military efficiency, strode by along the footpaths beneath her vantage. Their pace was casual enough, their expressions easy, but Shins had no doubt that they were more than capable.

They *had* to be, if they were going to dress like a colorblind monkey had selected the bulk of their wardrobe.

It had been years, now, since Widdershins had learned to sub-vocalize, to pitch her words to her divine partner in such a way that *nobody* could overhear; still, she lay against the stone, thinking flat thoughts, until the pair was well and truly gone.

"Cut that a little close, didn't we, Olgun?"

The tiny god from the far northlands, whom none now revered but the young woman herself, willed an indignant protest.

"Oh. You did suggest something like that was possible, yes." Widdershins chewed a lock of auburn hair that had fallen loose from her hood. "So, what? The other gods don't like you because you're a foreigner?"

For all their time together, some concepts were still difficult, still too complicated, for Olgun to easily convey. Shins got something about the sheer prevalence of faith and divinity interfering with other, unrelated faith and divinity, and at that point she stopped trying to figure it out before her brain packed its bags and quit her skull in a magnificent huff.

"Shall we do this already?" she asked, uncertain and frankly uncaring as to whether Olgun had finished or she was interrupting. "Or have we come to our senses and decided that this is all really, really stupid?"

A stubborn, insistent prod.

"I *know* it was my idea! That's why I get to decide if it's stupid! Trust me, I know a stupid idea when I have one! Just, maybe not right away . . ." And then, "If you say *one thing* about me having a lot of practice, I'm leaving you here and you can walk home. And stop looking at me like that."

A quick flex of arms and knees and she was on her feet. A second flex and she was off the wall and sailing earthward. Wind and snow scratched with kitten claws at her exposed cheeks; her dirty-gray cloak spread behind her like wings, briefly exposing the worn black leathers that would, by themselves, have cast her as a conspicuous shadow against the ambient white; and the not-quite-sound of Olgun's startled not-quite-gasp forced a delighted grin across her face.

She landed, snow crunching beneath her, and tumbled into a momentum-eating roll. When she was done, on her feet once more, she stood with such careful balance that her feet scarcely left imprints in the powder, and the trail left by her landing, while obvious, didn't resemble a person at all.

"What? Hey, it's not *my* fault you weren't ready! You're the one letting the divinininess of the place slow you down. Why should I have to wait for—It is *so* a word! I just said it, yes?"

It was only then that she realized she'd already bolted from her landing spot, taking shelter behind a nearby mausoleum in case her arrival had attracted any attention. Using the tiny etchings—ivy and holy icons, mostly—she was up atop the structure faster than most people could have managed a ladder. Once more on her belly, she waited, watching. . . .

Watching over a cemetery to shame even the richest that her home city of Davillon could boast. No simple tombstones here, not a one. No, the meanest, tiniest grave was still a crypt of stone rising like a handmade mountain from the earth and snow. The largest could have housed multiple families, and they *averaged* larger than most of the hovels or apartments Shins had lived in for most of her life.

All her life, save for those few blessed years under the roof of Alexandre Delacroix. . . .

It was a small city unto itself, really—a true and literal necropolis. The crypts were organized into blocks and neighborhoods, connected by winding paths superior to the roads in many villages through which she'd recently traveled. A few of those structures were plain, but most had at least the sorts of iconography she'd just used as a stepstool, and many were so ornate, they were themselves works of art. Sweeping eaves, graven columns, angels and gargoyles of granite or even marble. . . .

Honors paid the dead while the living suffered and starved. Widdershins felt her face abruptly warm, her heart pound, her fists clench. All she'd seen, all she'd endured, and these . . . these . . .

She fought him. Waves of peace swept through her—Olgun's efforts to calm her down, keep her head clear, a rising tide lapping at the edges of her anger. But she *wanted* that anger; clung to it as a rock, a shield.

Until she no longer could, and the flame went out.

Then she *had* no shield. Then she was in a graveyard—with nothing between her and the memories of *another* graveyard, half a year and hundreds of leagues behind her.

Broken tombstones and broken bodies . . .

Agony as the *thing* called Iruoch, creature out of nightmare and fairy tale, stripped ribbons of skin from her flesh. . . .

Frustration at a foe that would. Not. *Die!*

And another pain, even worse, as she cradled the lifeless body of a man she might, just *might*, have loved.

It was neither Widdershins's skill nor Olgun's small magics, but sheer and unadulterated luck that her sob was lost in a sudden gust of wind before anyone loitering nearby could have heard.

"I know!" She snapped it through clenched lips, her gritted teeth a cage to prevent the words from escaping as a full-on scream. "I know you only *meant* to help! You still *didn't!*"

Until Iruoch, until she'd left Davillon—until Julien—she'd never once felt Olgun recoil like a frightened puppy. Recoil from *her*. Since then . . .

"Oh, figs . . ." How many times? Half a dozen? More? She'd lost count. "Olgun?"

Nothing.

"Olgun, I'm sorry." *Don't cry. Can't cry. If I cry, the tears will freeze to my skin.*

If I cry, I have to keep remembering why *I'm crying.*

"I just . . ." Shins cleared her throat. "I need to be angry right now. It's holding me up."

Time hadn't done it. Distance hadn't done it. Her fury, only barely held at bay by a leash of iron will, was all that stood between her and Davillon; between her and the searing pain Davillon had become.

She all but gasped in relief at his response, the mere feel of his presence. Understanding, nurturing, protecting.

Relief enough that she was willing to pretend—as he seemed to want—not to notice the underlying hurt that even the mute godling could not entirely conceal.

"He wouldn't have wanted this, you know," she said a moment later, once more casting her gaze across the intricate monuments and looming statuary. "He'd have wanted something simple. Modest."

"What? Of *course* I think he's *worth* it. But he'd rather they'd spent—"

Another surge of warning, another sudden silence, as another pair of sentries rounded a nearby crypt and wandered by, oblivious to those who watched from none too far overhead. Thin snow and frozen dirt crackled beneath their boots, sounding much like a very slow fire, until they were well out of sight once more.

"Ever seen a cemetery this heavily guarded, Olgun?" A response, a roll of the eyes. "Of *course* I know. But this is Lourveaux; how many tomb-robbers can there—? Oh, hush! I am *not* a tomb-robber!"

And then, more softly, "That was one time, and it wasn't *really* a tomb, in the strictest sense. And it was an emergency. Shut up and help me figure out which way to go.

"You can *too* do both at once! What's the point of being a god if you can't even talk and be quiet at the same time?"

In point of fact, whether Olgun did indeed have the divine power of communicative shutting up, the unfortunate truth was that he currently had nothing of use to communicate. Judging by the faint sludge of emotion bubbling up through Widdershins's system like a bad breakfast, the graveyard's massive scale and mélange of faith had the god just as confused as she.

The result, then, was *hours* of wandering, almost aimlessly, as thief and deity struggled and failed to find one particular abode in a sea of final resting places. Racing across the tops of icy mausoleums, constantly sliding or dropping prone to avoid the roving eyes of equally roving sentries; clambering down to earth where the crypts grew too uneven or too far apart for easy travel, huddling behind corners until the way was clear for a quick dash across the roadway; all in the midst of flurries of a wind that Shins, despite Olgun's scoffing, was certain could inspire a polar bear to don a parka. By the start of hour three, her normally pale cheeks were flogged red by the cold, and she had become fully convinced that her cloak itself had actually frozen to death.

Until finally—after having avoided roughly a dozen guards or groundskeepers and having crossed over or past enough crypts to populate a thousand nightmares—purely by chance, they found it.

Neither the largest, nor the most ornate; that much, at least, the Church had done in accordance with the man he'd been.

It had a peaked roof, this particular tomb, clearly designed to look like a cathedral in miniature. It even had a steeple, which could not possibly serve any purpose beyond the decorative. Stained glass gleamed in several of the walls, reflecting the white snows despite the lack of any substantial sun, but only a few allowed that light into the mausoleum itself. The others were constructed against backings of solid stone—priceless art, deprived of both function and, for the most, any living audience to appreciate it.

Shins could have remained on the roof. Even-sloped and snow-slick, it was no perch she couldn't handle. Somehow, though, it seemed . . . wrong. She'd come all this way to see him, to talk to him, no matter how foolish she felt for it. No way could she bring herself to go through with it while squatting over his head.

Again she dropped to the snow, rolling back to her feet, then swiftly darted up beside the padlocked door—some sort of hardwood, inscribed and engraved, smelling faintly of old lacquer, and probably worth more than some whole tombs back home. Recessed a bit from the stone porch, overhung by scalloped eaves, it ought to provide sufficient shadow to conceal Widdershins from any passersby.

Well, it *might* provide sufficient shadow, anyway. That'd have to do.

Back pressed into a corner beside the door, the young thief slid downward until she sat, legs crossed, staring out at the other tombs, at the snow, at everything and nothing at all.

"Hello, William."

Unlike Widdershins's god, William de Laurent, archbishop of Chevareaux, declined to answer.

"You probably didn't expect to see me again, did you?" she asked the mausoleum at her back. Her voice was fuzzy, almost but not quite echoing in the recessed doorway and then flattened by the snow-choked air. "Long ways between Davillon and Lourveaux, yes? Bit of a hike just for chat with . . . Oh, this is *stupid*!"

Olgun let loose a startled bleat—or the emotional equivalent of a bleat, which was rather like a sudden urge to think about sheep—as Widdershins shot to her feet, pressed her shoulder to the side of the alcove, and began to peer about for guards.

"Because it's stupid," she repeated, in answer to his unspoken but hardly unfelt question. "He's dead. He's been dead a year! I'm talking to a wall, Olgun. And a door. And possibly a stoop, although I'm not sure, because I've never been clear on the difference between a stoop and a porch. So maybe a porch.

"Who I am *not* talking to is the only clergyman I ever met who was worth more than a mangy goat!"

An image floated toward the surface of her mind, rippling into focus. An image she didn't care to see.

"An *old* mangy goat!"

Olgun wouldn't stop; for all her efforts, the vision insisted on crystallizing, and Shins had nowhere to turn.

"An *incontinent* old mangy goat! An . . . Oh, figs . . ."

Once more she slumped to the stoop—or porch—this time with her legs splayed out crookedly before her, the image of a curly haired blonde woman foremost in her thoughts.

"Yes, I spoke to Genevieve a lot after she was gone. That was stupid, too."

It was petulant, and she knew it before Olgun could point it out, before the words were even out of her mouth. "I know, I know . . ." A long sigh, then, steaming in the cold. "It wasn't, was it? And she'd be cross with me for saying so. All right, well, we're here anyway, yes?"

She scooted a bit, so that this time she might at least address the mausoleum directly.

"Sorry about that, William. Haven't . . . really been myself recently." She chuckled, soft and blatantly forced. "Guess the fact that I'm here proves that, yes? I mean, I'd never been out of sight of Davillon's walls when we met. Now . . .

"Gods, how the hopping hens did I even *get* here? I didn't set out for Lourveaux. I just . . . walked. Didn't plan to come visit you; I decided to when I realized how close we were."

The back of her head rattled with what could only be called the clearing of a divine throat. Olgun's way, perhaps, of jogging her memory over the fact that it had been *his* suggestion, one that Shins had dismissed until she realized he wasn't about to give up.

She, of course, acknowledged no such thing and kept speaking, voice growing as brittle as the slender icicles hanging overhead.

"I had to get out. I *had* to, I . . . don't think you'd have been very proud of me, William. I messed things up. I tried to take care of everybody, I swear I did!" Her shoulders, indeed her whole body, had begun to shake, through no influence whatsoever of the winter chill. "But I let them all down. Robin, Renard . . . Oh, gods . . . Julien . . ."

Whatever was about to break loose, whatever torrent of white-water emotion might have overspilled the dam in that moment, for good or for ill, never had its chance. Her reverie, her fragility, shattered as though they, too, were stained glass, at the crunch of a footstep on the frost-covered stone behind her.

A footstep belonging to someone that Olgun *hadn't warned her about!*

CHAPTER TWO

"Maurice?!"

"Is this just how you normally greet people, Widdershins?" His words were tight, strangled, and more than a touch manic. "Because I have to confess that I assumed the last time was a fluke. I mean, it felt like a fluke to me. Did it feel like a fluke to you? I thought it was a fluke. But now I'm not so sure, and the ground is *really* cold, and I'm starting to have trouble breathing with you there, and that blade is *awfully* close to my face, when you think about it, so could you please let me up and say hello like a normal person?"

Her expression dazed and vaguely wide-eyed, not unlike a deer suddenly face-to-face with a shark, Widdershins rose. Maurice—Brother Maurice, properly, Order of Saint Bertrand and former assistant to the deceased archbishop of Chevareaux—practically inflated with a huge and desperate gasp. Whether it was relief that her knee was off his sternum, or that her rapier was no longer a mouse-stride from his eye, or both, was unclear. And, ultimately, unimportant, as the deep influx of winter air prompted a red-faced, chest-clutching coughing fit that lasted the better part of two minutes.

He looked very much as she remembered him: straw-colored hair cut in a tonsure; soft, but not remotely weak or decadent, features. The coarse brown of his traditional monk's robe was largely hidden beneath a thick white coat. His only adornment was the Eternal Eye, ultimate symbol of the Hallowed Pact, representing all 147 recognized gods of Galice.

And it stood out, primarily because—in utter disregard for the monastic traditions of simplicity and severity—it was crafted not from wood or ceramic or pewter, but from a silver that seemed to gleam without benefit of any sun in the sky.

Widdershins didn't even have to ask. She'd seen it before—not one like it, but that precise icon. For a moment her eyes flickered back to the stone façade of the mausoleum, and she could not quite repress a grin.

"He'd approve," she said softly, then merely shrugged at the monk's questioning blink. "Sorry about that," she said instead, though her tone suggested less genuine contrition than amused indifference. You snuck up on me."

"Oh, I'm—"

"*Why* the happy hopping horses did you sneak up on me?"

"Well, I wasn't entirely sure you were who I—"

"For that matter," Shins broke in again, brain finally catching up with the circumstances and her eyes beginning to narrow in suspicion, "*how* did you sneak up on me?"

"Uh, I'm not entirely sure what you . . ."

The indignant thief was, however, not listening to him at all anymore, but something else entirely.

"Oh, I see," she grumbled. "And this by you was funny, yes? Just because *you* knew he wasn't a threat wouldn't make him any less dead if I'd stuck something sharp through something squishy! I—Oh." She cast Maurice a tentative smile, genuinely apologetic now, when she finally noticed the gradual widening of his eyes and growing pallor of his face.

"We'll talk about this later," she murmured from an upturned corner of her mouth. Then, more loudly, "Uh, I'm not sure exactly how much you know about—"

"Not here, in the cold, please. The caretaker's hut isn't far from here. We can get out of the wind, have some hot tea . . ."

"And get me out of sight of the guards?"

It was Maurice's turn for a tentative, almost-sickly smile. "I could vouch for you, certainly, but there would be a lot of questions—you, um, didn't make your entrance in any proper manner, or I'd have been informed—and I'd just as soon not try to explain you right now. If I even could."

Shins chuckled. "All right. After you."

Nervously glancing back over his shoulder, as though afraid she might simply up and vanish, the monk guided her along the cemetery's many smaller footpaths, winding to one side of this crypt and behind that one, avoiding the main thoroughfares as often as he might. More than once he strode ahead to check that their way was clear, then held his visitor back until the nearby armsmen had moved on.

After the third such occasion, Shins padded up to stand directly behind her host, almost silent on the snow. "What's with all the guards, Maurice?" she whispered.

"Widdershins . . . I realize that you and I are acquainted, but it really would be more proper to call me 'Brother Maurice.' At least when on holy ground such as this."

"*William* didn't feel it was improper," she said pointedly. And then, "What's with all the guards, Maurice?"

The monk glowered for a moment, then simply sighed and turned once more into the dancing flurries. "Just in case any of the unrest should happen to pass into the cemetery."

"Unrest?"

Maurice's jaw dropped; she could tell from behind him. "Did you *not notice* the protesters shouting on every major street corner? The scrawled slogans and flyleaves that crop up all over? The city's had a bear of a time keeping up; they clean one block, the next just—"

"I avoided major street corners," she said with a shrug. "And major streets, in general. Beyond that? Just looked like Davillon to me, except even richer and more pretentious."

"Lourveaux," he insisted through gritted teeth, "is not Davillon. This is *not* normal here."

"Right. So why the 'unrest,' then?"

"We'll get to that. That's another 'out of the cold' conversation."
Their voices fell. The wind picked up.

Shins waited until it was quite clear he wasn't about to say more,
then asked, "So what's the *real* reason for the guards?"

Maurice jumped as though he'd just discovered a mole in his
small clothes. "What?!"

"Come on, *Brother* Maurice. You're a monk, and a devout one at
that. I could hear it in your voice and see it in your posture if you were
planning to lie to someone *tomorrow*."

"I wasn't lying," he protested in a soft grumble. "I was just . . .
waiting to tell you everything."

"Stop waiting."

Another sigh. "Fine. The guards . . ." He turned aside as a particularly brisk breeze hurled a few random flakes into his hood. "For the
same reason I was so cautious approaching you," he said, voice raised
just enough for her to hear him over the gusts. "We've had a number
of . . . suspicious characters here on and off over the past few months."

"And you're sure they weren't just family members visiting the
tomb of Lord Suspicious Character IV, or something?"

"We aren't *complete* fools here, Widdershins. Don't say it."

"I wasn't going to. Too easy."

Inside her head, Olgun was quietly having hysterics.

"They managed to pass themselves off as mourners initially,"
Maurice admitted. He drew them both to a halt, took a long moment
to peer both ways down a main road, struggling to see through the
gray, and then continued once more. "But we figured out fairly swiftly
that the same group of people were rotating through. This fellow one
day, that fellow the next, and so forth. I've no idea what they're doing
here—there's been no vandalism or robbery—and we haven't the
right to do anything but escort them out if they're here improperly.

"But . . ."

A long silence stretched between them.

"I think one of your sentences slipped its leash," she said finally.

He offered another sallow grin, then pointed through the snow to a small building—the same size as the more modest mausoleums but far less ornate. She nodded, and they both headed toward the door.

"But," Maurice continued, producing a large, iron key from within his robe, "I couldn't help notice that most of them have been spotted not too terribly far from His Eminence de Laurent's tomb. Could certainly be coincidence, and his is *far* from the richest mausoleum here, so I can't even say for sure . . ."

The monk continued, unlocking the door with a heavy *clonk*, ushering his guest inside, and locking it once more with equal volume, but Widdershins wasn't hearing his words anymore. The grounds-keeper's abode nicely retained the heat, and a small pile of embers still smoldered in the fireplace, but the refugee from Davillon felt a greater chill here than she had outside.

People—not a *lot* of people, but enough—knew that Widdershins and the archbishop had grown close, however briefly. If someone was watching for signs of *her* . . .

Was it possible? "Olgun? I'm being paranoid, right?"

His fretting, worried reply didn't precisely calm her down.

"Right. Make this snappy, Maurice," she said more loudly, spinning and nearly colliding with the startled young monk, two steaming mugs of tea in his hands. "I'm not going to be staying in Lourveaux very long."

Maurice blinked, twice, but apparently their first encounter, last year in Davillon, had rendered him at least partially immune to the confusion suffered by so many individuals who spoke to her. He merely nodded and placed the two mugs on the table.

Widdershins took a seat on one side of it—an old, simple, but remarkably well-preserved piece of carpentry, with lightly padded chairs to match—while Maurice took the other.

"I know about you," he said, sipping gingerly at his tea. "You and, ah, Olgun."

No real shock, there. Shins wrapped her fingers around her own teacup, more to warm them than out of any desire for a drink. "I'd wondered if William had the chance to tell you."

"He didn't, exactly. He . . . died very shortly after you left."

Two pairs of eyes gazed down at the table, then, rather than at each other.

"But," he continued gamely, "His Eminence and I had discussed *some* of his suppositions before he sent me to fetch you. Then, more recently, when Bishop Sicard came from Davillon to tell us about your . . . more recent troubles, the diocese asked me to consult. They knew I'd already met you, and much of the bishop's testimony was . . . difficult for some of them to believe."

"I was there," she said, voice suddenly small. "It's still difficult for *me* to believe."

Maurice began to reach across the table. "I'm truly sorry for your—"

Ceramic cracked in Widdershins's hands, leaking a steady dribble of tea onto the wood.

"Right," he said, drawing back. "Anyway, Sicard's story filled in the remaining gaps, or at least enough for me to have a basic idea of your situation."

"And does it bother you?"

"It might," he confessed, "had it clearly *not* bothered His Eminence. He trusted you, though—*and* Olgun, apparently. I can do no less."

"Thank you for that," she said, and meant it. "I . . . Wait. Didn't he also want you to transfer orders and become a priest yourself? I seem to recall . . ."

"I'm a servant, Widdershins. I don't *want* to lead anyone."

"Maybe that means you *should*."

This time, their eyes *did* meet; Maurice looked away first. Mumbling something Shins couldn't quite catch, he rose and returned with a towel to wipe up the spill. She, though she felt a faint pang of guilt for the teacup—it looked old—allowed him to do so without offering to help.

For a time, then, they spoke little of import. Maurice shared the latest news and rumor from Davillon, carried to Lourveaux by travelers who had left far more recently than Shins, but little of it interested her, or concerned anyone she knew. She, in turn, offered a brief account of her past six months, wandering Galice, but omitted most of the details—of the towns through which she'd passed, the threats she'd avoided, the few daring thefts that had allowed her to pay her way. And certainly she said nothing of her reasons for leaving Davillon at all.

So tired was she, so *accustomed* to being tired, that it wasn't until Olgun gently prodded her that she realized her eyelids had begun to drift shut, that she was on her dozenth yawn of the past hour.

"I'm sorry," she began, "I—"

"There's room for two here," Maurice offered. "Decently, I promise."

"Oh, thank you. I was *so* worried you were going to misbehave."

"Widdershins—"

"Thank you, Maurice. But no. I really need to go."

He rose, and for the first time she saw a flicker of iron in his expression. "It's dark. It's freezing. Whatever you fear, it won't find you here over one night."

"I . . ." She stumbled, then, slightly but notably, as a wave of exhaustion drained much of her remaining strength from her limbs. "Oh, don't you *dare*!"

Olgun's stern response—accompanied by a second wave of fatigue—felt very much like one of her father's "If you won't take care of yourself, you'll just have to live with how *I* do it" lectures from her childhood.

Surrendering—sullen, cursing up what for her was a storm and for others might qualify as a single raindrop, but resigned—she allowed Maurice to show her to her bed.

"So tell me about this 'unrest.'"

"*Gah!*" Maurice bolted upright, startled from a deep sleep, and promptly rolled off the side of his narrow cot in a muddle of sheets and gangly limbs. The hut reverberated with the dull thump of monk against floor.

Widdershins leaned idly against the wardrobe, the only other piece of furniture in the room, ankles and arms both crossed. It was the same spot she'd occupied—the same *pose*—since she'd finished packing up her few possessions in preparation to leave, over half an hour gone by. It was still almost that long again until dawn would peek in the windows to see if it might be welcome for breakfast, but the young woman had grown tired of waiting.

After another moment of tangled thrashing with no sign of an emergent Maurice, however, Shins felt a gentle, probing suggestion in her gut.

"Oh, come *on*, Olgun! It's a bedsheet and a three-foot fall! I'm sure even he can handle . . . Oh, *fine*." She pushed herself away from the wall, took two steps from the wardrobe, and abruptly froze.

"Um, Maurice?"

The thrashing ceased. "Yes?" The reply was oddly muffled, less by the weight of the linens, Shins guessed, than embarrassment.

"Do you need help?"

"It wouldn't be *un*appreciated. . . ."

"And," she continued, giving voice to the question that had stopped her in her tracks, "are you dressed?"

A moment. Two.

"I don't think I'll be needing any assistance, thank you."

The thief snorted and made a point of both stomping her feet and slamming the door so her host would know he was once more alone in his bedchamber.

By the time he emerged, she had taken an identical leaning posture, this time against the pantry. He was, thankfully, fully clad now—not in his traditional coarse robe, as she'd anticipated, but heavy, functional tunic and trousers.

"I didn't know you even *owned* normal clothes. Olgun, did you know he owned normal clothes? Don't monks burst into flame or turn into frogs or something if they own more than a robe, worn sandals, and a length of string?"

"Widdershins . . ."

"*Two* lengths of string, then, is it? The Church has gotten more relaxed, yes?"

"Did you want to talk about what's going on in Lourveaux right now or didn't you?" Maurice asked, his tone almost desperate.

Shins nodded once. "So?"

"Let me just brew up a pot of—"

"Oh, no!" Shins lurched away from the pantry, standing fully upright. "You've already used up your grace period, going off on that tangent about your wardrobe."

"*I* used it up?!"

"Well, of course. It's not as if *I* could choose how you spend *your* time, is it?" And then, "Olgun? Is the vein in his forehead supposed to do that?"

"It's been building for the better part of a year now," Maurice said, apparently having decided that answering his guest's questions was the safest route to maintaining at least a semblance of sanity. "Ever since the Church appointed His Eminence's successor as archbishop of Chevareaux."

Widdershins winced as William de Laurent sprang once more

to mind. A quick pivot and she began to pace the length of the tiny kitchen, past the pantry and stove in a handful of steps, and then back.

And then—whether she came to it herself or it was a nudge from Olgun, she couldn't fully say—it dawned on her where the monk must be leading.

"Oh, figs . . . Church politics, Maurice?"

"Um, well . . ."

"So nice to visit with you. Thanks for putting me up for the night. I'll be leaving now."

"Wait! Widdershins, please!"

She was already nearing the front door, ears all but deaf to Maurice's pleas—or Olgun's protestations of curiosity, for that matter—until something finally punched through the mental cotton she'd stuffed in her ears.

"Widdershins, she wants to see you!"

She stopped, one gloved hand inches from the latch. She felt her shoulders and back tensing, so tight they might just deflect a flint-lock ball. "Who wants to see me, Maurice?" Even *she* was frightened by the utter, icy calm in her voice.

"Her Eminence Archbishop Faranda. William de Laurent's successor."

It took Widdershins roughly three or four years to turn from the door to face her host once again. Perhaps another year or so before she could choke back her growing fury enough to be sure she could speak to him without violence. Olgun's suspicions simmered beneath her own, not yet ignited into the same fiery rage, but certainly starting to smolder and spark.

"And how does 'Her Eminence' know I'm here, Maurice?" Not so calm, now, her voice, but rather something approaching an animal snarl.

"What? Oh! No, no!" The monk held both hands out before

him, though whether the gesture was beseeching or defensive was far from clear. "I haven't told anyone you're here! I meant, she's wanted to meet you since she heard of you! Asked me to arrange it if, by any chance, I could. I told her I didn't expect to ever see you again, but . . . Well, I mean, you're here. . . ."

Somebody might as well have unstoppered a drain, so swiftly did Shins's anger diminish, leaving only a frustrated—and perhaps frightened—weariness. For a moment, it was almost enough to make her dizzy, and she could only smile her thanks when a quick surge of strength from her partner ensured that she kept her feet.

"I think," she said, carefully making her way to the table and lowering herself into the nearest chair, "that you'd better make that tea after all."

"'Nicolina Faranda'?" Widdershins repeated, transforming the name she'd just heard into a question. "That doesn't sound Galicien."

Maurice, seated opposite her once again, nodded through the herb-scented steam rising from his teacup. "It's not. She's from Rannanti."

Shins couldn't quite keep her jaw from dropping.

"The Hallowed Pact is hardly limited to our country. You must know that."

"I do, but . . ." She glanced down at her own drink—in a simple wooden cup this time, she'd noted with some amusement—and gathered her thoughts. "I thought all High Church clergy had to be Galicien?"

"That's been the custom, since the Basilica of the Waking Choir is here. Initially, it was just simpler to draw new officials from nearby, and eventually it became a matter of politics—"

"Everything does," she groused softly.

"—but it's not a rule in any formal sense," Maurice concluded.

"But . . . Rannanti?"

"You're hardly the only one to have gotten the impression that the Church has become a Galicien institution, in fact if not in name. The appointment of Her Eminence Faranda—"

"You know," Widdershins remarked casually, speaking to Olgun but quite deliberately pitching the comment loudly enough for her mortal companion to overhear, "he could talk at least twice as quickly if he didn't insist on using everybody's full title *every single time.*"

Maurice glared over his teacup, an effect largely ruined when he accidentally banged the rim into his teeth. ". . . of *Her Eminence* Faranda," he continued through his pained wince, "was meant to cut such growing sentiment off at the knees. To say nothing of, just perhaps, being the first step in an end to the rivalry between our nation and hers."

Widdershins didn't so much scoff as snort. "Galice and Rannanti have been rivals for—"

"Yes, thank you, I *did* study history in the monastery."

"I didn't study history anywhere, and *I* still know that! Going to take a bit more than a Church appointment to fix that, yes?"

It might have been her own mind, might have been Olgun, might have been a cooperative effort between them, but once again she found herself leaping ahead, realizing precisely where Maurice was leading.

"And you all just learned that the hard way, didn't you?"

Her host muttered something toward the table (which, despite being nearer than Widdershins, probably couldn't make it out, either).

"Figs and finches, Maurice! Did *nobody* at the basilica have the brains to realize this might make a few Galicians just a *wee* bit irritable? Pretty sure a lot of older folks still remember losing parents and grandparents—"

"I'm not one of the high officials, Widdershins. I don't know what they thought or didn't think! My *guess* is that they expected problems, but not to this extent."

"And the city guard? Lourveaux *does* have a city guard, yes?"

"Church soldiers. The, uh, the secular government is really just more of a recordkeeping bureaucracy than . . . Um . . ." He looked briefly like a turtle, trying to retract into its shell from Widdershins's level stare. (Olgun presented her with an alternate image to the turtle, accompanied by what could only be called a dirty-minded chortle of the soul, but she quickly shoved the image aside before she burst into laughter, blushed red as raspberry jam, or both.)

"So just to be clear," Shins said, drumming the fingers of one hand on the table and of the other on her teacup, "the Church appointed a new archbishop from Galice's oldest rival, took no steps to handle any resulting social unrest, and now has riots on its hands in the city that is *only* the seat of power for the entire Hallowed Pact. Have I left anything out?"

"They're not riots, not yet. Just a lot of protesting and vandalism, mostly." Again, he seemed suddenly to want to shrink away from her expression. "No, I . . . think you've got the gist of it."

"Are you sure? None of the bishops decided to poke a few sleeping bears? Throw darts at a grimoire and read random passages?"

"I believe that's on next year's agenda."

The wisecrack, unexpected as it was, silenced her for a moment—which, a gleefully snickering Olgun assured her, was almost certainly the monk's whole point.

"She wants your *help*, Widdershins. At least if she decides you can be trusted."

"She?" Shins shook her head, trying to throw off a sudden daze or perhaps dislodge an insect buzzing in her hair. "She who? Wants what? Who what?"

"Her Eminence. We're fairly sure there's someone orchestrating at least some of the unrest, and they're far too adept at ferreting out anyone we send to find them. The archbishop was hoping that you might—"

Widdershins shoved herself back from the table and stood, knocking the chair over behind her; spun on her heel and all but dashed for the exit. This time, the monk's pleas for her to wait didn't even slow her as she hauled open the door and threw herself into the blustery winter winds.

CHAPTER THREE

Lourveaux really was very much like Davillon, except for the ways in which it wasn't.

Here, in the poorer neighborhoods and back alleys, as distant from the beating heart of the Church of the Hallowed Pact as one could be and still stand within the city proper, things looked almost familiar. Streets caked with dirty-gray snow, passersby in threadbare coats and worn shoes; the same scent of cheap woods and even less pleasant fuels, smoldering away in a desperate defensive line against winter's advance; the same sorts of buildings, blocky and bordering on decrepit without ever *quite* threatening to just give up the ghost and collapse like a bad soufflé.

Even here were differences, however. The roads were paved far more often than not, in even the meanest neighborhoods, and more frequently with brick than with cobblestone. The architecture was just a *bit* more ornate, more ostentatious; flared eaves here, an artfully rounded corner there. The clothes had, on average, been just slightly nicer before they'd been ravaged by use and time.

And then there were those moments, when the clustered buildings and winding streets collaborated with the clouds above and the winter haze below, to part all at once. Then, for a sun-drenched moment, even from the ugliest outskirts of Lourveaux, a passerby could see the center.

The center of the city. The center of the Church.

Great arches and bridges of gleaming, white granite. Marble pillars and windows of exquisite glass. Spires and domes and steeples of classical styles, atop which flapped 147 different pennants, each with the unique icon of a god.

And towering above it all, a single cupola, large enough to have given birth to any handful of the others, gleaming silver despite the overcast. Unengraved and unadorned, save for the repeating motif of the Eternal Eye.

Beating heart and quickened soul of the Hallowed Pact, focal point of the world's largest religion. The Basilica of the Waking Choir.

Widdershins couldn't flee swiftly enough.

The streets, though far from empty, were remarkably uncrowded for early morning—though whether that was unusual for Lourveaux or just another difference between here and Davillon, Shins couldn't have guessed even if she'd cared enough to try. Where the gaps in the traffic of people and horses and carts were wide enough—as they usually were—she slipped through without so much as brushing against anyone. Where they were not, either Olgun reached out to prod someone into a mild stumble or sidestep, clearing a path, or else Shins simply pushed around whoever was in her way with just enough muttered apology not to be *entirely* rude.

She made no deliberate effort to avoid the young monk who'd come racing after her, panting breath sending little puffs through the cold air, struggling to get his arm through the sleeve of a heavy coat—but neither had she bothered to slow down for him.

"Widdershins, please! For the gods' sakes, would you—"

"Not the gods, Maurice," she snapped without turning. "The Church. For the Church's sake. And I've had enough of church people and Church politics in my life! Just leave me *out* of it!"

"What have you got against the Church, any*uuunnngghk!*"

Widdershins didn't even remember reacting; reaching; moving. For a single heartbeat that dragged on forever, she wasn't in Lourveaux, wasn't seeing the semibustling roadway before her.

She was seeing an orphanage, whose caretakers—clergymen and -women, all—had lost the ability to care over hard and thankless years.

A religious zealot, the demon he'd summoned, and the trail of corpses they'd left behind—including an entire room of her friends and brethren; including William de Laurent; including the man who'd been a second father to her, Alexandre Delacroix.

A foolish priest who'd meddled with powers he couldn't remotely comprehend, who had drawn the murderous Iruoch to Davillon.

The bodies . . . Gods, so many bodies, consumed by that horrible fae *creature* and the chorus of phantom laughter that surrounded him. Adults, children . . .

Julien.

She saw them all. She heard their screams. She smelled the blood; it choked her, winding through her nostrils and lungs, a serpent bent on poisoning her from the inside.

Just as swiftly, they were gone. The images, the sounds, the asphyxiating miasma—washed away by a gentle stream, clear, cold, happily burbling.

A stream named Olgun.

When her vision cleared, she found her fists wrapped in Maurice's tunic, his back shoved hard against the façade of a building that— when last she remembered seeing the world around her as it actually was—had been a good few yards away.

From the wild, panicked glaze in the monk's eyes, she guessed his journey across the street, driven by her hands and her fury, hadn't been pleasant.

"I'm sorry. I . . ." She wanted to pretend the sudden rush of shame, the heat in her cheeks that even the breeze couldn't cool, was more of her divine companion's doing. Wanted to, but couldn't; she knew better.

"I'm sorry, Maurice." And then, more softly, "And you, too.

"This . . ." she continued, voice slightly raised once more. "This isn't . . . I just . . . Please don't ask me about this anymore. I can't help you. I can't work with your archbishop. I *can't*. I—"

The back of her neck twitched, as if her skin had just been crawled over by a bumblebee in satin socks. Her hackles rose, and she didn't so much hear a call of warning as abruptly discover that she, for some reason, was *expecting* to hear one.

One of Olgun's "cries," that, one she'd experienced enough times to know precisely what it meant.

"Who?" she demanded, already spinning away from the startled figure half-slumped against the wall. Her eyes scanned the crowd—smaller now even than it had been, as many had fled when it appeared she was assaulting her companion. Those who remained all stared at her as intently as she did them, clearly wondering if she was a mad-woman. It should have been impossible to pick one individual from the throng, one man watching her with a very different intent, and had she been alone, it would have been. With Olgun guiding her eyes, however, she noted the faint narrowing of his own; the posture minutely, invisibly tensed; the way he examined her, knowing, studying, rather than wondering.

And now she couldn't help but wonder, herself. Had she seen him many minutes ago, loitering about when she left the cemetery? She'd hardly been paying attention, couldn't say for certain, but she was fairly sure she had.

"Maurice?" She muttered from the side of her mouth, allowing her attention to wander past the man she'd pinpointed. "Left side of the street. Blue-and-yellow coat, tarnished buckles on his boots, hair that looks like cheap twine."

Whatever else he might think of her at the moment, the monk clearly recognized the importance of her tone. "He looks vaguely familiar. I think . . ."

"Think faster, yes?"

"I think he's one of the grief-stricken children of Lord Suspicious Character we talked about."

Shins nodded, turning slowly back toward her quarry—and then not so slowly, when the man abruptly bolted, tearing back down the road as though he was late for his mother-in-law's funeral. Many of those nearby turned to watch him go; the others were still fixated on Widdershins herself.

She'd been so cautious! What had tipped him . . . ?

Oh.

The young woman and her god both rolled their eyes at Maurice (or Olgun did, at least, the spiritual equivalent), who had been staring openly at the fellow he'd been asked to examine, and then they swiftly leapt to pursue, leaving their less savvy companion behind.

The befuddled citizens of Lourveaux all but fell from her path as she neared, clearly willing to let the crazy lady pass unmolested. The notion that, so far as they were concerned, she had just attacked one innocent passerby for no good reason and then launched herself after a second like a wolf made of springs only barely flitted across her mind before she cast it aside as unnecessary weight.

It would have been so easy, in Davillon. She could have taken to the rooftops, knowing with absolute certainty where she could intercept him based on which corners he turned; could have darted through courtyards between buildings, or even some of the buildings themselves, and known precisely where she'd emerge; might very well even have anticipated his final destination, based on his general direction. She could have kept up until he slowed, utterly undetectable, and then tailed him until she knew who'd sent him, or could confront him at a site of her own choosing.

In Davillon.

In Lourveaux, she knew almost nothing of the streets, nothing of the layout, nothing of the interiors. In Lourveaux, the more ornate and more frequently sloped buildings made hopping from one to the next a slower, riskier proposition. In Lourveaux . . .

All she could do was call on Olgun to help her outrace and outlast her prey, and run.

She felt the familiar tingle over her skin, followed by a surge of strength in her legs, a soothing balm in her coldly burning lungs. The buildings and passersby to either side surged past her, her hair writhed in a brown pennant behind her, in defiance of the wind. So fast did her feet fly, the crunching beneath her boots sounded less like snow and more like a carpeting of dead beetles.

It surely wasn't as swift as it felt; Olgun's magics reached only so far, could drive her body only to amazing feats, not impossible ones. But it *felt* glorious and, more to the point, it enabled Shins—despite her ignorance of these streets, despite winding through people who didn't clear her way swiftly enough, despite leaping *over* a small cart that trundled into her path—to close on her target in a matter of moments.

When the disreputable fellow made a sidelong dash into what even a newcomer to the city could tell was a blind alley, she knew she had him.

"Oh, don't be a ninny!" she snipped at the warning image parading before her inner eye. "Of *course* I know. Are *you* ready?"

Olgun's reply, translated as nearly as possible from emotion and imagery to actual vocabulary, was, "Don't be a ninny!"

Widdershins hit the mouth of the alley at a dead run and dropped, leaning back at a nigh-impossible angle. Her momentum carried her forward on her knees, digging parallel trenches in the ash-gray snow, cloak and hair billowing behind her. The sharp crack of a flintlock bounced around her ears, and she was certain she actually *saw* the ball fly overhead, punching through the space her torso would have occupied had she remained upright.

A flex of both legs—she ignored the brief agony of protesting joints; hadn't this sort of thing been easier when she was more of a child?—and she was standing once more, launched upright by muscle both her own and Olgun's. She stood several paces before her quarry, drawing her rapier—a weapon won from one of the world's finest duelists, who had decided at least temporarily to cease trying to kill her—with a theatrical flourish.

He produced a blade as well—something between a large knife and a short sabre—but the expression on his face, which strongly suggested he had just mistaken a chamber pot for a washbasin, was evidence enough that they both knew precisely how this fight would end.

"This doesn't need to be painful," Shins told him. The tip of her rapier sliced tiny patterns in the air between them, so swift and so complex that she could have been knitting with it. "The only thing pointed we *have* to exchange are questions . . . Oh, figs."

With a cry rather more desperate than fearsome, the stranger lunged, sword held high.

"Why is *everyone* but me stupid, Olgun?" The thief pivoted on one heel, letting her opponent's charge carry him clear past her— then continued her spin, rapier extended, so the tip sank just half a finger's worth into the man's left buttock.

One more long step, closing even as he toppled with a porcine squeal, brought her near enough to slap the weapon from his hand before he hit the dusty bricks.

"I'd have that looked at," she told him, gesturing idly at his rear end with her rapier before wiping it clean on his coat. "Assuming you can find anyone willing to look that close." With the blade free of blood, she slashed a corner from that coat, making him wince and yelp before he realized he hadn't been cut. She handed him the wad of fabric; he stared for a moment in utter incomprehension.

"Oh, for . . . You'd prefer *not* to bleed to death from your backside, yes? If nothing else, that'd be a seriously embarrassing epitaph!"

Grumbling something made unintelligible by humiliation, anger, pain, and—well, grumbling—he pressed the makeshift bandage to the wound in a motion that apparently struck the tiny northern god with no small measure of amusement.

"No!" she insisted in response to Olgun's newest image, "I will *not* make a joke about that! Holy hopping horses, when did *I* become the mature one on this team?!"

Choosing, after a long and indecisive moment, not to answer the unspoken questions—or assumptions of lunacy—written clearly across her opponent's face, Shins sheathed her rapier with a flourish even more dramatic than when she'd drawn it. "This," she told him almost thoughtfully, as though picking up on a conversation inconveniently interrupted, "doesn't need to be any *more* painful. Agreed?"

He nodded vigorously, then winced; apparently even that tiny jostle tugged at the new addition to his hindquarters.

"Oh, a *smart* decision! I'm *so* glad. I was afraid that wound I gave you might've caused brain damage."

Olgun burst into silent hysterics.

"Hmm . . ." Idly tapping a nail against her teeth, making an obvious show of her nonchalance, Shins allowed herself a moment to examine the alleyway in which they'd been fighting. (If, Olgun pointed out in a surge of amused contempt, one could call what the fellow had offered a "fight.") Other than cheap brick rather than cheap cobblestone or unpaved dirt, it was . . . well, an alley. Close-leaning, decrepit buildings, lots of grime, smatters of garbage, and the stench of same—though rather less overwhelming, in the winter cold and blanket of snow, than in warmer seasons.

It had, indeed, been a poor choice of ground to hold; yards from the mouth, the narrow lane ended in a high fence, presumably marking the border of some courtyard or other private land beyond.

"Dived in without looking," she commented, idly pacing. "Got more than you expected, yes?"

She'd meant it as a throwaway comment, a casual taunt at a big, rugged-looking fellow who had just been laid low (and made to sit funny) by a teenage girl. It required neither Olgun's aid, however, nor her years of experience dealing with the most disreputable scum

Davillon could belch up, to recognize the knowing, almost guilty look that flickered across his grimacing face.

"But you *did* expect it, didn't you?" It wasn't a surprise to her, really. She'd known from Olgun's earliest warning that he'd been deliberately following them, and a lifetime of what some might call paranoia but others would recognize as hard-won experience had suggested the target probably *wasn't* the young monk.

Yet, for all that she'd expected it, she felt her stomach clench and her soul shrivel at the implications; felt the embers of rage she'd been nursing since Davillon, fueled by guilt and fanned by hate, flare once more.

"Why were you following me?" She only realized after she'd spoken that her voice had dropped to little more than a whisper—or a soft growl.

"Following? No, I wasn't! I was just—"

Shins took two steps to the side, flipped the man's discarded blade into the air with a foot, then—accompanied by the telltale prickle of Olgun's assistance—caught it and hurled it in the same movement. It sank into the road by his left hand, sliding so perfectly between the bricks that the handle scarcely quivered before coming to a full stop.

"Paid to," he said then, nearly stumbling over the words. "Bunch of us, supposed to watch for you, or at least a girl of your description, warned you were dangerous, none of us believed it . . ."

"And you were told to watch Wil . . . the archbishop's tomb?"

Had the thug nodded any more frantically, Shins would have expected that his head was trying to pop loose and make a run for safety while she was distracted by the rest of him.

Any grim amusement at the thought, however, was brief enough. *Who in Lourveaux knew her that well?*

Even back in Davillon, the people who would likely have thought to watch for her here numbered less than a dozen, at least so far as she knew. Almost none of them had the means to acquire eyes *here*, let alone the motive. . . .

Maurice . . . ?

Shins and Olgun both dismissed the thought almost as soon as it surfaced. The monk didn't have a dishonest bone in his body; his mere presence made *other* people's bones more trustworthy. Besides, it'd been him who warned her of the watchers in the first place, and while Shins had encountered people whose schemes were convoluted enough to involve that manner of deception—including a few clergymen—again, Maurice wasn't remotely one of them. So . . .

"Who?" The young woman dropped into a crouch, the better to lock eyes with the wounded man. "Who hired you to—"

"There! That's her!"

"Oh, come *on!*" Shins didn't even need to turn to know what she'd see, though she did so anyway. Several of the citizens who'd seen her almost attack Maurice, and then take off after this fellow here; and along with them, a small patrol of the Church guard. They wore red tabards and simple breastplates, rather than the blinding and puffy garb she'd seen before—perhaps they dressed like mating birds only when guarding holy sites?—but they carried the same halberds, and did so with the same apparent skill.

And these particular guards were carrying their weapons in Widdershins's direction, rather rapidly.

"Olgun? This is your doing, yes? Some sort of a prank?"

She knew, of course, that it wasn't; was already fleeing down the alley before she even sensed his answer. But it almost wouldn't have surprised her if he *had* claimed credit. Of all the lousy timing . . .

The soldiers didn't bother to increase their pace. What would be the point? They were only steps behind her, and in the time it would take even a skilled climber to top the fence . . .

"Little assistance, Olgun?"

Her next step came down on nothing at all, a boost from nonexistent hands. She soared, higher than any normal leap could take her, angled not toward the fence—which was still too high to clear—but the wall beside it. The sole of one boot slapped against old wood, Olgun's power tingled in the air yet again, and Widdershins literally kicked off the wall, launching herself higher still.

She heard the sprinting guardsmen break into a bout of very un-Church-like cursing as she sailed easily over the fence, landed in a crouch in the dirt of what might once have been someone's vegetable garden, and raced away into the streets of Lourveaux. . . .

Wondering just how far she'd have to go from Davillon to escape this sort of thing, and who the frogs and fishes was after her *this* time!

CHAPTER FOUR

"Tell me again," the monk growled around a mouthful of gummy sludge, "why I agreed to accompany you to this revolting establishment?" He was still garbed in clothes that could, with extreme accuracy, be described as un-monk-like; nonetheless, he stood out in this rougher crowd like a maypole in a graveyard.

Shins looked up from the scuffed and discolored table, grateful for the excuse to turn her attention away from her own—and she used the word loosely—"meal." The goop in the bowl purported to be stew, but the young woman was quite sure it was lying on that score; she could just tell, by the expression on its face. Even Olgun seemed borderline nauseated, and he neither ate nor even possessed a stomach to upset.

"Because you agreed to help me figure out who's looking for me," she reminded him, "and you said this was the only place your . . . secret contact"—she barely kept the snicker from her voice—"would meet you."

"And why am I helping you, instead of fleeing back to the cemetery or the basilica as fast as my sandals can stand?"

"Because you're wearing boots, for one thing." Shins took a sip of watery ale, which was absolutely vile but still three steps above the pseudo-stew, then added, her voice friendly, "And second, because if you won't help me, I'll just have to scour Lourveaux for answers all on my own." She didn't even attempt to make the eyelash flutter that followed appear at all genuine.

Olgun guffawed in her head, and she was hard pressed to keep from joining in, at Maurice's horrified shudder—not at fear for her

45

safety, she well knew, but at the thought of what might happen to Lourveaux with her loose in its borders. He glared at Shins for a long moment and then, with what sounded like an honest-to-gods "harrumph," turned his face back to his bowl.

"Did he just choose eating more of that unholy corruption over talking to us, Olgun? I think I might be insulted! Are you insulted? *I* feel insulted. You should smite him. Are you allowed to smite monks of other religions? Or is that, I don't know, rude or something?"

For some time she went on, nattering at Olgun—and Maurice, when he wasn't sufficiently blatant about ignoring her—but all the while, her eyes flickered left and right, her casual gestures and shifts allowing her to survey the room.

She was not especially taken with what she saw.

It was, in a word, tavernish. This, in itself, was hardly surprising, what with it being a tavern and all. Shins hadn't been able to read the sign on the way in, but then, nobody could, as it hung, face turned inward, from a single chain that had long since rusted. The inside was a labyrinth of mismatched tables, rickety chairs, sagging floorboards, and rafters whose population of rats probably kept the place well stocked in stew meat. The patrons ranged from merely down on their luck to genuinely and even proudly disreputable, which at least had the advantage of producing enough body odor to overpower the so-called food.

Given the sorts of establishments she'd frequented in Davillon— the Flippant Witch was more upscale than this place, but not by terribly much, and she'd *run* that one for a while—Widdershins felt right at home.

And that, in essence, was the problem. She knew enough to recognize that at least a few of the people here could prove dangerous, but she hadn't the first notion of who was connected to whom, what factions might be at play, or what the local underworld etiquette might be.

The more she thought about it, the less amused Widdershins grew. When Maurice had begun talking clandestine meetings and shifty dealings, she had literally laughed until she cried. Even minutes ago, it had taken everything she had not to do so again. But she'd been expecting silly, upper-class-slumming sordid.

This place? This was *authentic* sordid. An honest monk shouldn't know people who knew people who knew people who would frequent this place!

"Maurice . . ." Then, when he appeared to still be ignoring her, "*Maurice!*" That, and a well-aimed spoon bouncing off the bridge of his nose, finally snagged his attention. "Maybe you'd better tell me about this 'contact' of yours, yes?"

"I thought we agreed that you weren't going to ask any questions."

"That was back when I didn't take you seriously. Now I'm un-agreeing."

Maurice appeared to be chewing his cheek, but perhaps he was simply struggling not to lose the so-called stew he'd foolishly so-called eaten; Shins couldn't be certain from across the table. Several times his lips began to part, he drew breath to speak, and several times he clearly decided against whatever he was going to say.

"That's all right, Maurice." Shins leaned back in her chair, arms crossed, smiling cheerfully. "I'll just follow him after our meeting. We can learn all we need that way, can't we, Olgun?"

The monk looked as if he'd just seen a ghost, and realized he owed it money. "You can't!"

"Uh . . . Actually, it seems pretty simple, yes? Just watch him and walk where he does."

"Widdershins . . ." So distracted was he, Maurice had actually begun fidgeting with the bit of stew left in his bowl. The thief was moderately horrified to realize that it was briefly retaining whatever shape her companion's fingers molded it into. "I know you're good. I know Olgun makes you better."

She sniffed, but didn't interrupt.

"But you don't know Lourveaux. He does. And he's pretty good at this, too. He'll spot you."

"Doubt it. But if so . . ." She tried to shrug, a gesture that did little more than make the chair quiver. "I'll just ask him directly."

"You have no idea the damage you could do!" Maurice all but whined.

"Not a clue," she acknowledged, voice chipper. "Gods know *what* I'll be interfering with." Then, in response to an unspoken comment, "What? Um, no. Do *you* know? Well, then I didn't mean *all* gods, did I?"

And back to her less-intangible conversation partner: "Stop looking at me like I'm crazy."

"Why, is it supposed to be a secret?"

Widdershins was too busy waiting for Olgun's guffaws to stop filling her head to actually respond to Maurice.

By the time her thoughts cleared and she regained the presence of mind to glare, Maurice had clearly come to a decision.

"I won't tell you his name," he said firmly. "But he's . . . Um . . ."

"Not the *most* informative thing you've told me, that."

"He's a . . . purveyor, and former acquirer, of . . . exotic wares."

"He's an ex-thief and smuggler, and now a fence," she translated.

Maurice could offer only a grin more watery than the ale. "Well, yes."

Widdershins threw her hands up, very nearly knocking her chair, and herself, entirely over backward. "Why didn't you just *say* so? It's not like you're going to offend *my* sensibilities. . . ." She trailed to a halt, slowly cocking her head to one side. "And since my brain's finally caught up with my mouth, you shouldn't even *know* anyone like that! Why doesn't he offend *your* sensibilities?"

"Who says he doesn't?"

Whatever comment she was about to make was brought up short

by the thread of bitterness suddenly winding its way through the monk's voice. She merely nodded instead, not so much urging as allowing him to continue.

Apparently done fidgeting with the food, Maurice was now absently turning and sliding the bowl in which it lived. "The Church has . . . lost a lot over the centuries. Texts. Holy relics. Art." *Twist, slide. Slide, twist.* "Sometimes pieces can't be located—or, once located, retrieved—by, um, entirely legitimate means." *Twist, slide.* "So, the guard looks the other way regarding this man's illegal activities, so long as he keeps them subtle and bloodless, and in return, on occasion . . ." *Slide, twist.*

"He provides stolen goods for you." Widdershins hadn't thought she had a high enough opinion of the Church to be disappointed any further. Something about the sheer mundaneness of this all, however, made it worse.

"*Recovered* goods," Maurice corrected her, but it was a halfhearted protest at best. *Twist. Slide.*

"Uh-huh. Typical. Just . . . typical. And how do *you* know all this?"

For the first time—not merely in *this* conversation, but any and all of those she'd had with him—the monk's features went stiff, his eyes hard.

"There aren't many saints in this world, Widdershins. Even good men sometimes have to get their hands a little dirty. Or at least their assistant's hands."

It was Olgun—wasn't it always Olgun, these days?—who kept her from lunging from the chair, hauling off, and smacking the man across from her. The god's spiritual whispers, downy and soothing, damped down her anger enough that it passed *before* she did something idiotic, rather than after.

How dare he?! How dare he talk about William that way?

Except . . . Maurice had known the archbishop closely, served him for years. Shins had known the man for an evening.

Might be a bit *of a pedestal I've put him on, yes?*

Whether she'd spoken to Olgun or merely thought it, she wasn't certain, and ultimately it didn't matter. Before the little deity could respond, assuming he'd heard her at all, the guest whom they'd awaited finally deigned to arrive.

He wore the sort of finery that ensured he stood out in a dive like this one without standing out at all. That is, fancier than everyone else here, but not so bright, so rich, so colorful that he appeared to come from a different world. Just a member of the downtrodden who happened to make it good. The gazes that followed him were envious, the mutters of those who stepped aside for him just a tiny bit annoyed, but none crossed the unseen border into "hostile."

Otherwise, unremarkable. Taller than average, perhaps. Hair, beard, eyes, all of darker shades largely undefinable in the dimness of the common room.

He reminded her, she realized, a little of Renard, her friend and former mentor back in Davillon. If, that is, Renard were about a third taller and at *least* a third less flamboyant.

"If I'd known you were bringing a companion," he began, "I'd have recommended a slightly higher-class establishment." Had his voice been any more carefully and deliberately cultured, it would have thickened into yogurt. Still, there was something behind it, beneath it, a flinty tone that Widdershins recognized from her own life on the streets. Though she kept her expression neutral, even bland, her attention had drifted subtly toward his blade; even Olgun's not-quite-murmurs in her head sounded abruptly mistrustful.

"Are there any higher-class establishments that'll let you in?" Maurice snipped.

The man's only response was a soft chuckle. "And you, my dear?" He offered Widdershins a shallow bow. "What do I call you? Besides lovely?"

Shins suddenly felt like she needed a bath. Shins suddenly felt like *Olgun* needed a bath. "Madeleine," she said stiffly. "And *just* Madeleine. Not dear. Not lovely."

"You wound me."

"Oh, no. Trust me. When *that* happens, you'll know it."

The newcomer drew himself up, his smile slipping for the first time. "Were you both planning to be this rude for our entire meeting?"

"No plan," she told him. "It just seems to come quite by instinct." A pause, then, "Or, at least, *I* didn't plan to be rude. Maurice, did you plan to be rude?"

"Umm . . . No?"

"There, see?" Shins waved a hand dismissively. "Maurice didn't plan to be rude, either. You must just bring it out of people, yes?"

Two sets of jaws worked soundlessly as two men gawped at the young woman beside them. Until, finally, the stranger chuckled again and pulled up a seat. "I could get to like you," he admitted to her.

"Oh, I could never ask you to trouble yourself."

Another chuckle, a faint sniff at a nearby ale followed by an upturned lip, and Maurice's contact was abruptly all business. "So . . . What does our beloved Church of the Hallowed Pact require of me now?"

A lifetime of deception allowed Widdershins to keep any trace of expression off her face, but internally, her startled gasp was as genuine as the one she felt from her divine companion.

It made sense, certainly. This man wasn't likely to have gone out of his way to do a lone monk a favor; if Maurice had implied that this meeting was Church business, well, that was just the smart way to go about it.

She just wouldn't have expected William's old assistant to even think of something like that, much less be willing to act on it. Perhaps the archbishop wasn't the only one about whom she was more ignorant than she thought.

". . . be required," Maurice was telling their guest when she focused once more on the discussion. "Today, all we really need is someone with an ear to the goings-on of Lourveaux. The, um, less overt, less legitimate goings-on."

"Crimes, schemes, conspiracies, intrigue," Widdershins clarified jauntily. "You know, the stuff the Church has to pretend it's not involved in."

If looks could kill, Maurice's would have . . . well, been a moderately severe flesh wound, at worst. Coming from *him*, however, that was vicious enough.

Their guest raised an imaginary goblet in toast to Shins's comment, lips bent in a crooked and oddly mischievous smile. "All right, that should be simple enough."

"Mm. Right. So, Wid—uh, Madeleine has been in the city less than three days, yet she seems to have enemies here."

"Shocking," the other man murmured—and then seemed genuinely shocked in turn when Widdershins's response was to stick her tongue out at him.

"It's true that she does have a penchant for attracting hostile intent," Maurice said, earning his own stuck-out tongue in turn, "but in this case, these men were watching for her long before she turned up. We've no idea how they knew she was coming, let alone why they want her."

"*I* didn't know I was coming until recently," Shins added. "And I didn't tell anybody." Then, more softly, "You don't count as 'anybody.' Oh, you're not insulted. You do too know what I meant!"

Again she came back to the conversation halfway through a sentence, ". . . pretty sure I'd know if any of the underground guilds or major gangs had their eye out for someone in specific," the fence was saying. "Obviously I can't be positive, and there are always freelancers and smaller bands whose doings remain secret simply because nobody's noticed them yet. But if I had to wager, it'd be that you're not looking for someone in the community of the extra-legally inclined. Or if you are, they're nothing more than hired watchers for someone else."

Extra-legally inclined. Need to remember that one. . . . "So who, then?" Shins asked.

Something passed over the man's expression as he studied her, something invisible and yet nearly tangible enough to dislodge his hat. Something that looked an awful lot like understanding.

Oh, figs . . . "Olgun . . ." It wasn't even a breath, the syllables scarcely vocalized at all. "I think he just figured out we're not here on Church business."

From somewhere just behind and to the left of her soul, she felt the god's reply; agreement, and acknowledgment that he was ready for whatever was about to happen.

Except that neither of them were. Without so much as the flicker of an eyelid, he resumed speaking, answering the question Shins had all but forgotten she'd asked.

"You may have noticed," he suggested, "that the city's in a bit of an uproar at the moment?"

"In the same way this place is 'a bit' unappetizing, yes." *Why are you still helping us?* Had she read his expression wrong? Was he planning some sort of double cross? Or had he simply decided that, as the request had come from a clergyman and he was here anyway, he might as well see it through?

"The craft guilds and the Houses have noticed, too. There's more political maneuvering, backbiting, intrigue, and manipulation going on in Lourveaux—and indeed, across Galice, so long as Church and government eyes are distracted—than there are diseases in a brothel."

Charming.

"I've heard nothing of this!" Maurice protested. "The Church wouldn't—"

"Wouldn't tell just anyone even if they knew," Shins interjected. "Not when they don't have the manpower to do anything about it."

"Precisely!" Again the stranger offered an imaginary toast. "Assuming your 'spies' are anything more than the result of a personal vendetta, I find it far more likely that your enemy is political—House or guild—than criminal."

"Same thing, aren't they?" Blandly as she spoke, her mind was racing. She'd accrued more than enough personal vendettas in her life—but all were local to Davillon. Even if one of her ... . misunderstandings . . . had been enough to inspire a hunt for her across Galice, she could think of nobody who had both the means and the slightest chance of knowing she might visit de Laurent's grave.

Then again, how the happy frog would any of the Houses have known to look for me here, or even wanted to?

She could just leave. Get out of Lourveaux and vanish once again into the back roads and small towns of Galice. Get so lost that it wouldn't *matter* who was looking for her.

And spend the rest of her life wondering who *else* was out to get her, and why.

Gods, I'm so tired of politics. . . .

"I think," she sighed, "that you'd better tell us what you've heard. . . ."

The next hour was spent hunched over, so near the table they could *smell* the stains in the wood, engaged in low, raspy, sometimes nigh-inaudible conversation.

Nigh-inaudible, and definitely—at least for Widdershins—incomprehensible. House Blah had bribed a city council seat away from House Whatsis. Parties unknown were slowly buying out the properties and goods of the Someone Guild. This craftsman was broke; that House was losing everything; and none of it meant the first thing to Widdershins, who was barely keeping awake, let alone following along. Surely none of this had the slightest thing to do with her. . . .

A name, vaguely familiar, finally hooked her attention like a trout.

"I'm sorry, House What?"

Maurice and the fence both jumped, apparently having grown accustomed to the idea that they basically had the conversation to themselves. "Carnot," the stranger repeated. "House Carnot."

A shudder ran through thief and god both. House Carnot had bloodlines in almost every major city, Davillon included. Gaston Carnot, the marquis de Brielles, had died in the bloodbath that had forced Adrienne Satti to adopt a new name and had left her the final surviving worshipper of an obscure, foreign deity.

They'd never been close, Gaston and Widdershins, but she wasn't likely ever to forget—him or any of the others.

Still, the Carnots *were* spread far and wide. The fact that she recognized the House meant absolutely nothing.

"And they're doing what?"

"I was just getting to that. Using means both legitimate and il-, they've more or less been crushing a long-term rival into the dust. Buying out properties, hiring away workers, stripping city permits, cutting off access to government contacts, undercutting prices, and the like. They didn't have much presence left in Lourveaux, so it wasn't hard for the Carnots to drive them completely from influence—and from the city entirely, if rumor is to be believed."

"Uh-huh." Widdershins found her attention, and even consciousness, starting to wander once more. More out of obligation than interest, she forced the last question out. "And which rival House have they been stomping all over?"

"Um . . . That'd be House Delacroix, I believe."

Widdershins knew, with absolute certainty, that she spoke for Olgun as well as herself when all she could say was, "Of course it is."

But at least she wasn't sleepy anymore.

INTERLUDE: DAVILLON

Mugs clinked, dishes clanked, servers bustled, customers babbled. Individual sounds, largely of contentment and satiation if not happiness; together, however, they became far more. This was the voice, the song, and the easy, relieved sigh of the Flippant Witch.

Stained but not filthy, worn but not dilapidated, old but not yet sickly, the tavern played host to several dozen patrons, lost in drink or conversation. They, like the establishment itself, were enjoying the best season Davillon had known in over a year. The displeasure of the Church and the interdiction on trade no longer weighed upon the citizens' shoulders; trade and travel thrived; and if the custom at the Flippant Witch couldn't yet compare to its glory days under the late and lamented Genevieve Marguilles, then at least the tavern had regained its health.

Now that the city was in a better way—and now that *she* wasn't running the place.

That was the only way Robin allowed herself to contemplate her absent friend: as "she." As "her." Actually hearing that name, saying that name, *thinking* that name was enough to make her feel too much that she'd sworn to herself she'd never feel again.

It was a vow she renewed every time she cried herself to sleep, utterly determined that *this* time would be the last—but at least that was only once or twice a week, now, rather than nightly.

To most of her patrons and friends, Robin looked well enough. Although still painfully slender, still more girl than woman, she'd begun to truly shed the last vestiges of childhood: gawky becoming graceful; freckles lightening a bit, though surely they would never vanish against the pallor of her skin. She still chopped her hair raggedly but, either by choice or by inattention, had allowed it to grow longer than was her wont, so that it now hung just past her shoulders.

That, when added to her position of authority over the Flippant Witch, had begun attracting attention of boys and men that even the most drab, baggy, unflattering apparel couldn't deflect.

Gods, it's obnoxious!

"Pardon?"

Robin glanced up into the red-bearded face of Gerard, one of the Witch's oldest employees, slightly embarrassed. "Sorry. Didn't mean to say that out loud."

He offered her a grin that she knew, from experience, was a friendly one—despite teeth so discolored and uneven he looked as though a mountain range sprouted from his gums.

"You did, though. So *what's*—oh, three more of those for the teamsters in the back—what's obnoxious?"

"Nosey employees," she huffed in feigned exasperation, "who eavesdrop on conversations so private, they involve fewer than two people." An exaggerated flounce carried her to the barrels stacked behind the counter; she returned with fistfuls of foaming tankards that she thrust at Gerard along with a mischievous wink. The beefy server chuckled, wiped an imaginary splash of ale from his faded blue tunic, and vanished amongst the tables with the drinks.

It was all an act, and they both well knew it. Robin pretended to be cheerful; Gerard, and the others, pretended to believe it. In truth, she'd had precious few reasons to be cheerful in half a year and more.

"Hey, Robin!"

Few. Not none.

The young woman's smile grew broader and far more genuine as she turned, recognizing that voice despite the distorting sounds of the semicrowded room. "Faustine!"

The newcomer—one of several, as customers continually came

and went, passing through the Witch's doors—offered a bashful smile of her own in return. The flickering of the fire in the hearth across the chamber and the various smoking lamps cast flowing hair, normally only a slightly blonder hue than moonlight, in dancing shades of orange. Faustine slipped through the crowd, gracefully if not nearly as effortlessly as Wi—as *she* would have done, and slipped up to the bar. A quick flip of her skirts, long enough to be fashionable without keeping her from the constant running required of her, and she perched upon a rickety stool that had just been vacated by a staggering drunk.

Shoving a few more tankards out of the way, and ignoring the occasional call for drink or food, Robin sidled along behind the counter, then took Faustine's hands in her own. Faustine's face flushed, eyes darting to either side. She clearly started to pull away, and just as clearly stopped herself. Looking down at the countertop, she instead squeezed her own fingers tight around Robin's.

"I didn't expect to see you today," the tavern keep told her, delight and excitement just audible in a voice no longer accustomed to conveying them.

"I . . . Oh . . ." Although Robin's elder by half a decade or more, it was the new arrival who continued to stammer, bashful as a schoolgirl. "I . . . didn't actually expect it. To be here, I mean. Tonight." Then, at the younger woman's puzzled blink, she mustered up an apologetic smile. "I'm here working. Not . . . Not that I'm not glad to be here . . ."

Robin nodded, thoughtful . . . And then waited. And waited.

"Faustine?"

"Oh!" The courier laughed nervously, then released Robin's hands to dig into the small pouch all but hidden by her vest and skirts. The paper she handed over was thick, cheap, sealed in wax without the slightest hint of sigil or signature.

"Who'd be messaging me?"

It was a rhetorical question; one that—like her earlier outburst—

she hadn't meant to speak aloud. Still, Faustine shrugged. "I don't know, Robin. Came home after a crosstown delivery and found it on the stoop, along with my standard fee and an open note that just said 'Sorry I missed you.' It's not really the sort of thing I usually courier, but . . ." Another shrug, another bashful smile.

Robin nodded, cracked the wax, flipped open the paper . . . And would almost certainly have sprouted icicles had she frozen any more thoroughly.

Genevieve's grave. Now. Please.

"Robin?"

The girl barely heard. All she could do was stare.

"Robin, what's wrong?"

Was that *her* handwriting? It didn't *quite* seem to be—and Robin had spent more than long enough staring at that damned note *she'd* left behind when she ran away—but it was close. A little rough, a little sloppy . . .

Just the sort of difference one might expect in a missive dashed off in frightened haste.

"Please . . . Robin, you're scaring me!"

She finally looked up, and wondered what her own face must look like, to have Faustine's looking so stricken.

"I have to go." *Is that* my *voice? It sounds too hollow to be mine. . . .*

"Go where? What does it *say*?!"

"I'm sorry. I can't, I . . . have to go."

Without another word to anyone, without a glance at the unserved customers, without so much as stopping to find her coat, Robin was out in the chill of the evening, skinny legs carrying her far faster than it appeared they ever should.

For the briefest instant, Faustine and Gerard caught one another's gaze. He knew Robin well enough; she had heard the stories more than frequently enough; neither had the slightest doubt who could inspire the girl to such haste.

Though her lips quivered ever so slightly and every muscle in her face went taut, Faustine bolted from her seat and followed.

Robin grew only vaguely aware that Faustine was following, could scarcely even register it as important. Nor did she attach any significance to the fact that the courier, who spent hours a day walking if not running across Davillon, struggled to keep up with her.

Her lungs burned with effort and chill; her breath steamed; people came and went in flashes of shocked or angry faces, shouting or cursing the girl who brushed past them or, in one or two cases, shoved them aside with a strength that belied her size.

None of it registered, none of it mattered. There was no world beyond her destination, the road she traveled, and the maelstrom of emotion that roiled around her mind, threatening to drag it under and drown it. Fear and anger and hurt and worry and more love than she wanted to admit and just maybe a tiny flickering ember of hate. . . .

She knew she neared the cemetery by the smell, the scent of soil and growing things, otherwise alien to this time of year. The city and the Church made every effort to keep the various graveyards (or the wealthier ones, at any rate) lush or at least passable, regardless of season, though their efforts were often symbolic at best. It was another half minute before the gate itself hove into view.

Robin skidded to a halt, her chest heaving, her whole body shaking for reasons utterly unrelated to the cold. She braced herself against the iron with a hand, bent almost double, and still felt herself starting to collapse. . . .

She didn't see or even feel the hands catching her until she hung almost limp from their grip. "I've got you, sweetie."

"F-Faustine?" Was Faustine even supposed to be here? Was that a good idea? She couldn't think past the pounding in her head and heart . . .

"It's me. Come on."

Arms wrapped around Robin's shoulders, helping her stand straight once more. Slowly the spots began to fade from her eyes, the agony and nausea from her gut.

"Faustine, I—"

"It's her, isn't it?"

Robin had swallowed enough tears of her own to recognize them unshed in someone else; the tremor of a word, the twitch of a face. Fully cognizant of everything around her for the first time since she'd read those words, she lightly brushed a finger across the other woman's cheek.

"I think it is," she said simply. "And I *have* to."

"I know."

"Will you . . . come with me?"

Robin hadn't known a human visage could twist in that many emotions at once, but when Faustine's finally settled, it was on a sad and gentle smile. "Came this far . . ."

Arms around each other, they passed through the gate and made their way along the snow-lined footpaths.

It was only a bit later that Robin finally thought to wonder why nobody had asked their business. The cemetery gates didn't precisely close at sunset, but they always picked up a guardsman or two to watch until they *did* shut, after dark.

Must've just missed them. . . . She was too exhausted, too distracted, to consider anything else.

She'd have known the resting place of Genevieve Marguilles even had she not been here multiple times before, both on her own and with . . . *her.* Unlike every other grave around it, the grasses that grew on that grave, the flowers that blossomed around the stone and the ivy that crawled along its surfaces, truly *were* evergreen. Something *she* and Olgun had done. . . .

Except this time, it wasn't just a minor god's magic sustaining the

foliage where Genevieve's body lay. It was the blood of four *additional*
corpses, scattered across the grave and the nearby grass, their deaths recent
enough that the wounds still oozed in the rapidly cooling air. Browning
streaks marred the headstone; flowers lay crushed beneath the dead.

"Oh, gods . . ."

Robin staggered from Faustine's grip, reaching out as though she
could somehow wipe away the desecration with a swipe of her palm.
The world blurred behind burgeoning tears, which she could only
just blink away.

She heard the rustle of the courier's skirts, a faint scrape of leather,
and then Faustine was again at her side, dagger in one hand, small-
barreled flintlock in the other.

The woman *did* run around Davillon day and night, after all.

"Aww, how cute. I didn't expect *two* of you."

Both women spun to stare at a figure across the path, in the lee of
a small mausoleum; little more than a smaller shadow in the larger.
Robin had the vague sense of a hooded cloak, but precious little else.

"What have you *done?!*" That last was a shriek, but she couldn't
contain it.

"Two pheasants with one shot," the woman—woman? Yes, the
voice was definitely female—informed them. "First, just a bit of a
message." A hand-shaped blur waggled at the bodies. "Recognize any
of them?

"No? Huh. Must not be much family resemblance. That aristocratic and dignified corpse there on top is one Gurrerre Marguilles,
patriarch of his house—until recently—and father of poor, rotting,
beetle-infested Genevieve. Gurrerre declined an opportunity I offered
him and, well, I think this rather makes a statement."

Robin felt like she couldn't breathe, couldn't think, could only
wait as two conflicting urges battled within her soul: to break down
in tears, and to make every effort to strangle the stranger with her
bare hands.

"Who *are* you?" She was startled that she'd managed to force the words out and only then realized it was Faustine who'd asked.

"Just a traveler finally come home." Robin could *hear* the smarmy grin in her voice. "And by the way, if you take that shot, you *will* miss. And I'll be irritated."

The barrel of the courier's pistol began to quiver.

"And your . . . second pheasant?" the younger woman finally demanded.

"Oh, getting you here, you skinny little worm. See, I have a *second* message—a very private, personal one—and you're going to deliver it for me."

Robin would have sworn the woman didn't move at all, so fast was her lunge. It carried her from across the path to Faustine's side in the beat of a moth's wing, a bolt of lightning sculpted from shade.

The flintlock discharged harmlessly, batted to one side with a casual backhand; the woman's other fist drove hard into the courier's stomach, sending her to all fours, retching a sour-smelling sludge tinged pink with blood.

Robin's horrified scream had barely begun to emerge, little more than a piercing squeak, when the woman was on her as well. Steel glinted in her fist, reflecting the early moonlight from the snow, and Robin recognized Faustine's own dagger in the instant before it vanished from her line of sight, pressed against her throat.

Red. It was the strangest observation for her to make at the time, but a lock of the woman's hair had slipped from her hood; it was red.

And her eyes shone far too wide, and too white.

"I could just kill you," she hissed, breath warm against Robin's face. "That'd be nice and agonizing. But it's not exactly clear, is it? I mean, so *many* people could just *kill* you. . . ."

A smile, now, as white as those eyes in the blackness of the hood.

"The gunshot's probably attracted attention," she said, "and your friend there might be able to stand in another few minutes. If you're lucky, little worm, you won't bleed to death."

"Wh-what . . . ?"

Fingers clenched in ragged brown hair, yanking the girl back and off-balance . . . and the cloaked woman plunged Faustine's dagger, hilt deep, into Robin's upper thigh.

Agony, like nothing she'd known, nothing she'd imagined; a thick and somehow-viscous nausea at the sight of the blood pumping from the wound, at the slick feel of the steel inside her flesh. She didn't remember collapsing to the snow, which swiftly grew crimson around her; didn't remember clutching, flailing madly, at her leg; didn't recognize the sound that stabbed at her ears and throat as her own voice.

"Yes . . ." the woman murmured almost sensually, sliding back into the darkness. "I'm pretty sure she'll understand *that*. . . ."

Flashes of red and white: smears flashed across her vision, or blood and snow?

She saw Faustine dragging herself toward her, mouth agape in horror, reaching . . .

And then the pain, mercifully, began to fade. Consciousness fading, Robin found herself wondering, with disturbing calm, whether she would wake up again or not. And what *she*—what Widdershins—might think if she didn't.

CHAPTER FIVE

Hooves pounded divots into cold-hardened soil; great flanks heaved and sweated beneath saddles of ornate leather. Cyrille Delacroix leaned forward, nearly standing in the stirrups, relishing in the feel of the chill air over his face even as he prayed to Cevora and the rest of the Pact that they might arrive before too much ground had been lost.

Mother hadn't wanted to send him out, to lead the quartet of household armsmen riding in a cluster around him, that much he knew. He was "too inexperienced." "Too hotheaded." "Too unreliable." "Too young." Plus a wide variety of other *too*s he'd heard from Mother and his older siblings more times than he could count. But none of *them* had been available, had they? When the field hand had come running into the main house at dusk, bellowing about another "cursed blight," he'd been the only one of the Delacroix scions unoccupied elsewhere. And given how little they yet understood about these spreading pools of rot, and how many their fields had already suffered, Mother wasn't *about* to trust this outing to servants alone.

Well, good! This was his opportunity to prove his mettle, to stand equal to his brothers and sisters (well, *most* of his brothers and sisters) in the matriarch's esteem. He could only imagine the dashing figure he must cut; russet destrier galloping under him, his navy coat and night-black hair sweeping behind him, custom-fitted cuirass— unsullied, as yet, by any genuine use—gleaming beneath the gibbous moon. It was straight out of a storybook, or at least he imagined it to be. He glanced southeast, hoping for the silhouette of old Castle Pauvril against the stars and sky—it would've completed the illustration perfectly—but alas, the night proved too dark. No matter, though; he'd just—

"Master Cyrille, *stop*!"

The young aristocrat hauled back on the reins, painfully twisting his mount's head. The animal screamed, skidding to a stop, rearing violently. It was luck and tight stirrups, rather than any skill on Cyrille's part, that prevented an unscheduled and inappropriately strenuous dismount.

Once he'd guided the horse around in a tight circle, leaning forward to mutter soothingly at the beast and pat its neck—and, not coincidentally, to give his own breathing and heart rate the opportunity to slow from their own headlong gallop—he turned angry (and still frightfully wide) eyes on the guard who'd shouted.

"What was the meaning of *that*, Jourdain?!"

Clad in a much thicker doublet and a tabard boasting the masked lion sigil of House Delacroix, the soldier guided his mount forward a few paces and idly pointed with one hand, stroking his mustache with the other.

"Oh." Cyrille desperately hoped the tint of moonlight made the sudden flush in his cheeks invisible, or else that Jourdain and the others would attribute it to the cold. Then again, it didn't much matter. He knew they laughed internally, though they were too disciplined to show it; and he know Mother would hear all about it.

"Good eyes," he commented gruffly. Then, casually as he could manage, he slid from his saddle, took an oil lantern one of his guards had just lit, and knelt to examine the hard earth onto which, in his self-glorifying reverie, he'd almost blindly charged.

Or rather, what *should*—like the rest of the field at this time of year—have been hard earth.

Instead, the soil on the surface was a glutinous slop, seemingly an amalgam of pus and the residue left behind when vegetables were allowed to rot indoors. The vapors wafting from the morass stung the eyes and lungs like those of old cat urine. Cyrille gagged, his gorge rising and his throat tightening, a combination that could well prove lethal if permitted to go to extremes.

Worms and beetles of every sort, even those normally unseen in winter, lay scattered across the surface of the muck. A few still twitched. Most were long dead. Cyrille knew, from past example, that any grasses or plants to have survived the cold would have perished as well—and worse, that the soil would be dried, grainy, utterly unsuitable for farming of any kind.

And the longer he waited, the more land would be lost.

"It's definitely the blight," he announced, rising from his knee and trying to command through scratchy voice and burning throat. He chose to interpret Jourdain's muffled cough as a result of the fumes, rather than cover for a mocking snort. "Send someone back to the house for more hands. The rest of you, break out the tools."

For all their contempt (or at least what Cyrille *assumed* was poorly hidden contempt), the Delacroix guards snapped into motion at his command. Jourdain barked at one of them to ride for the manor, while the others began yanking open saddlebags that looked packed enough for leagues rather than a quick sprint across the property.

Shovels and picks from a couple; waterskins and bottles from others. The glistening around the mouths of those skins and bottles was evidence enough that they did *not*, in fact, contain water.

"You two, spread out. Figure out where best to start the trench." He glanced down again at the vile sludge, which seemed almost to absorb the light of the lantern. Yes, it had definitely advanced a few fingers' widths just in the moments since they'd arrived. A bit of very rough estimation, then, "I suggest you start at *least* five feet out. Probably more; we'll have help soon enough, but that ground is tough.

"Jourdain, you and I are on the oil." He grabbed the straps of several waterskins and began to stride around the decay in the opposite direction, assuming the armsman would keep up. "I don't think we have enough to cover the whole contagion, but I think if we can sear it all the way around, that should do until—"

"Master Cyrille!" Intense but hushed, it was somewhere between a whisper and a snarl. The young man and older soldier turned toward the two guards they had just dispatched the other way, now jogging swiftly toward them.

"I believe I assigned the both of you a task—" Cyrille began haughtily.

"There's someone else here!"

Jourdain's hand was to his belt and then held out before him as fast as the stars twinkled, fist full of an ornately etched flintlock. Cyrille's rapier slid from its sheath only a second later, his fingers clutching the hilt in a textbook dueling grip. Then, after sliding shut the aperture on the lantern with a soft *click*, "Show me."

All four of them, aristocrat and armsmen, slipped across the desolate field, allowing their eyes to adjust, the moon alone to guide their way. Careful, silent, barely a scrape of boot on rocky soil; it appeared, initially, that they'd caught their quarry unawares.

Clad in an ashen cloak and hood, presumably against the chill, the figure was otherwise unidentifiable, undefinable. Cyrille could tell only that it was shorter than he—and, if the muffled buzz drifting his way was any indication, softly mumbling to itself.

A mumble that sprouted, flowerlike, into articulate words just as Jourdain drew breath to speak.

"Hello, guys. Was wondering who'd come along. Any idea what all this is? It's not precisely natural, you know."

Cyrille could only blink. How had she—at least, judging by the voice, "she"—known they were here? Who was she? And what in Cevora's name was she *talking* about?

"Dumb question," she continued. "You'd have to be stupid or blind not to know, yes? Or maybe both. It looks like the bottom of a plague's chamber pot around here."

The young aristocrat found himself utterly at a loss. "Who the hell . . . ?"

"A *sickly* plague," she added helpfully.

Jourdain raised and aimed his pistol. "Turn around and identify yourself!"

"An *incontinent* sickly plague."

"*I said turn and identify!*"

"Wow, all right. Touchy. And *loud*."

Slowly she turned, slowly she raised dark-gloved hands to lower the hood from her head . . . and Cyrille felt as though he'd just been punched in the chest. And the gut. And then each had turned and punched the other.

She wasn't the most beautiful girl he'd ever seen, not even close. Dwelling among the aristocracy, the young Delacroix had known women of noble blood and meticulous upbringing whose entire lives seemed devoted to the refinement and ultimate perfection of personal beauty.

This stranger? Pretty enough, certainly, but hardly exquisite. Features a little too sharp, hair a little too uneven. Her eyes and cheeks were just the tiniest bit sunken, touched by the ravages of recent travail.

And she talked funny.

But there was something about her, an allure of the genuine that Cyrille had never seen before. She was *real*, where every aristocrat he'd ever known, family or otherwise, wore at least a patina of the artificial.

It wasn't until the pain of the emotional blow in his chest grew even worse, and the roar of an excited crowd or perhaps an angry sea filled his ears, that he remembered to breathe.

". . . any good if I gave you my name," the stranger was explaining to Jourdain, clearly exasperated and apparently utterly unperturbed by the pistol pointing her way. "You don't *know* me. So what difference does it make? Wouldn't you rather talk about—"

"Oh, for Cevora's sake!" Was Cyrille imagining things, or did the woman flinch at the guard's outburst? "That's it. You're coming with us!"

"I am?" She actually put her hands on her hips and cocked her head; Cyrille wasn't sure if he wanted to laugh or sigh aloud. "I don't seem to recall this particular discussion. Did I miss a meeting?"

"Until we determine your involvement in the poisoning of the House Delacroix fields—"

"Do I *look* like an incontinent plague to you?"

Jourdain actually sputtered to a halt, gesticulating wildly with the flintlock. Cyrille bit his lip to keep from guffawing openly. His whole body, even the blade of his rapier, quivered with his suppressed mirth.

Then the elder guardsman ordered "Take her!" and Cyrille wasn't amused anymore.

"Now hold on a minute. Surely that's not—"

Nobody was listening. Jourdain's weapon was shifting back to cover the woman once more. The other two armsmen were approaching from either side, hands raised, blades loose in their scabbards. The breeze kicked up over the field, sending shivers across every patch of exposed skin, as winter itself seemed to tense up.

And though he knew he must be mistaken, Cyrille could have *sworn* that he heard the stranger mutter something very much like, "Oh, figs."

He could make even less sense of what happened next.

The hammer on Jourdain's weapon fell with a loud clunk when it was mere inches off target, discharging its ball harmlessly into the diseased bog. The guard jumped, wide-eyed, nearly fumbling the gun. The other two turned their heads to gawp his way, perhaps unaware it had been a misfire, wondering what he was shooting at.

In that tiny span of distraction, shorter than the twitch of a dreaming dog's paw, the stranger moved.

She crossed the distance between them at a pace Cyrille wasn't sure the horses could have hoped to match. Her hands closed on Jourdain's shoulders before he seemed fully aware she was coming. A short jump, braced with that grip, brought both her knees up, hard and fast. The first sank into Jourdain's gut, the second uncomfortably lower. The leather padding of his uniform absorbed the worst of it—but what remained was clearly bad enough. He tumbled to all fours, gasping and dry heaving.

The woman pushed off him as he fell, coming to rest facing Cyrille. She held in her right fist a rapier with a brass bell guard; stood planted in a stance that would've gotten Cyrille reprimanded by his instructors—and which, he had no doubt, would get him dead if she wanted it to. His own rapier hung limp at his side, and the young Delacroix scion offered the insightful and most pertinent observation he could manage.

"Did you know the jewel's missing from your pommel?"

And then he could only laugh, albeit somewhat hysterically, at the utterly bemused expression flitting across her face. Then she was running again, the other two guards in pursuit, and Cyrille was left staring, largely unawares, at the whimpering Jourdain.

Briefly. Sucking in his breath, struggling to bring his laughter and his shock under control, he turned to follow.

Only once did he stumble in the dim light of the moon, foot catching on Cevora knew what, but he was up and running again with only dirty breeches and a slightly skinned palm to show for it.

It took him no time at all to catch up; pursuers and pursued had gotten only as far as where Cyrille and the guards had left the horses. In those mere moments, however, the woman had already dropped one of the two guards. He lay on the hard earth, moaning and clutching at an arm that gleamed wetly in the ambient luminescence.

As far as the other . . .

Again Cyrille could only stare in unabashed awe. The woman

tumbled backward out of the path of the armsman's swinging blade, leaping so that she rolled on her back across the saddle of a skittish, nervously prancing horse. He saw the beast's eyes go wide, but it was too well trained to bolt. She cleared the saddle completely, vanishing briefly behind the animal's flank.

And reappeared from *beneath* it, daring its hooves as only a lunatic might, snagging the guard by the knees before he'd taken two steps. A swift jerk and he was on his back with a grunt, lying supine beneath the stirrup.

Once more she vanished into the shadows, once more reappearing, this time leaping clear *over* the horse, not so much as touching it, flipping in midair. A single slash with her rapier as she hung upside down at the apex of her flight, and the heavy canvas saddlebag dropped from the horse to land square on the guard's upturned face.

Everything from that point was basically a formality. After sheathing her blade, she casually strode to the dazed armsman, yanked the saddlebag down so it wrapped his head, chest, and arms. She cinched it tight, then kicked his sword away into the darkness of the field. She knelt by the wounded man next, ripped a length of fabric off his tabard to stanch the bleeding from his arm, then tied his hands with a length of bridle.

Finally, just as casually, she strode over to Cyrille himself.

"Sword."

"I—what?"

She rolled her eyes, an expression he couldn't help but find strangely endearing. "Your sword. Give."

Cyrille looked down, surprised to find the weapon still in his hand; he'd utterly forgotten about it. But . . .

"No."

"Did he say no?" Cyrille hadn't the first notion to whom she might be speaking, but it clearly wasn't him. "I'm sure I heard him say no. Did you hear him say no?"

"I . . ." *What in the gods' names . . . ?* "This blade was entrusted to me by my family. I cannot hand it over to just anyone."

"I'm not *just* anyone," she insisted. "I'm anyone, and a bunch of other stuff, too!"

A long pause. "What?"

"Do they teach all upper-class children that wit, or are you gifted?"

Another long pause. "What?"

The woman's sigh was very much how Cyrille might have imagined a deflating ox might sound, had he ever had occasion to imagine deflating oxen. "Sheathe it," she ordered him. "Just . . . You understand that if I see even a mouse tail's width of steel, you're going to lose *so* much more than your sword, yes?"

"Um . . ." His rapier slid home with a dull slither and thump. "Yes."

"Good." She turned, idly rubbing her chin, to examine the two bound men. "There's nothing out here that's going to eat them any time soon, is there?"

"I don't think so. Maybe wolves, if we left them long enough, but probably not even then."

"We'll try not to leave them long enough, then. Now let's go talk to your man with the itchy trigger finger, so I can pointedly note that if I was the bad guy, he wouldn't still be alive enough to hear me deny being the bad guy."

"I'm a little bit worried that I followed that," he offered with a shy smile.

"I don't care if you followed that. Just follow me."

Still pondering the labyrinthine twists of the stranger's logic, and thoughts, and speech, he rather eagerly did precisely that.

❋

"Olgun?" Widdershins's throat and lips scarcely budged, so deep beneath her breath did she speak, so that the upper-class whelp trudging along behind her wouldn't hear. "Why do half the people I meet try to hit me with something?

"Yeah, yeah, I know, you don't even have to say it. 'Because the other half don't know me that well yet.' Ha, ha, flapping ha. Remind me to leave you in a basket on the stoop of an orphanage somewhere." She halted so abruptly, the man behind her had to draw up short with a gasp or risk stumbling into her. As though it were the most urgent question asked in human history, she whispered, "Come to think of it, do gods even *have* parents? And if you never did, are you still considered an orphan for not having them now?"

Olgun's empathic response clearly carried the image of patting Widdershins patronizingly on the head, then sternly pointing in the direction ahead of them.

"Fine!" she humphed. "See if I answer any of *your* theological questions!"

A couple more steps, and something else occurred to her. "Hey, you! Um . . . What's your name?"

"Cyrille Delacroix, of House Delacroix," the aristocrat told her.

"Do you realize how redundant that is?"

". . . What?"

"Never mind. Your other guard, the older one. What's *his* name?"

"Jourdain."

"All right. Olgun?"

A faint tingle of power, a crawling in the air, and Shins knew her voice would carry well ahead of her, without sounding clear across the open field.

"Hey, Jourdain! I'm coming your way. Cyrille's with me. He's fine.

"You won't believe me. You won't believe when I tell you your men are fine, too. Cyrille will back me up. You'll assume I've threatened him. I'll send him over to stand beside you, well away from me. He's still going to back me up. You're going to grumble, and doubt, and look for an excuse, but you're going to be *just* convinced enough to listen to what I have to say, especially when he orders you to stand down! So can we just skip all that and talk like civilized people, or at least Galicians?"

"What makes you so sure I'd order him to stand down?" Cyrille asked from behind her.

"You want to hear what I have to say," she told him.

"Yes, but what makes you so sure of *that?*"

"The fact that you were going to tell Jourdain to stand down, obviously."

That, at least, shut him up again.

Dirt crunched and Jourdain appeared from the darkness, flint-lock in one hand, sword in the other, and—for *some* reason—walking with short, almost squeamish steps. "Master Cyrille?"

"Everything she said is true, Jourdain. I'm fairly certain she's not the enemy, at this point."

"I wouldn't be so quick to—"

"And I *am* instructing you to stand down, as she anticipated."

Widdershins smirked, openly smug, while Jourdain—despite looking as though he wanted to chew through his lip until he could brush his teeth with his mustache—lowered his weapons.

"You realize," he growled, "that the blight has spread farther than it would have, thanks to your interference."

"I'm not the one who pointed a pistol at me and chased me." Rather than letting the nascent argument mature into adulthood, she continued, "So what do you know about this gunk?"

Cyrille opened his mouth to answer, but the guard beat him to it. "You say you're not our enemy, why don't *you* start with what you know about it?"

"Hmm. I know it's not natural. . . ."

"Stunning deduction," Jourdain muttered. Cyrille shushed him.

"But it's not . . ." She paused, casting about for words. "It's not *normal* magic," she told them, wincing internally at how stupid a statement that actually was.

It was also the best she could do, though. Although not precisely an expert, she'd encountered a few unnatural effects and entities—the latter, mostly—in her time. From the moment they'd encountered this "blight," Olgun had been insistent that this was nothing like the others.

He had been rather less able to convey to Widdershins what it *was*. All she'd gotten was a mixture of confusion and frustration; he didn't fully understand it, and what he *did* comprehend, apparently, simply couldn't be rendered effectively in imagery and emotion.

"Look," she snapped, his own frustration feeding hers, "I know what that sounds like. Just trust me, it's magic, but it's not like *other* magic. That I've seen. Or heard of."

Cyrille's gaze flickered, albeit only briefly, from her to Jourdain. "The Thousand Crows?"

The guard made a brief scoffing noise. When Widdershins just stood waiting, however, arms crossed and foot tapping the soil, he sighed and said, "Local gang of thugs and criminals in Aubier. Rumor has it they've a sorcerer among their ranks. It's nonsense, of course."

"Oh, of course." Absently, directed mostly to Olgun and herself but loud enough for the others to hear, "Six months from home, and I still can't get away from these hopping thieves' guilds!"

Jourdain's snort was even more contemptuous. "Why am I unsurprised? But calling the Thousand Crows a 'guild' would be a joke. They're not big enough or organized enough, and frankly the city's probably too small to support such a thing."

"You'd be surprised," she muttered. "But assuming it's *not* nonsense, they'd have to have a reason for coming after House Delacroix in particular, right?"

This time, it was Cyrille shaking his head. "I don't see why—or how, for that matter. Ever since this started, we've had guards patrolling our lands day and night. The blight's hit us only in our textile-related fields—flax, grazing for sheep—not any of the food crops, so we've been particularly focused there. Nobody could have slipped past our people *that* many times!"

"I could." Then, at Jourdain's narrowed glare, "I *didn't*. Well, I mean, other than tonight, to take a look. Just saying I *could*. I'm here, after all."

"One person, one time. Not the same thing. My men are better than that, and they haven't even *seen* any trace of trespassers."

"Except the big blotches of diseased soil, yes?"

"At *any* rate," the young aristocrat broke in, seemingly trying to head off another conflict, "even if they *could*, the Thousand Crows would have no *reason* to target us. We've received no demands; we devote no more of our household guard to peacekeeping and law enforcement than any other house in Aubier—"

"They could be working with House Carnot, couldn't they?"

The sheer disbelief wafting from the two men was nearly enough to sweep Olgun away in into nonexistence.

"Why in Cevora's name would you think *that*?!" Cyrille finally forced out.

"Uh . . . Rival House? Taking steps to cripple Delacroix influence? *Some* of this must sound familiar, yes?"

"I don't know what House politics look like where you're from, uh . . . You never gave us your name?"

"Widdershins," she mumbled absently, and immediately cursed herself (or at least called herself all manner of animals and fruit). She'd had every intention of going by "Madeleine" here—as a name, it would stand out a lot less—but she'd been so distracted. . . .

If Cyrille was thrown, however, it took no form she could spot in the gloom or hear in his voice. "All right, Widdershins. The situation may be different where you're from, but here? House Carnot's presence in Aubier is minimal, and they hold no real power. They're not a rival; they're barely *noticeable*. And we'd certainly have noticed if they brought in the sort of manpower or resources a major move would require."

Shins really, *really* wanted to sit down. "Olgun?"

His response was, emotionally, a bewildered shrug.

It made no sense. None. She'd spent days in Lourveaux, looking into House Carnot after Maurice's contact had dropped their name as enemies of House Delacroix. She'd learned they had moved against their rivals fiercely, not just in Lourveaux but elsewhere. She'd learned that the Delacroix who lived in Lourveaux had left, heading for the Outer Hespelene region and Aubier in particular, perhaps the last city in which the Delacroix held any real influence.

And she'd learned that Lazare Carnot, patriarch of the House in Lourveaux, and the bulk of his people, had left on a journey of "family business" not long afterward, leaving only a few cousins and a handful of servants to maintain the estate until their return.

They *must* have been on their way here, to finish the task. They must!

Mustn't they?

"I don't understand," she admitted finally. "Didn't they at least *tell* you what was going on with the Carnots?"

"They?"

"The Lourveaux Delacroix bloodline!" she all but shouted. Were they *all* idiots out here in the Outer Hespelene, or . . . ?

"Widdershins," Cyrille said gently, "we haven't hosted anyone from other branches of the family in a couple of years, now."

"Oh, figs . . ." *They hadn't made it. . . . None of them had made it. . . .*

The first shouts and hoofbeats of the approaching Delacroix field hands echoed out of the darkness. In that one heartbeat when Cyrille and Jourdain both looked away, Shins all but fell back into the shadows, vanishing from their sight. Normally, she'd have relished imagining, or even watching, the expressions on their faces, would have laughed inside, and Olgun with her.

Tonight, she and Olgun both had too much to think about, new information and old, and not a bit of it remotely good.

CHAPTER SIX

She didn't look precisely "matriarchal," at least as popular archetype would have it.

She was neither gaunt and hatchet-like, nor rotund and imposing. Her hair had only just begun to gray at the temples, leaving the bulk of it her original rose-tinged blonde. Her height, her features, even—as she was not currently out and about in public—her attire . . . All were remarkably mundane. She was a woman who, in all *physical* respects, could enter a crowded room and attract the attention of absolutely nobody.

Until she turned her shriveling gaze or iron-laced voice on someone. Then, *then* there could be no doubt that Calanthe Delacroix, matron of House Delacroix in Aubier and the entirety of the Outer Hespelene, was a woman accustomed to being obeyed.

At the moment, clad in somber blues and violets barely a step away from mourning garb, she sat in a high-backed chair of plush cushions and red velvet, her fingers laced together in her lap, her eyes unblinking. Bookshelves, small doors, and portraits in gilded frames occupied two of the chamber's walls; a great curtained window, a sprawling fireplace, a banner boasting the leonine symbol of Cevora, and a suit of old armor, the third; the heavier door and a pair of statue-still servants, the last.

Cyrille and Jourdain stood before her—both clad in new outfits, unbesmirched by the dirt and sweat of their recent endeavors—slightly breathless and parched from talking. And around them—standing, sitting, or sprawling throughout the library, attentions fixed either on the speakers or the matriarch, depending on their inclination—were most of the other Delacroix scions.

Malgier, arms crossed and back ramrod straight, standing at his mother's side as was his wont. Arluin, slowly stroking his thick and almost-untamed beard, the only facial hair to be seen in the room beyond Jourdain's mustache. Anouska, the spitting image of her mother as a young woman, taking in every word and every gesture with eyes as cold and as flat as ice, scarcely blinking. Josephine, her tight curls bobbing and casting shadows in the light of a tiny glass lantern with lenses of various hues—a toy to which she apparently paid far more attention than she did the goings-on around her. The twins Chandler and Helaine, sitting beside one another on a futon, absently rolling glass marbles across and between their knuckles, perfectly synchronized.

Only Marjolaine, the sole sibling younger than Cyrille himself, was absent, a fact that surprised none of them whatsoever.

Marbles clacked together. The clock on the mantelpiece ticked its rhythm. The fire crackled, occasionally popped as a bit more wood gave up the ghost. And for long breaths, these were the room's only sounds.

Calanthe raised a hand, up and back. Instantly, one of the servants was beside her, placing a long-stemmed goblet in her fingers. Two delicate sips, which somehow managed to drain every drop of wine from the vessel, and she handed it back to the servant, who promptly returned to his spot against the wall. All without a word spoken; all without once lifting the weight of her regard from Cyrille's cringing, tensing shoulders.

"I had hoped," she finally intoned, "that my son had finally outgrown his foolish years. Clearly we have a few birthdays ahead of us yet, before that blessed day arrives."

Malgier sneered, the twins both chortled openly, and Josephine looked up from her shiny lenses long enough to ask, "Wait, whose birthday is it?"

"Nobody's, Fifi." This from bearded Arluin, his voice gentle. "Go back to playing."

"And leave the conversation to the adults," Malgier added through his grimace.

"Hey! I *am* an adult!"

Chandler chortled again. "Physically, maybe, but—"

"Enough!" It wasn't a shout, just the slightest raising of the matriarch's voice, but every other mouth snapped shut as tight as the visor on the antique suit of armor.

"I can at least comprehend," Calanthe continued, "where Cyrille's idiocy comes from, though I expect better of a Delacroix, regardless of age. But you, Jourdain . . . You've been at this for years. *You* know better."

"This . . . *woman*," the armsman protested, as angrily as protocol would permit, "incapacitated both my men—"

"And we'll be having words regarding that, as well, rest assured," the matriarch said stiffly. Half the others were smirking, now, cruelly amused at the notion of the guards coming out second in such a "fight."

"I ordered him to stand down!" Cyrille finally burst in, unable to contain himself. "Widdershins isn't the enemy, Mother. She could've killed us all, and she didn't. She's trying to help, and I think we could use it. She wants to figure this out as much as—"

"*Silence!*" The matriarch all but lunged to her feet, and everyone in the room flinched openly. "Cevora deliver us," she growled, "from smitten children!"

"Mother, I—"

"You will not speak again until directed to, Cyrille."

"But—"

Malgier took a step forward, snarling, hand raised. Cyrille cringed away from the coming blow, but Calanthe raised her own hand in signal.

"I don't believe that'll be necessary this time, Malgier. Will it, Cyrille?" Then, at his questioning look, "I asked. You may answer."

"No, Mother, it won't."

"Good." Gracefully, she resumed her seat, Malgier returning to his place at her side. "This . . . 'Widdershins.'" The contempt she infused into that single word would have poisoned an entire flower garden. "Clearly not of refined blood or breeding. No woman who was would call herself that."

Cyrille opened his mouth, closed it again.

"A mercenary, perhaps? A criminal? Few people develop the sorts of talents you describe for honest goals. Professional soldiers, for the most part, and she sounds like no soldier to me. You two may have very well had your hands on our enemy and allowed her to go!"

Jourdain shifted his weight to his other foot, the closest the guard would come to overt fidgeting. "Madam, I . . . Apologies, may I speak?"

"My instruction was to Cyrille, not to you."

"Of course. Madam, while I am the first to agree with you that your son's judgment is somewhat . . . impaired on this matter . . ." If he noticed Cyrille's glare, he offered no sign of it. ". . . I do have to say, I believe he may be correct about this woman not being the foe we seek. It's true that she could have slain any or all of us, and clearly made a point not to do so. She seemed genuinely curious about the blight, and I saw no sign that she possessed any sort of magic that would allow—"

"Are you so modest, Jourdain," Anouska asked; her voice, like her face, was nigh identical to her mother's, "that you've kept your sorcerous expertise from us all these years?"

A glower from Calanthe was enough to silence both her eldest daughter and the snickers that followed, but the point had been made. "I'm no expert, of course—" Jourdain began, his cheeks flushed.

"Yes, I believe we've just covered that," the matriarch said dryly. No snickers, this time; nobody would dare.

"You *have* been doing this a long while," she continued, "and I know your instincts, in general, to be good. So I'm inclined to think there is at least a *chance* that you are correct, that this Widdershins is not the source of our difficulties."

Cyrille began a deep sigh of relief, a sound and a sensation both swiftly interrupted.

"Which does *not*," Calanthe announced, "in any way make her our ally. She might represent a rival, looking to take advantage. She might be some hoodlum seeking her own profit, or some drifter hoping we'll reward her 'assistance.' And it might just be that our good guardsman is mistaken about her."

The grinding of Cyrille's teeth nearly drowned out the twins' glass marbles.

"I do not trust her presence. I do not trust her motives. I *certainly* do not trust her judgment!" The woman shook her head, not dislodging so much as a curl or ringlet of hair. "The Carnots. Really! Even a cursory understanding of Aubier would have inspired her to choose a more likely culprit as her scapegoat.

"I want to know who she is, where she is, why she's here. And until I am *convinced* her efforts are neither hostile nor detrimental, I want whatever she's doing stopped."

Then, "Oh, speak your mind, Cyrille. You're beginning to sound like a teapot."

The breath all but exploded from him. "Mother, we shouldn't waste this opportunity. She could be of great help to us! She could assist in determining what *is* happening to our fields! She could—"

"Warm your blankets for a few nights, Brother?" Helaine taunted, snapping a marble into the air and catching it again as it fell.

"Serving girls not good enough for you?" her twin added.

Again Josephine—Fifi—looked up from her gaudy lantern. "What's wrong with extra quilts and a bed warmer?"

At least the sudden silence that accompanied the incredulous stares turned her way made it unnecessary for Calanthe to shush her children yet *again*.

"Cyrille . . ." She no longer even sounded angry, just exasperated and perhaps a bit tired.

"Yes, Mother?"

"Gather some of the guards and groundskeepers, and go and supervise the cleanup of this latest blight."

Jaw held rigid, the young man nodded, turned on a heel with almost military stiffness, and pushed past the servants on his way through the door.

"Josephine, go assist him in gathering what he needs for another night ride, and then go to your room and go to bed."

"Yes, Mother." Fifi gathered up her lantern; offered Arluin a friendly smile, all the others a puzzled blink; and followed Cyrille from the room.

"As for the rest of you," she continued, gaze sweeping the chamber, somehow seeming to meet everyone else's eyes simultaneously, "it appears we need to have yet another chat about behavior and decorum. . . ."

❁

Head down, clinging to the wall like a lizard—albeit a lizard with long hair, a cloak, and battered leathers—Widdershins drew back from the curtain-covered glass. She felt her ears tingle, or rather she felt them *cease* tingling with anything but winter's chill, as the influence Olgun had extended to assist in her eavesdropping fully receded.

"Are we absolutely certain Alexandre was related by blood to these people?" she inquired of the god, disbelief and revulsion soaking her words despite how softly she spoke. "Because I'm not entirely convinced they're related by *species*."

She crept along the side of the manor, hand over hand, foot over foot. Her pace was slow, lest fingers chilled by wind, or brick made slick by frost, overcome even her own ingrained talent and divine assistance.

Not that a fall from this height would remotely endanger her. It'd just be embarrassing, especially in front of Olgun. And since she was *always* in front of Olgun . . .

"Yes, Olgun." This reply, to his latest surge of memory, came with the obligatory eye roll. "I *have* met a few hoity-toity high-and-mighty myself, you know. That's the funny thing about stealing money—it always seems to be the rich people who have the most of it. I knew full well what to expect when we came out here."

She flipped heels over head, pushing off from the wall to land on her feet in the dirt-stained snow, then glanced back over a gray-cloaked shoulder. It was, indeed, an aristocrat's home. The stone walls, whitewashed (if perhaps beginning to flake); the sweeping eaves; the glimmering windows of glass . . . While it might have been slightly smaller and more worn, it would have fit quite well with the manors of Davillon's Rising Bend district.

More so, to Widdershins's urban mind, than it did here. The house loafed like an old cat, not on an estate of gardens and fountains and winding paths, surrounded by stone walls or iron fences, but in the midst of the Delacroix farmlands. Rolling fields stretched out in most directions, broken only by the occasional copse of trees or half-frozen stream, smelling—even in the midst of these frigid months—of loam. Shins found the juxtaposition almost dizzying.

Or maybe that, too, was just her revulsion at the behavior of a good man's distant and not-so-good relatives.

"I know, I know," she reassured the little god as she swept across the fields, leaving no trail that would last until morning, easily side-stepping the patrolling guards. "They're not *all* that bad. Cyrille seems like he might be a decent sort, I suppose. A little dim, though, yes? And maybe a few of the others, but most of them . . . ? Guh!" The shudder began as exaggeration, then turned real thanks to a gust of winter. "I'd rather give muscle rubs at a leper colony than live with those people."

More imagery from Olgun, and this time Shins didn't have it in her to be sarcastic. Over a year after his death, over three since they'd parted ways, the memories of her father-in-all-but-blood still pierced her. "I know. We're not here for them. We're here for him. I'm not quitting, Olgun. I'm just . . . You think we could *hire* someone to help them so we could leave?

"What? I don't *know* how we'd pay them! Maybe steal something? I've heard I'm good at that. I suppose we could sell your body, if you were willing to stoop that low . . . and had a body. . . .

"Oh, shut up. You and your nonsense ideas." A final glance around to ensure none of the Delacroix patrols were near—the distant castle, made ghostly in the silvery light, appeared to be reaching desperately for the half-clouded moon overhead—and then she darted into the nearby trees. Here, the shadows were so deep, the guards could very literally have stepped over her and never known she was there.

"C'mon, Olgun. They don't believe the Carnots are involved? Let's go gather them their proof so we can get *out* of this nest of rats and vipers before we get . . . I don't know, venomous fleas or something.

"It *could* happen!

"Shut up. We have evidence to find."

"How can there not be *any evidence?!*"

Widdershins, who had long since mastered the paradoxical art of ranting and raving under her breath, in almost complete silence, ranted and raved under her breath in almost complete silence.

She was perched on a rooftop, now, rather than clinging to a wall, half-crouched over a shingled peak, steady as she might have been on solid ground. Both her ratty cloak and a weathervane (the latter of which would have looked far more appropriate out in the farmlands, perhaps atop the Delacroix manor, than it did here) twisted fiercely in the wind, which was unbroken at this height by walls or trees. It brought tears to her eyes, tiny gnawing teeth of cold to her cheeks and ears, but she would neither blink nor flinch—less out of any need to prove a point than because she was just that annoyed.

Or, perhaps, to prove the point that she was just that annoyed.

From here, she could observe much of Aubier, at least so thoroughly as the moonlight and the occasional lanterns permitted. As had been the case with the domicile on which she perched—a three-story cube of stone with a roof, larger and nicer than many she could see, but nowhere near either the size or quality of the Delacroix estate—she found herself less than impressed with what she saw.

Aubier couldn't decide if it was a town bloated to the size of a small city, or a small city that still nostalgically called itself a town. Roads alternated in no discernible pattern from cobbled to frozen dirt; from short and straight to as crooked and winding as a snake eating a worm. Homes ranged from shabby but honest shacks to pretentious houses larger than they needed to be but smaller than they clearly wanted to be. Open spaces of dirt might, in warmer seasons, have served as parks or public gardens within the town-slash-city limits, or as more farmland without.

And the lack of any genuine sewer system, such as Davillon and Lourveaux boasted, contributed to a bouquet that was foul enough even in winter. In summer, Shins just knew she'd be asking Olgun if he could temporarily remove her nose, or at least turn it inside out.

None of which was the actual reason for the frustration that burned the young thief like a virulent rash, threatening to tether her to this backwater place and miserable family for far longer than she'd hoped.

"Seriously, Olgun! I'm actually asking. Use your divinitiness. Knowledge unobtainable to mortals. How can we have found *nothing?*"

As Shins was "actually asking," Olgun actually answered. Where Widdershins had refused to squint against the frigid gusts, her eyes narrowed sharply against the god's images.

"Don't even say that! The Carnots *are* involved; nothing else makes sense! Well . . . All right, you didn't *say* it, but . . . Don't do what it is you do instead of saying it.

"We *know* they moved against House Delacroix, drove them out of Lourveaux, yes? We know that a whole gaggle of the family left Lourveaux not long after the last Delacroix, who never made it here. Lazare Carnot was one of them. House patriarchs don't just wander off, so where the flopping hens *are they*?"

Because they *certainly* were not here, in the ancestral home of the Carnot bloodline in Aubier. Widdershins had scoured every room, every hallway, every nook, every cranny. The Carnots, at least locally, were largely dull and unobservant, the epitome of the laziness that could overcome an aristocrat when ambitions were all but extinguished. Guards and servants were few, and easily avoided. Only once had she even come *near* to being discovered, by a man she believed to be head of the household staff. And at no point had she discovered any sort of secret more incriminating or sinister than an illicit liaison or a bit of cheating on local taxes.

She had even located a hidden cupboard, one that blended so well with the surrounding walls that the family itself clearly had forgotten its existence. The dust within was more than enough proof that at no point in generations could a house patriarch, or anyone else, have been concealed within. The old furniture and somewhat faded finery belied any recent influx of coin or influence, and the fact that the bulk of the family appeared content to laze around the house did not inspire Shins to believe they were engaged in some great conspiracy of nobles. She'd gone ahead and gathered the addresses of the few other properties—several shops and a small warehouse—the Carnots owned in Aubier, and she'd check them all just to be sure, but none of them struck her as a likely hideout.

In short, as she'd bemoaned to Olgun multiple times in a scant few minutes, they had no proof, not even the tiniest shred of evidence, of anything whatsoever.

Some unnatural union of a growl, a sigh, and a groan rolled from her throat, almost freezing on her tongue before it fell away to vanish in the night. "I don't know, Olgun. Maybe we *are* on the wrong track? I mean, this *could* be coincidence, yes? The Carnots can't be the only rivals of the Delacroix trying to take advantage of all the Church nonsense and political silliness. I guess we ought to at least check some of the other . . .

"What? No, I *don't* know how many Houses have a presence in Aubier, or which ones are competitors! How would I possibly know that? And where would you have been when I learned it? Napping? Bath time? Napping during bath time? I . . . Do gods bathe? I mean, you don't really have a body to wash, I suppose. . . ."

Another growl-sigh-groan. "Point is, yes. I know it'll take forever if we have to look into all of this House by House, but what choice do we have?"

At which point the first smile in many hours began to lurch hesitantly across Widdershins's face as she abruptly realized *exactly* what choice they had.

CHAPTER SEVEN

"Name's Jourdain, right?"

The mustached armsman turned, as did the trio of others whom he led. The street was only moderately crowded, most of the market-goers having run their errands earlier in the day and most of the vendors having not yet closed up, but still it took Jourdain a moment to spot the source of that voice.

Unsurprising, perhaps, given that she wasn't standing in the street at all but was perched on a windowsill some feet above him, cast in growing shadow by the angle of the lazily setting sun.

"Widdershins," he said, his voice neutral. The other guards stirred; no doubt they'd been told to watch for a strange woman with that stranger moniker. "Not precisely the most inconspicuous place for a conversation."

"*You* missed me until I called your name, yes? Besides, who says I'm trying to be inconspicuous? Maybe my entire goal is to . . . conspic."

Jourdain's face remained straight, but the other three guards blinked almost perfectly in unison. "What do you want?" the elder soldier asked.

"Just to ask you a few questions. Well, and also hear some answers. I mean, it'd be a bit wasteful to *only* want to ask questions and *not* get any answers, yes?"

Jourdain openly glanced around him. While most passersby were blind to the young woman's presence and too far to hear the conversation over the din of the market, some few had indeed stopped to watch in puzzlement as four armed household guards conversed with what was either a very peculiar person or an even more peculiar win-dowsill. "So come down here and talk to us like a normal person."

Shins's laugh was almost more of a bark. "Like a normal person that half of you think is your enemy, and the other half are still under orders to question? I think I'm going to decline."

"What? How—?"

"If it helps, I'm declining regretfully."

"How did you know our orders—?"

"Sorrowfully, even. I might cry."

In point of fact, it was taking all she had not to laugh—not least because Olgun was "humming" a tune of mournful disappointment as accompaniment to her "regrets."

Two of the Delacroix guards reached for their pistols, but a raised hand and an eyebrow-creasing glower from Jourdain halted them in their tracks. "Why would I answer any of your questions?"

"Uh, because I'm trying to help your employers? Maybe?"

"I still have strenuous doubts as to your motives."

"Oh!" Widdershins slapped and rubbed her gloved hands together, hoping to restore a bit of the warmth that even the leathers had failed to retain, then waited for a small cluster of evening shop-pers to pass between her and the guards. "That's not a problem. I *don't* doubt my motives, and since I'm the one you're telling, that makes it perfectly safe."

This time Jourdain *did* blink, along with the other two guards.

"So where," she continued before they could react any further, "would I find the Thousand Crows? Or any of Aubier's organized criminal guilds, really. I'm not picky."

Jourdain's face began to darken.

"Only, I've already visited something like two hundred and ninety inns and taverns . . ."

Olgun gently corrected her with what could only be described as the emotional equivalent of *eleven*. Widdershins gently ignored him.

". . . and even the occasional bathhouse, gods have mercy on my eyes, seeing as how they, or at least the neighborhoods you find them in, are usually the best place to uncover your more unsavory sorts. Even tried one across town, uh . . . Kind of grungy? Caters openly and specifically to strangers to Aubier?"

"All inns cater to foreigners and strangers—" Jourdain began, but one of the others cleared his throat.

"She means the Open Door, sir. Makes a big show of being friendly to outsiders. Wide menu, lots of servant types, welcome banners for them that reads, and overcharges for the lot."

"Right," the young woman confirmed. "That one. Went there, even though the people I'm looking for are local. Found nothing. Whole *lot* of nothing. Enough nothing to choke a . . . um . . . Well, it doesn't matter *what* it would choke, because enough nothing to choke *anything* is certainly something!"

This time, the blinking from the guards and the small assembled audience was nearly enough to generate a noticeable breeze.

"I told you before," Jourdain snarled, "this business of a 'sorcerer' is rubbish. Even if it weren't, the Crows are nothing but a band of thugs. I haven't the slightest idea where to find them, and I doubt most of *them* know where they're going to be from one miserable night to the next. And Aubier *has* no organized crime. That I know of," he added, withering just a touch beneath Widdershins's incredulous and mildly contemptuous sneer.

"Uh-huh." She watched the three guards for a moment, quickly studied the growing crowd, then back to Jourdain. "And you wouldn't tell me if you knew?"

"That's entirely possible."

"Jourdain, who are the other major gangs besides the Thousand Crows?"

The guard captain could barely be bothered to shrug. "I have no idea. Most of them come and go."

"Mm-hm. So if the Crows are just another gang, the stories of a sorcerer are nonsense, and there's nothing special about them, why are *they* the ones that you—and everyone else, it seems—have heard of?"

"Chance," he snapped at her, but some of the blustery certainty had washed away.

Widdershins opened her mouth to say something else—a gesture that stretched itself into a broad smile at the sudden tingle of Olgun's magics, and the clattering and cursing as someone was "encouraged" to trip headlong over the detritus in the old apartment behind her.

Did they really *think I hadn't noticed when they sent the fourth guard away a few minutes ago?*

Meant it was time to go, though, before someone down there decided to draw again.

"Olgun?"

An answering surge of anticipation, and then Widdershins rose to her full height on the narrow ledge, offered Jourdain a jaunty wave, and leapt. The by-now familiar surge of power and the feel of a semisolid boost in midair more than allowed her to clear the gap to the window of the next apartment over; a second such surge, and she landed smoothly and securely on a stretch of wood a cat might have had difficulty crossing. Widdershins slipped through the window, made a beeline for the door, and had blended into the streets of Aubier before Jourdain and his men had so much as reached the second floor.

※

"Are you insane, woman?" The jowly tavern keep leaned over the bar—seeming almost to engulf portions of it in his grimy shirt and pudding-like flesh—to breathe some truly unique fumes into Widdershins's face. Clearly the man was not averse to sampling his own wares; he could almost certainly have cleaned the countertop of grime and stains simply by exhaling on it a time or three.

"Probably," she replied. She'd long since given up on trying to maintain the friendly smile with which she'd begun the day. All she managed now was to keep the snarl of frustrated anger from her countenance, and even with that less ambitious goal, her jaw and her back teeth ached from the effort. "But it's a simple enough question, yes?"

"You think you can just walk up to a fellow and ask something like that?" Shins found the wobbling of his fleshy face almost horrifyingly hypnotic. "You trying to get me in trouble with *both* sides of the law?"

"Oh, for the love of pastries . . . Look, I've been to about two hundred and ninety of these stupid places . . ."

Eleven, Olgun corrected again.

"At every single one of them, I've done everything but hang a sign around my neck. Tried all the signals and hand signs and slouches I learned to get the local thieves' attention, but I'm not *from* here, so I don't know the local cant and people probably just thought I was twitching from slow poison. Even picked a few pockets here and there, *almost* obviously enough for even a *city guardsman* to notice! You have any idea how hard it is to be that careless on purpose?"

Olgun mildly suggested that the barkeep probably did not, as it no doubt came far more naturally to him.

"So yes!" Her rant now teetered on a knife's edge between exasperation and simmering rage. "I barking well *am* asking you! Just point me to someone in this dungheap who can tell me what I—!"

"You need to leave, lady," the man hiding behind the jowls insisted. "Now!"

It wasn't the stares or the low mumbles of the common room's patrons, all of whom had now abandoned drink and conversation to turn her way. It wasn't even the soothing balm of Olgun's presence, which—despite his obvious efforts at calming her down—was tinged with an unmistakable anger of its own.

No, it was the barkeep's face—the quivering lip, the bulging eyes, the fearful shake of his head as he retreated from whatever it was he saw in her own twisting expression—that quenched her fury like a sudden rain.

Gods, what is wrong *with me?*

She spun and all but fled the tavern, holding her breath until she was through the door so that she couldn't accidentally utter a single word that might make things worse. She was blocks away—she didn't even know in which direction she'd turned—before she stopped shoving through the evening traffic and slowed herself long enough to think.

"Olgun?" Her whispers came between heaving breaths, gasps from exertion far more emotional than physical. "What's happening to me? I wanted to pull steel on that man!"

A flicker of imagery and emotion, reminiscent of the energies she felt anytime they worked in unison.

"But . . . it's never been like *this*," she told him. "Me being sad makes you sad which makes me sad, me being reckless makes you reckless which makes me reckless, and all that. We've known that for a while now, yes? We've both been angry before, though, and it's never made me want to . . . to . . ."

"Do you think Iruoch did something to us before we killed him? To me? He was magic; he could have infected us or something! Couldn't he?"

The deity's reply made it quite clear that, no, he did not attribute their shared anger to that murderous creature of the fae. What he *did* attribute it to, however, was a concept too complex to accurately convey in emotion and imagery. Widdershins couldn't begin to understand it.

Or maybe, she *almost* admitted to herself, she just didn't want to.

She was neither *so* distracted, however, nor so introspective, as to miss the obvious. Or even the not so obvious.

"I see them," she assured an abruptly nervous Olgun. "Three that

I've noticed. Probably at least twice that many in total, yes? Don't suppose you can tell if they're Thousand Crows or someone else?

"Well, *I* don't know how you'd know! Maybe they have tattoos or custom-brocaded smallclothes you might have spotted! I'm just asking! Oooh, you . . . Any witchcraft or sorcery, anyway?"

None, or so his answering emanations suggested. None he could *sense*, anyway, which was, after his confusion over the spreading blight on the Delacroix property, rather less reassuring than Shins might otherwise have found it.

"Another alleyway, do you think? Or maybe . . . Oh, figs . . . Olgun, is the street clearing out because it's getting dark, or do you think the good folks of the neighborhood have some idea what's coming?"

"Right. Me, neither." A quick scouring of the street, eyes flitting like a drunken moth, until . . . "There. You ready? Right. Me, neither."

A shallow grin, a slight quickening of breath, and Widdershins abruptly burst into a run, angling across the haphazardly cobbled street toward the heavy wooden structure she'd selected. The sound of pounding feet, shoving bodies, and curses rather more vicious than "figs" all conspired to inform her, in no uncertain terms, that her pursuers had abandoned any semblance of stealth.

Really hope those shutters are as flimsy as they look. . . . "Olgun?"

The air tingled and tickled appropriately in response; Widdershins took one more sprinting step, and dove.

Wooden slats split with a series of cracks, like a mouthful of broken teeth. Widdershins erupted from a cloud of splinters, a leather-clad brunette cannonball, untouched by the jagged bits save for a few shallow rents in her gloves. A second cloud, this one of dirt, erupted as she hit and rolled across the packed earthen floor. Surging back to her feet, she took in the entire structure at a glance before dashing quickly to the left.

As she'd suspected from outside on the street, she found herself in a smithy, recently used—judging by the aromas hanging in the air and the lingering warmth of the forge—but now closed up for the night. Cinder- and soot-choked hearth, which Shins was fairly certain should have been cleaned out before now; anvils of various sizes atop old wooden stumps; racks of tools, against the walls and free-standing both. One row of tools even hung high above the hearth, perhaps older implements rarely used but not yet deserving of disposal.

A step on the dirt, a second on the anvil, and again Shins was airborne. Twisting to the horizontal, she landed on the sloped chimney above the hearth, slipping beneath the dangling tools without disturbing a single handle. There, braced with one hand and one foot against the edge to keep herself from sliding, at least partly hidden by shadow and steel, she waited.

The first of her pursuers followed through the window a moment later, firing a flintlock blindly over the sill, presumably to ensure she wasn't waiting immediately to one side. He clambered through and moved toward the door, unbarring it for three more of his companions, while a fifth also availed himself of Widdershins's makeshift ingress. All were clearly typical bruisers and underground muscle. She'd met more than enough of their type in her years to recognize the breed.

Only five. Either she'd overestimated, or more waited outside in case she made a break for it. Better to assume the latter.

"A few seconds more . . ." So under her breath, nobody would have heard even had they been living in her throat at the time. "Just one more . . ."

The thugs began to fan out, pistols or brutal knives in hand, peering and poking into any obvious hiding spots. . . .

Widdershins kicked, launching herself with both her free foot and the one that had been bracing her. Both fists closed on the rack of tools, toppling it from atop the forge. Propelled by her momentum,

Olgun-augmented strength, and its own impressive weight, it ripped free of its flimsy bolts and plummeted into the room. The clatter of toppling tools, a veritable orchestra from hell, wasn't quite deafening enough to obscure the abortive scream and breaking bones of the ruffian on whom they landed.

He'd probably recover, but Shins wouldn't have wanted to be him for the next . . . ever.

Attention snared by the toppling rack, utterly unprepared for Widdershins's speed, the others might as well have been wrapped in cobweb. A handspring launched her from the heap of metal before the tools had even begun to settle. She felt her calves close around the head of the next nearest thug; a quick twist, hurling herself to the side, yanked him from his feet to bounce his head rather painfully off the closest anvil. Shins swore his eyes actually rolled in opposite directions before closing in unconsciousness.

And then there were three. . . .

She landed in a crouch, one hand on the floor, facing back the way she'd come—and facing, too, a trio of bruisers, all of whom looked very much as though they'd expected a bunny and snagged a bear.

The first to react, a scraggly beanpole of a man, raised a broadbarreled flintlock—a situation Widdershins and Olgun had faced so often she scarcely even had to whisper his name. Power surged, powder sparked, and the weapon discharged itself a heartbeat early, the lead ball gauging a chunk out of a stump before flattening itself in the wood.

Shins straightened upright and casually began slapping the dirt from her gloves as she asked, "Can we call this a night, yet, boys?"

Albeit at a much more wary pace than before, all three stepped toward her.

"Thought not," she sighed.

Widdershins jammed the toe of one boot beneath a hammer that had bounced loose from the fallen rack, kicked it up into the air, snagged it with one hand, and—with yet another boost from her own personal god—hurled it across the smithy.

At which point there were *three* thugs collapsed and bleeding, and only two still standing.

The first lunged at her, stabbing at her gut with his fighting knife. She spun past, deflecting it with the rapier she knew her opponents hadn't even seen her draw. Steel scraped on steel and she was behind him, lunging not in his direction but at the other. Circling around, clearly having planned to get behind her, he could only gawp, caught flat-footed, as the tip of her sword punched into his side. Not deep, almost certainly not enough to kill, but *more* than sufficient to put him down.

Widdershins came out of her spin, ready to parry once more, and found no need. All she saw was the sole of one boot as he fled back through the door, and that only for the barest instant before he slammed it shut behind him.

"Ha!" Widdershins knelt beside the wounded man, reached out to grab a handful of shirt to wipe his blood from her rapier. "Did all right for ourselves, didn't we, Olg—?"

A ceramic decanter, roughly the size of Widdershins's head, hurtled through the window to shatter against the stone of the hearth—and from it burst a cloud of russet dust that spread rapidly through the air of the smithy.

Shins felt as though she'd just attempted to inhale the detritus coating the inside of the forge. Her throat closed up as though someone had stuck a cork in it. Only a rasped appeal to Olgun enabled her to breathe at all; she felt the swelling fade beneath a breath of his magics, not much but just enough. Her eyes stung, beginning to tear, as did the insides of her nose and mouth. Gasping, choking, hand pressed tight to her face, she stumbled toward the door . . .

Reaching it just in time to hear something else—something that sounded very much, but not precisely, like the first ceramic projectile—disintegrate against the wood.

A musty, rotten stench, foul enough for the thief to smell despite barely breathing at all, accompanied a gooey sheen. It seeped around the wood, *through* the wood, which began visibly, if only slightly, to rot.

To rot . . . And, as though it had absorbed the moisture of a dozen autumns at once, to swell. Widdershins didn't have to hear the creak of the door against the frame to know that she wouldn't be opening it any time soon.

"Figs . . ."

Or at least, that's what she *thought* she said. It came out as such a jagged croak, even she couldn't be certain.

No choice, then. Back to the window, no matter who or what waited outside. She was staggering by the time she made it across the smithy once more. Her arms shook and threatened to give out as she hauled herself bodily over the sill. Still, when she collapsed in a heap in the road outside, huddled, hacking, vomiting, it was a relief compared to what had come before.

"Jean says we should've shot you as you came through the window." It took her a moment to register the voice. Deep, sneering, somehow slimy; if the sludge from the bed of a stagnant swamp were to suddenly speak, it might well sound like this. "But I wanted to see you for myself. See who's dumb enough to come looking for us but scary enough to put five men down. Right now, I have to say, I'm only seeing the first half."

Behind her violent coughs, Widdershins almost smiled—not at anything the stranger had said, though she was always thrilled to be underestimated, but at the faint charge running through her skin, her lungs. Now that they were out of that hellish cloud, Olgun's power should enable her to recover a *lot* faster than these people would expect. Just keep them talking a little while . . .

Blinking away the tears, she achingly raised her head.

And would have sworn, initially, that she was looking at a ghost. A big, ugly, rancid-smelling ghost.

Brock?!

But no. As her vision began to clear, Widdershins realized this very much was not the Finders' Guild enforcer who had made her life so miserable, had brutally assaulted her best friend—and whose dead body she'd seen with her own eyes a year gone by. He *was*, however, very much of a kind with the late and utterly unlamented Brock.

He was a brick wall mistakenly born into a man's body—so tall that Shins almost felt the need to take a break while looking up from his feet to his head, broad enough of shoulder to stand in yoke and haul a wagon under his own power.

His waist, however, was oddly slender for his size, his neck *just* long enough to be notably peculiar. Not a brick wall, then, she decided. The offspring of Brock and a large snake with especially poor standards.

Scattered behind him were a half dozen or so thugs and bruisers, all clearly cut from the same cloth (or perhaps burlap) as the men she'd ambushed.

"Hello," he said, smirking down at her. "I am Ivon. This is Fingerbone."

Only then did Widdershins notice the other man, standing behind Ivon—"in the lee of Ivon" would have been more apt—but ahead of the others. All she could make out was fancy clothing now gone shabby, hanging loosely from a dark-skinned body so hideously gaunt he might have inspired a skeleton to eat a loaf of bread.

And it was then she realized that what she'd mistaken for a faint ringing in her ears, perhaps caused by whatever substance they'd tossed into the smithy, was in fact this "Fingerbone," sniggering constantly through a phlegm-coated throat.

"Now that we've been gentlemanly enough to present ourselves," Ivon continued, "who the shit-soaked burbling hell are *you?*"

"Oh, yes. Very gentlemanly. Refined, even." She still sounded as though she were speaking *through* an irate bullfrog, but at least her words were intelligible again. She gave brief thought to lying, decided there was no real point. "Widdershins."

"Widder-what, now?"

"Widdershins. My name."

"What the hell kind of name is 'Widdershins'?"

She waved vaguely with one hand, allowing it to flop, appearing far more dazed and bleary than she truly was. "What kind of name is . . . um, is . . . ?"

"Fingerbone," the wall-snake-man sneered.

"Oh, no, I meant 'Ivon.'" Shins offered him a pert little smile. "By the way, are you at all bothered by the fact that you just suffocated four of your own men in there? Almost makes one question your commitment to your people, yes?"

Ivon's sneer slipped and slid into a snarl. Fingers began tapping at the hilt of the weapon slung at his waist—not a hammer, as Brock had carried, but what appeared to be a massive chopping blade, as much forester's tool as armament. If the average dagger could expect to grow up into the average sword, this was the adult form of the standard kitchen cleaver.

"Isn't lethal." Fingerbone swayed out from behind his presumed boss, his words the scratch and screech one might expect from a creature so corpse-like. Shins saw, now, that he dragged behind a decrepit wood wagon, clearly sized for a child's toy. Inside it sat a number of ceramic vessels, all similar to the one that had released the toxic powder. "Ugly, choking, tearing, gasping. But not killing." He tittered—a high, ear-grating, brain-scratching sound. "Not killing."

"Most of the time," Ivon added. "Long as you're in good health. Any of my boys dead in there, well . . . Probably weren't all that useful anyway, were they?"

"That's why the 'Thousand Crows,' then? Left that many people behind?"

She hadn't been *certain*, of course—they could have been some other gang, having caught wind of her activity—but it had seemed a fairly safe bet. Especially given the peculiar magic of the smothering dust and whatever they'd done to the smithy door. When Ivon didn't correct her, she took that as confirmation enough.

"I'm going to ask you one time," the gang leader said, all trace of false amity dropping away, fist now firmly clenched on his sword. "Then we're going to take you somewhere private and encourage you to be a little more forthcoming. Think a lot of my crows'd like it better the second way, but it's your call for another ten seconds. *Why have you been asking around about us?*"

Because my plan had been to locate and single out one of you—or knock a bunch of you silly, then single out someone who came looking *for you—and follow him back to wherever it is you loiter to figure out if you're the ones poisoning the Delacroix fields, and if so, why.* Which, while truthful, was not an answer that Widdershins felt would go over particularly well, or do her much good in the long run.

Seven-to-one odds, and she wasn't quite back to her best, yet. But she'd faced worse, and they couldn't possibly be expecting . . .

"No, we're not running!" she hissed in response to Olgun's hesitant query. "I want answers so I can get *out* of this stupid town! So . . . You ready?"

The god's answer was nervous, true, but also carried a strong sense of anticipation.

Widdershins tensed, gathering herself to move . . .

Fingerbone shrieked, something between a scream and a manic chortle. Just about as swiftly as Shins had ever seen anyone move (without divine assistance) he yanked a decanter from the wagon without even looking back at it and hurled the projectile her way.

Shins had no idea what had given her away—perhaps nothing, and the apparent madman was gifted with some lunatic insight— and for the nonce, it didn't remotely matter. Legs uncoiling like a goosed viper, she hurled herself aside just before the ceramic struck and shattered.

At the corners of her vision, as she rolled, she watched the filth-gray sludge begin to splash—and then to congeal and grow rigid, similar to hardening wax. She'd no way of knowing what the stuff *was*, but the effects were clear enough; had she been even a second slower, she'd be partly encased in it. Helpless. Likely for only a moment, until she broke her way free, but a moment with Ivon and his people was more than sufficient.

Now they were ready, knew she wasn't nearly as incapacitated as she should have been. Now the nearby doorways disgorged additional Crows, until they numbered almost thrice their starting strength. Now Ivon had his brutal chopper drawn and held aloft, and Fingerbone was already reaching for another pot.

"And then again," she murmured, "we could run."

The young thief took to her heels, through a city she didn't know, a pack of murderous thugs—and possibly one sorcerer—baying and clacking blades as they gave chase.

CHAPTER EIGHT

"All right, Olgun." So far, Shins's breath came easily despite the sprint, but at a flat-out run such as this, even with the god's aid, it wouldn't be for long. "We need to pick a destination a tad bit more specific than 'away,' yes? 'Cause we, uh . . . I think we've *reached* 'away,' and those seams of britches appear to have the same destination in mind."

Many of Aubier's roads were unnecessarily broad, the turns often gradual; a bad place in which to shake a pursuit, especially when those chasing her knew those streets *far* better than she. First Lourveaux, now this.

"Seriously, is there some patron god of footraces I was supposed to sacrifice to? Because if you can get me his name, I'll find him a goat. Or a virgin.

"Or a virgin goat."

If there *was* such a deity, Olgun appeared not to know his name either.

Thus far, the almost impossible speeds at which she ran had kept her far ahead of the Thousand Crows, and she'd lost sight of many, but she'd never managed to shake them entirely. The fastest of them, Ivon included, always seemed to appear behind her just as she began to wonder if she was finally safe. At least they hadn't opened fire, but as silver linings went, that was a thin patina indeed. The streets were now almost deserted—from the hour, the presence of the Crows, or both, Shins couldn't say. She had little doubt that the moment the risk of civilian casualties (and thus official government attention) reached an acceptable threshold, she would start to hear the thunderous retort of flintlocks.

No allies. No refuge. No crowds in which to vanish. No idea where she ought to go, or how she would get there if she did.

She'd been in worse situations, certainly. But not recently.

Her feet ached from slapping so hard against the cold-hardened earth of the roadways. Her lungs were finally starting to burn. She was quite certain she must, by this point, smell much like a mendicant who had taken a vow against bathing. And was also a baboon.

Gods, if she could just get a *minute* to catch her breath, get her bearings . . . to *think* . . .

An image—crisp, clear, specific—flashed across her mind.

"Are you . . . sure?" she asked around ever-more-frequent gasps. "The buildings here . . . aren't as—"

Olgun was *quite* sure, a fact he expressed in no uncertain lack of words.

"All right. On three . . ."

Widdershins broke right, scarcely waiting for the familiar tingle of power before leaping for a second-story windowsill. From there she cleared a narrow alley to the next structure, grabbing hold of sloped shingles, vaulting up on the roof, and leaping once more. She found herself atop the building, staring out over a large swathe of Aubier illuminated primarily by lanterns and torches in the windows below.

Olgun had, indeed, been right. While Aubier was far more spread out than Lourveaux or Davillon, the particular sequence of blocks stretching out toward the northeast were near enough to one another that Widdershins could cross most of the gaps without difficulty.

For a few moments, at least, she had a clear path—one that Ivon and the Crows could not easily follow, one that should allow her to gain some distance even if she couldn't lose them completely.

"So what the frogs and fishes *was* that?" she demanded as she set off once more, keeping to a slower pace long enough for her breathing to steady. "That . . . stuff? That powder, and waxy gunk? I've never seen magic like that."

And then, "It's *not*? So what *is* it?"

Again, Olgun proved unable to convey what he wanted to; Widdershins had the sense that he was trying to explain something he only barely understood, and for which she had no reference at all.

It was, however, a *familiar* confusion she sensed.

"Same as the blight, then?"

Uncertainty, but a sense of growing conviction.

"So, probably. All right, that's one question answered. Now we just have to live long enough to tell . . ."

Her voice trailed away, though her jaw continued to work, seemingly chewing on a new idea. Would that work? Were *they* her way out of this? Would they even still be there?

Well . . . Better than fleeing aimlessly.

Widdershins grinned shallowly, turned to face a little more east than north, and broke once more into a dead sprint.

"See? I told you they'd stay open late if we asked nicely."

Cyrille sighed, though he maintained enough self-control to avoid visibly rolling his eyes at his sister. "That wasn't my point, though, Fifi."

"Oh?" The young woman finally looked up from the ornate platter she was studying, part of the set they'd just purchased to replace a few dishes Marjolaine had smashed during the most recent of her many screaming arguments with Malgier. She was not, for a change, carrying her lantern; jaunts into town were among the few occasions where she traveled anywhere without the silly thing.

"We . . . we're Delacroix. They'd have stayed open for us whether we'd asked nicely or not. But it wasn't *polite* to ask it of them."

Fifi's whole face was a rounded mask of bewilderment. "Why?"

A second sigh, even bigger than the first. Cyrille glanced around, met Jourdain's gaze; the old guard only shrugged. The rest of the soldiers either kept looking straight ahead—the more professional ones—or scarcely smothered snickers, directed either at Fifi or at Cyrille, depending on their own opinions regarding the proper use of aristocratic authority.

"Never mind, Fifi."

"Oh, no, go ahead and explain, Cyrille." Widdershins dropped to the street directly beside the two Delacroix siblings. "Gods know nobody *else* is ever going to do it, yes?"

The next minute or so was absolute chaos: weapons clearing sheaths, guards screaming at her, Cyrille and Jourdain shouting at the guards, Cyrille and Jourdain shouting at each other. It was almost funny.

Still, the thief kept only half her attention on the fracas, peering intently over and around the madly shifting guards, Olgun's vision augmenting her own.

And there they were. Glaring at her from the shadows of the nearby streets, Ivon and several of the Thousand Crows, lips twisted in frustrated fury. As she'd hoped, then—they outnumbered the guards, but the Crows weren't *about* to risk an open attack on a cadre of House soldiers.

Satisfied she was safe, at least for the moment, she returned her focus fully to those around her.

Um . . . Safe from the Crows, *at any rate*, she amended.

None of the blades or pistols were currently pointed directly at her, but neither had they been put away. All the guards were silent, now, glaring her way; the only voices left were Cyrille's and Jourdain's.

"If you two gentlemen could stop fighting over me for a bit, perhaps we can discuss this like rational adults?"

Two gaping jaws turned her way. She shrugged.

"At least *similar* to rational adults? I know I've met one or two at *some* point. I think I can fake it."

"How do I know you're not here to harm Cyrille or Josephine?" Jourdain demanded, his mustache practically bristling.

"Um, because I didn't harm Cyrille or Josephine? Despite appearing right next to them in what would have to be the most salmon-headed assassination attempt in history?

"Besides, you know better than that, after the other night."

"Do I?"

"Oh, of course you do!" Cyrille finally broke in. "Would all of you *please* put your damn swords away? She's not going to hurt anyone. And I'm assuming," he added, "that this is important if she was willing to risk having to beat the stuffing out of the lot of you, so maybe we should hear her out?"

Widdershins smile was a weak one as resentment flickered over the faces of the armsmen. "Cyrille? Stop being on my side."

He looked perplexed, perhaps even hurt, but Jourdain's irate façade cracked in a faint chuckle, despite his obvious strain to prevent it. A bit of tension fled from the assembled guards, breath coming easier, shoulders starting to relax . . .

"Is this the girl Mother got *so* angry at you for helping?" Fifi asked nervously.

Every one of the armsmen, Jourdain included, went rigid, exchanging swift glances before their gazes turned icy. Cyrille's shoulders visibly slumped.

"She has a point," Jourdain told them, once again all business. "I really think we need to take this young woman to see Lady Delacroix."

Boots and armor creaked as the guards shifted, ready to take hold of either Widdershins or their weapons, as needed. Shins tensed, unsure of what her next move should be but prepared to make it all the same.

"No."

Widdershins gawped at Cyrille, and she very much was not the only one.

"You cannot countermand your mother's orders—" the elder guardsman began.

"I'm not. None of your orders were to take Widdershins prisoner—illegally, I might add. You were to find out what she's up to. I'd hazard a guess that hearing her out would tell us more of that than trying—and I do stress *trying*—to hold her against her will."

"I'm starting to think he's not that dim after all," Shins whispered to Olgun.

"Cyrille . . ." Jourdain tried again.

"We are going to get off the street," the young Delacroix continued. "Perhaps to one of our properties in town. And we are going to discuss this . . ." He grinned sidelong at Widdershins. ". . . *somewhat* like rational adults."

Jourdain's face had enough expressions for any four other men. The rest of the guards, and Josephine, just looked confused. Again. "I really think we need Lady Delacroix's instruction . . ." he muttered, as uncertain as Widdershins, at least, had ever heard him.

"Fine," Cyrille snapped. "You need to go home, go. Take Fifi. Widdershins and I will talk."

"I can't leave you in town unprotected!"

"Well, then, you seem to have a decision to make. Please do so quickly."

Shins whispered so only her divine partner might hear, "I had no idea he had that in him. Seemed a little more like a puppy that first night, yes?"

And then, with a series of bewildered blinks, "Me? Don't be silly! Why the happy horses would he care about impressing *me*?"

Whatever answer Olgun might have offered, if any, was interrupted by the conclusion of the ongoing argument. Jourdain and half the guards would return to the manor with Fifi in tow; the others would accompany Cyrille. Confused as a bat in a bakery, Fifi watched her brother over her shoulder until the lot of them were out of sight.

"So, where are we going?" Widdershins asked brightly. "Hideout? Bolt-hole? Sanctum? I've always wanted to see a sanctum."

"Uh . . . No, I . . . That is, my family owns several properties in Aubier. We lease them to vendors or craftsman, for shops and apartments. Pretty sure there are a few who aren't using the apartments, so . . ."

"Oh. That'll do, I suppose. How come nobody ever has a sanctum?"

They passed several blocks, seemingly the only traffic in the road this late. The back of Widdershins's scalp itched, and she swore she saw Crows lurking everywhere, but no trouble manifested. The guards, clearly uncomfortable with the situation, remained silent, so it fell to Cyrille and Shins herself to hold the silence at bay—which she did by asking questions about Aubier at speeds that threatened to shake her lips loose from her face, and by occasionally allowing her native guide enough time to answer.

". . . mostly run by the Houses working together," he explained. "No real baron or mayor or anything. Just a reeve, and he's really more of a symbolic tradition. Most of the government is, well, us . . ."

"The castle? Pauvril. Castle Pauvril. Baronial seat when there *was* a baron, generations ago. Now, it's mostly left alone, except for the occasional ceremony or big house meeting . . ."

"No, not really growing anymore. We're still on some major trade routes, but not as many as we used to be, not since things got tense with Rannanti again. It's not going to wither anytime soon— well, assuming the damn blight doesn't spread—but we're all pretty sure Aubier's done expanding. It's one of the reasons competition between Houses has gotten fiercer lately . . ."

"Uh . . . We do have a lot of them, given Aubier's size. I guess because we *are* on trade routes, and because Aubier's sort of the cultural center of the Outer Hespelene. But I don't think there's actually two hundred and ninety-one of them."

Twelve, Olgun corrected gleefully.

And so it went, until Cyrille suggested they had reached their destination. It wasn't much—a rough wooden building no different than any of the others nearby. Downstairs was a small shop, selling paper, parchment, and canvas; inks and paints; brushes and quills; anything to do with calligraphy, art, or otherwise leaving colorful stains on flimsy surfaces. Not a lot of demand for such things in any but the richest neighborhoods of Aubier, but apparently the proprietor had *just* enough custom from a handful of regulars to remain in business.

Or so the young Delacroix explained. All Widdershins could tell for certain was that the place was tightly shuttered and smelled of turpentine.

"The proprietor lives with his sister, in a room over *her* shop," Cyrille continued. "So he pays us rent on only the lower floor. The upper's empty. After you, m'lady."

Shins managed to turn away before smirking at the boy's clumsy flattery, and preceded him up the narrow stairs that climbed the side of the building. It was only when they reached a small landing and Cyrille began to reach for the latch that he abruptly froze.

"Um . . ." Even in the dim light of the sporadic streetlamps, Shins could see his cheeks flush a shade of red that would have been the envy of any apple. "I, uh . . ."

It took everything the young thief had not to slap herself in the forehead so hard that the guards behind her would feel it. "You don't actually have a key, do you?"

"Well, I hadn't expected to . . . I didn't think . . ."

"Oh, for the love of pastries. Move over." Shins dropped to a knee by the lock, slipped a wire from inside her belt, muttered a request for better night vision—which Olgun readily obliged—and had the door open in under a minute.

"After you," she said brightly.

"Thank you . . ."

The poor boy sounded so *crushed*. "I feel like I just kicked a kitten," Widdershins admitted to Olgun.

She managed to swallow a giggle at the god's response—an intense image of Cyrille with whiskers and fur-tufted ears, propelled into the air by the tip of Shins's boot to his rear—but it was a near thing.

It became a bit easier when she stepped into a room so dusty a single good sneeze would make the place almost as suffocating as the Thousand Crow's unnatural powder. As it was, she began to cough, until Olgun was able to soothe her already-inflamed throat just enough.

"Be fine," she croaked in response to Cyrille's worried glance. "Just . . . stuffy in here, yes?" She made an exaggerated point of examining the space around her. "Also cramped. How friendly are you with your guards?"

Indeed, though the room was devoid of furniture—save for a rickety stool and a bed with a mattress that looked about as firm and supportive as peat—it wouldn't hold more than two at all comfortably, and no more than thrice that number unless they were prepared to lean on one another and possibly synchronize their breathing.

Shins slumped onto the stool—she didn't entirely trust the mattress not to either swallow her whole or seep into her clothes—and proceeded to ignore the inevitable argument occurring in the doorway. The guards didn't trust her, were hesitant to leave Cyrille alone with her, were worried of what might happen if Jourdain found out they'd done so, and were positively terrified of what might happen if Lady Delacroix discovered same.

When all was said—and shouted—and done, however, the bottom line was that Cyrille Delacroix was one of their employers. Perhaps his orders were subordinate to almost every other member of the family's, perhaps it was an authority they were unaccustomed to him exercising, but the fact remained that if he told them to wait outside, that's what they were bound to do.

By the time Cyrille had slammed the door and turned back her way, Widdershins had ditched her ragged cloak and worn gloves, tossing both over the headboard where they hopefully dangled out of reach of the mattress that, to her mind, was looking hungrier by the moment. Her rapier stood against the wall, within easy reach. She prodded gingerly at herself, checking the various lacerations and bruises she'd acquired over the course of the evening. Nothing serious—with Olgun's aid, they ought to have all but faded completely by morning—but still, better to check.

Especially when she still hadn't the first idea what else, if anything, that choking cloud might have done to her.

"All right, Widdershins." Cyrille stepped around her and planted himself on the bed; if he mistrusted the thing at all, he showed no sign of it. His attentions seemed locked on her. "What the hell's going on?"

She told him, minus a few—read: any—personal details, only sporadically interrupted by her gradually easing cough. Her eavesdropping on the family conversation, her failure to find any proof of Carnot complicity, her earlier conversation with Jourdain, her search through two hundred and ninety-one (*twelve*) taverns and inns for any sign of the Thousand Crows.

And, of course, her battle and near escape when the Crows found her, as well as her near certainty that the strange magic they'd employed against her was related to the blights afflicting Delacroix lands.

"But you're still not going to tell me *why* you want to help us, are you?" Cyrille asked, almost pouting.

She shook her head, flexing her right elbow as she squeezed with her other hand, trying to work out a bit of stiffness. "Personal reasons," she said.

"You know, it'd be easier to convince Mother of your sincerity if I had *some* idea why—"

"Personal! Reasons!"

"Fine!" The wood of the bed frame squeaked a bit as he almost violently crossed his arms. He'd had to have stuck his tongue out to appear any more petulant; Widdershins couldn't decide if she wanted to laugh or smack him on the back of his head.

Boys. No wonder I fell for someone older, like Julien. . . .

The thought was a fist, one that nearly sent her reeling from her seat. It wasn't the first time she'd thought of the young guardsman since she'd left Davillon, not even remotely. But she honestly couldn't recall if she'd ever, until that moment, actually described her affection to herself, actually put any words to how she had felt, *still* felt . . .

"How do you do it?"

"I . . . What?" It took an effort to drag herself back from the recesses of her mind, to look once more through her own eyes at the room in which she sat, and the young aristocrat who'd just spoken. She actually envisioned herself reaching out, snagging his question like a lifeline. "Do what?"

"Everything you do. I've never seen anyone move the way you do, fight the way you do. Cevora's sake, I've never even *heard* of it, outside a few legends!"

He failed to notice her brief shudder at his invocation of Cevora.

"It's sure as hell not just special training," he continued. "The human body can't do that. Not, uh, even one as impressive . . ." The sentence trailed off into an inaudible mumble.

And Olgun pinch her if she wasn't seriously tempted. It'd be so nice, after all this time, to have someone she could *truly* talk to about everything. She hadn't realized, until her brief visit with Brother Maurice, how much she missed that. Maybe even needed it.

For all that, she couldn't do it. How well did she truly know Cyrille? When push came to shove, if it truly came down to deciding between his family or her, which way would he jump? How devout was his devotion to Cevora and the rest of the Hallowed Pact? Would he even *believe* her?

Or might he believe too much? Would his first true experience with divinity be enough to inspire worship? Would she lose her unique bond to Olgun when she most desperately needed him?

She'd tried to share her faith once before, with Robin, and failed. She knew she should do so again, knew that he was as mortal as she so long as he had only a single worshipper. But this . . . This wasn't the right time. It couldn't be.

She needed it not to be.

"Sacred ritual," she not *quite* lied, "with an element of genuine mysticism. From when I was younger."

"You're not serious!" Cyrille's incredulity practically left imprints on the dusty floor. "Are you serious?"

The thief shrugged. "You asked."

"But . . . Who? Why? How? Why you?"

Again she could only envision the man who'd taken her in, who'd changed her entire world, who'd introduced her into the sect of the god who now traveled everywhere at her side. "Family," she said simply.

To that, the young Delacroix scion nodded in understanding, and pressed no further.

"Widdershins . . ." he began hesitantly, after a bit of silence.

"Shins is fine," she muttered absently, thoughts and plans for her next step ricocheting through her skull, a barrage of mental ammunition.

"Uh, all right. Shins . . ." Was Cyrille nervous? He sure looked it, rolling a fold of the mattress fabric between his fingers and scuffing the toe of one boot on the floor, but for the life of her the young woman couldn't begin to guess why. "So, um . . . I haven't, we haven't known each other very long, but—"

"Shh!" Widdershins's hand shot up, gesturing for silence.

The aristocrat actually recoiled. "What? You could at least hear—!"

But Shins was focused on something else entirely, the faint scrape of movement Olgun had directed to her ears. "I said *hush!*"

This time, Cyrille recognized the warning in her voice. Or maybe it was the fact that she was quietly reaching for the sword beside her stool.

"How loyal are your household guards?" she whispered.

"Completely." Cyrille's fist closed on the hilt of his own weapon. "They'd lay down their lives for the family. Uh . . . Why do you ask?"

Shins didn't need Olgun's enhancement any longer; she could hear it quite clearly on her own.

"Because we never heard a single shout or trace of combat," she told him calmly, "and there are at least a dozen pairs of boots tromping up those steps outside."

CHAPTER NINE

"So what do we do?" Cyrille's words were too steady, almost monotonous. It was clearly either that or let them shake uncontrollably. Shins found herself just a tiny bit impressed; it was more than some experienced fighters could have done. "Out the window, maybe?"

She glanced at the tiny thing, rickety shutters in a wan, warped frame, and shook her head. They could probably both slip through it, but sliding smoothly from that to climbing the wall outside . . . Well, it wasn't *too* far down, but she still wasn't especially optimistic about Cyrille's odds.

"It's a narrow doorway," she observed, her own voice rising to be heard over the increasingly loud juddering of the stairs. "I can hold off a good number of people, if you're ready to take any who get past me, yes?"

"Uh . . . 'Take' . . . ? I'm not sure—"

"And assuming they don't just open fire, of course," she continued. "Or *light* a fire, for that matter. This whole building feels like the kind of wood you'd use if you were having trouble lighting kindling."

"Gghlrrk!" Cyrille informed her.

"Hopefully they won't want to go that far. Otherwise, we'll have to risk the win—"

Voices wafted to Widdershins's ears, hauled from the maelstrom of boots and creaking steps in Olgun's grasp. The thief briefly sagged, then drew herself fully erect.

"Or," she said, striding toward the door, hand reaching for the knob, "we can just let them in and get this over with. Had to happen eventually, yes?"

"Who . . . What are you *talking* about?" Cyrille might not be on the edge of panic, but he was certainly edging out toward the face of the cliff.

"Jourdain must have sent one of his men ahead at a full gallop for this to happen so quickly. Your mother's here."

"Oh." A pause, long enough for Shins's hand to fall on the latch, start to turn. "Is it too late to go back to the 'being set on fire' option?"

Widdershins flashed him an impish grin, yanked the door open, and leapt back, hands held *well* away from her sides—and any weapons, concealed or otherwise, she might attempt to draw. The first of the Delacroix guards, who had apparently been preparing to put his shoulder to the door, blinked in puzzlement as a handful of others flooded in around him.

Or rather, attempted to. The rather intimate confines of the room capped that "handful" at two, if they had any intention whatsoever of brandishing swords. The pair seemed a bit uncertain now that they were here; others milled about on the steps or the small landing, trying to peer inside and wondering how to make themselves useful.

It was, all in all, assuredly not the household soldiers' finest moment. It was only her understanding of how much worse it would make her circumstances that kept Widdershins from laughing outright.

The fact that Olgun *was* doing so, or at least the emotional equivalent, didn't make it any easier.

When the gruff bark of Jourdain's orders burst through the doorway, accompanied by a waft of expensive perfume strong enough to overpower the miasma of leather, oiled steel, and sweat, Widdershins's mirth turned to vinegar. She knew what was coming.

Guards snapped to attention, pushing themselves against the outer wall or banister to provide a pathway for their captain, Jourdain—and for their employer and matriarch, Calanthe Delacroix.

She was garbed in a fashionable full skirt and colorful blouse, but the leather jerkin she wore over it was clearly no mere accessory, and she held a gold-filigreed flintlock very much as one who knew how to use it.

One of the two guards in the room stepped—squeezed—out, so Jourdain could take his place. The Lady Delacroix remained on the landing, framed in the doorway. Her expression might well have inspired a snowman to put on a coat.

"Are you well, Cyrille?"

In her life, Shins had personally encountered not one, but two utterly inhuman creatures out of the depths of nightmare. The matriarch's voice, in that moment, was very nearly as disturbing.

"Mother, Widdershins isn't here to—"

"I don't want to hear that name out of your mouth again."

"But—"

"I asked you a question, boy."

Cyrille, without the slightest slump of his shoulders or exhalation of breath, somehow managed to convey the distinct impression of a sigh. "Yes, Mother. I'm perfectly fine."

"Good. If I hear one more word out of you before we return to the house, you will regret it for *weeks*."

No mere impression, this time. Cyrille gasped openly, his cheeks going red, the rest of his face corpse-pale. His lips moved soundlessly, first toward his mother, then Widdershins. Finally he stepped back, as near to the far corner as he could without actually cramming himself into it, his gaze downcast.

"My lady," Shins began, drawing on everything she'd learned in her days both as, and then imitating, an aristocrat, "I can assure you, your son did nothing—"

The rest of the sentence was crushed beneath a strange, shocked gurgling noise as the matriarch's pistol rose sharply, gaping at Widdershins's head. She felt something from Olgun somewhere between a startled yelp and an angry growl. Even the Delacroix guards, Jourdain included, drew back half a step.

"I should put you down right here," the older woman hissed, "as I would any other stray to come sniffing about where it's not welcome."

"Mother, no!" Cyrille had either forgotten or ceased to care about her earlier threat. At the same time, Jourdain began, "My lady, I'm not so certain—"

"Were you truly foolish enough to believe," she demanded, "that you would be permitted to interfere with this family without repercussion?"

"I'm not interfering with your stupid family! I'm trying to *help* you! Which," she added more softly, "I suppose *is* interfering, by strict definition, but—"

Cyrille and Jourdain both stared at her as though she'd sneezed an elk.

"*Even* if that's true," the matriarch interrupted, "and I'm not remotely convinced of it, so what? Do you think we can't see through you?" Then, with a withering glower at her son, "Most of us, anyway."

"See through . . . What?"

"A common trollop." The scorn was a cocoon around Calanthe's words, thick, nearly obscuring. "Were you hoping for coin? Perhaps Cyrille's hand, or that of one of my other sons? For what? Was a useless offer of assistance with a problem you cannot possibly comprehend supposed to make us overlook your lower birth and lower character? Feeble, even as such schemes go."

"You arrogant . . . ungrateful . . ." The blood pounding in Widdershins's temples was a war prayer, a furious call to violence. Every bit of calm and control she'd fought for over the past weeks evaporated in a single puff; she felt Olgun's rage burning alongside her own, the overlapping whole threatening to consume her. She wanted desperately to lash out, to draw steel across flesh and through blood. Anything to wipe the condescension off that woman's face, out of her tone. . . .

Even get yourself killed in the process?

She almost didn't care, all but ignored that faintest voice of reason in the back of her head, a voice she *almost* recognized. . . .

And get Olgun killed, too?

Her surroundings, the entire room, became ice water. "No . . ."

Then don't. Gentle, yet stern; refined, but in no way snooty. No surprise, she realized, that her conscience might select *his* voice, out of all the possibilities. And no surprise that, though he would no doubt be disappointed in the behavior of his distant cousins, he'd be even more so if Widdershins allowed them, or anyone else, to make her into something lesser than she was.

For him, she reminded herself, this time thinking in her own voice. *You're here for him, not for them.*

She could not begin to guess how long the internal tug-of-war had taken, but it couldn't have been all that long. When she blinked herself back to the room, seeing reality as it was rather than through a haze of crimson, nobody's expression had shifted. Calanthe glared, clearly awaiting the end of Widdershins's insult.

The thief, instead, crossed her arms and glared right back.

It was not the response the matriarch wanted, apparently, though Widdershins couldn't imagine what *would* have been. "Jourdain!"

"Yes, my lady!"

"I want this . . . *vagabond* in chains!"

It was Shins, this time—clinging to the memory of Alexandre by her soul's fingernails—working to calm Olgun's thunderburst of fury. "No." Whispered, words barely even dripping from her lips. "Not yet . . . Patience . . ."

"Uh, my lady . . ." The guardsman, grown old and experienced in his work, actually sounded nervous. "I'm not sure we have the legal—"

"Oh, for Cevora's . . . Act in your capacity as law enforcement, not household guard! You *do* have that authority, even when it's not our House's turn to provide the reeve's manpower. Unless you're about to try to explain that you understand city law better than I?"

"No, of course not, my lady. But—"

"Abduction and assault of one of the nobility."

"Mother!" Cyrille's cry was high, almost boyish. "She did no such—"

"I said *silence*! Trespassing on Delacroix lands. And on suspicion, at least, of being involved in the attacks on our House. To start with."

Jourdain frowned, mustache crinkling, but stepped forward, hand outstretched . . .

Cyrille crossed the tiny room in two running steps to stand between the thief and the guard. "No! Gods damn it, she didn't—"

For the first time, Calanthe's anger traveled in harness with a growing uncertainty. "Cyrille! Stop this at once!"

"No, Mother."

In spite of everything, Shins found herself chuckling at the twin expressions of utter shock on both the Delacroix's faces, one at hearing such a thing, one at saying it.

"Jourdain, kindly prevent my son from doing himself any further injury." The order was no less forceful, for all that it trembled around the edges.

The two armsmen advanced, the misgiving obvious in their expressions showing not one whit in their posture or their movement.

At the very least, the boy wasn't foolish enough to draw steel. His first punch connected with the younger guard's chin, sending him staggering, more shocked than pained. Yet Jourdain was on Cyrille before he'd even recovered from the swing, arms winding about the aristocrat's own arms and neck in what must have been a painful, but presumably undamaging, wrestler's hold.

And Shins knew *precisely* what she needed to do.

"Trust me," she whispered, for all she knew Olgun would never do otherwise, then lunged for the grappling pair.

Slowly, clumsily—at least for her.

The soldier Cyrille had struck grabbed her from behind, just as she'd figured he would. She thrashed, kicked, put on what she hoped was a believable show—all the while, her hands fluttering behind her back, fingers dancing unseen and unfelt along the armsman's belt.

Yes, that'll do. . . .

It took, all told, less than a minute until Cyrille and Shins were both held fast—or, in the latter case, *apparently* held fast—before the matriarch.

"Well done," the woman said, her tone once again iron. "Take them both back to the manor, and—"

"Apologies, my lady. I can't do that."

Cyrille would have had to twist his neck enough to make an owl wince to stare at Jourdain, but that certainly didn't stop the others.

"I beg your pardon?"

"As you ordered, I've placed Widdershins under arrest in my capacity as a servant of Aubier. That means I'm legally bound to turn her over to the reeve for imprisonment and trial."

"This doesn't concern her!" If a particularly dignified possum ever began to lose its patience, Shins imagined it would sound something like the matriarch in that moment. "I've given you your instructions!"

"I'm sorry, truly. But it does, now—and I, with utmost regret, cannot obey."

Widdershins hoped, for Cyrille's sake, that his mother didn't catch the slight twitching of his lips at her obvious discombobulation.

After a moment of fierce—and blatantly obvious—inner battle, Calanthe shook her head. "Fine. Turn her over for now. I'll discuss specifics with Veroche tomorrow. Make sure Cyrille gets home and *stays* home until I've the opportunity to deal with him."

The swirl of her skirt as she spun might have been more dramatic had the hem not slapped against the ankles of three different guards in the process. She pushed past her men toward the steps, and was gone from view.

A handful of the guards hustled Cyrille along on her heels. He had time for only a single plaintive look at Widdershins before he, too, was gone.

Jourdain studied the prisoner for a long moment, his expression unreadable. Then, "Search her. She's a tricky one." Somewhat more softly, "I do apologize. My men will be professional."

"No worries," she told him brightly. "I've been groped under cover of authority before. Besides . . ." Her smile widened, her face lit up even further. "If I feel any hands where they shouldn't be, I'll break them. Twice."

The men started to snicker, then stopped when it became very clear that Jourdain wasn't joining them.

"See?" she told them. "Ask your boss if I can do it, yes?"

Jourdain nodded slowly. "I do believe she can. And if she has need to, I do believe I'll let her. Now make this quick."

It was, indeed, quick. And thorough.

And very, very polite.

They took from her not only her rapier and the obvious tools on her belt, but the belt itself, the picks hidden in her gloves, her gloves themselves, a small file hidden in her boot, and her cloak.

"Be careful with that sword, please," she requested. "It was handed down to me by some guy who wanted to kill me with it."

In the end, they had everything that could possibly have doubled as either a weapon or a tool. Widdershins, in turn, had leaned back into the man holding her and snapped one of the many decorative bits off his employer-provided belt—one she'd pinpointed earlier, during her imperceptible examination. A roughly shaped lion of copper, it wasn't much, but Shins—and Olgun—didn't need much. It vanished up one sleeve, where the armsmen had already searched, and sat snugly against her skin as they gathered up her belongings and began marching her across Aubier once again.

✾

"As gaols go, I have to say we've been in better." Shins followed up with a clucking *tsk-tsk* sound.

Olgun grumbled something empathically.

"Well, yes, but it's the *principle* of the thing! Where's the challenge in breaking out of a place like this? Where's the fun in complaining that there's nobody I can brag to about it if it's not worth wishing I could brag about?"

Olgun either agreed with that logic or—more likely—abruptly had to find somewhere to lie down and let the dizziness pass. Either way, no response proved forthcoming, and Widdershins returned her attention to the rather underwrought "prison" around her.

The gaol was a simple open building, attached to the offices, archives, and meeting chambers of those few members of city government who were not also people of influence in a noble House. Crude, to say the least, it consisted of a few tables and chairs for the constables on duty, some padlocked chests for prisoners' belongings, and of course the cells themselves. These latter ran along the length of one wall, separated from the guards' area and from one another by thick, iron bars. Each cell contained only a wooden cot with a moth-eaten blanket, and a chamber pot that had apparently been cleaned by the expedient method of showing it running water from afar.

There *had* to be some other prison in Aubier, something more secure and *certainly* larger. Perhaps this was simply a way station for people on the way there, or to trial? At the moment, small as it might be, this one was almost empty. Other than Shins herself—and Olgun, if he counted—the only other inmate was a scrawny, slovenly fellow two cells down, flopped bonelessly on his cot and making sounds not unlike a hog gobbling up a small foundry. The sour reek of alcohol was almost overpowering even from here. Anyone actually in the cell with him would most probably be drunk from the fumes alone.

Widdershins was uncertain just how long she'd been here, as she'd taken the opportunity to catch up on some missing sleep. She knew it had been hours, though; could tell both by the sunlight streaming in through the narrow, barred window, and by the single constable sitting at the table and idly doodling on the wood with a stick of charcoal. He had not been on duty when she arrived, was not one of the Delacroix armsmen or anyone she'd seen before.

"When's lunch?" she called cheerfully. "And is there a menu?"

The guard looked up and over. "At lunchtime. And yes, you have a selection of two options today: Take it or leave it."

"Aww, I just had those for dinner last night."

He quickly turned away, but not before she spotted the chuckle peering out from behind his teeth.

"All right, Olgun, what do you think? Wait until nightfall, yes? If they've changed shifts by then, the new guard might be more alert, but—"

"'ey! I know you!"

Even had the drunk not been the only other person present, even if she hadn't glanced over her shoulder to see his face pressed against and between the bars of his own cell, she'd have had no difficulty figuring out who'd addressed her.

"Could you breathe in the other direction?" she asked him. "My eyes are watering, my throat stings, and I'm pretty sure at least one of my teeth is melting as we speak."

A few bleary blinks—and even those appeared to tax the fellow's remaining coordination—and then, "Huh?"

"Never mind. No, I don't think we've met. If we had, I'd *still* be having difficulty breathing and a hangover."

"Yeah!" If he shoved his face any farther between the bars, Shins was certain his eyes would pop out and soar across the room. "You're the girl ashk—asking about the Thoushand Crows! We're shu—supposed to-to keep a lookout for you!"

"Oh. Well, here I am. Better go report me, yes?"

"Right!"

He blinked again and proceeded, with some alacrity, to stay precisely where he was.

"Olgun? That thing you do, where I hear or see a little better than normal? Does that work with the other senses, and can you reverse it?"

A particularly peculiar tingle—she felt as though she could almost smell it, as opposed to merely feeling—and the rancid aroma faded to only somewhat nauseating levels.

"Thank you *so* much." Then, more loudly, "So you've got your ear to the street, yes? You know what's what, and who's who, and when's when?"

Vigorous nodding, only mildly confused. At one point, he thumped his head against the iron hard enough for the bar to ring, but he didn't even notice. "Yeah, I do. When'm not in here, anyways. . . ."

"Oooh . . ." Had she forced any more sycophantic awe, her voice might well have offered to go fetch her a drink. "And you were supposed to tell the Crows about me?"

"All are," he said, chest puffing out. "Anyone who sees you. Maline wantsh you pretty bad . . ."

"Maline?"

"Ivon Maline. Boss."

Shins nodded. "I didn't know that," she cooed.

The drunkard's chest puffed up farther still—but only for a moment, until he remembered he still had to breathe.

"And how were you supposed to tell the Crows about me? I guess a fellow like you must have a standing invite to their headquarters, yes?"

"Don't think they have one," he admitted, "'cept for whatever member's flat they're meeting at this week. Naw, just go to one of the plashes—places they go to drink. Find one if I know him, otherwishe let 'em find me. Always do seem to know when I got shomething good to tell 'em."

"Like magic? Everyone tells stories . . ."

"What, Fingerbone? Shcarecrow-looking freak, that one. Nah, no magic. Achemly."

It was, finally, Widdershins's turn for a bit of confused blinking. "What?"

"Achemly," he repeated firmly.

The young woman's mind whirled, stretching back to what little formal education she'd received under Alexandre Delacroix. A word, a term, something she'd come across in passing while studying histories and largely ignored.

"You mean 'alchemy'?" she asked eventually.

"That'sh what I said! Achemly! Deaf doxy . . ."

Shins slumped down on the cot, chin resting on one fist, struggling to dredge it all up. "Why the happy hopping hens didn't I pay more attention to the tutors? Don't even *think* about answering that, or I'll tell Calanthe Delacroix about you. Wouldn't it be fun being *their* household patron?"

She would have assumed it required an actual corporeal body to shudder, but Olgun made a pretty good show of it anyway.

"All right, so . . ." Whether it was speaking aloud or Olgun nudging at her thoughts, it slowly began to come back. "It's an old, old practice, yes? Science right on the cusp of magic? Cauldrons and tubes and boiling sludge. Acids and preservatives, poisons and cures, changing lead into gold and flesh into stone, all that." She paused. "Is *that* what you were trying to explain to me? The blight on Delacroix lands and that choking stuff in the smithy? That was all alchemy?"

The god offered up a tentative, uncertain yes.

"Nobody practices that anymore," Shins muttered. "I *know* I read that. That's why it was in a history treatise. So what the figs is a gang of common cutthroats at the rear end of civilization doing with it?"

If Olgun didn't require a body with which to shudder, he most assuredly didn't need one in order to shrug.

"Fat lot of help you are. All right, patience." She leaned back against the cell's only true wall, softly scraping the copper adornment over the stone, gradually mashing it into a thinner, more useful shape. "Picking the lock should be simple enough. We just need to watch for our chance . . ."

In point of fact, they *didn't* need to watch for their chance, for it was only a few hours later when . . .

"What do you mean, 'free to go'?!"

It was a middle-aged woman to whom that incredulous—and rather shrill—question was directed. Her graying hair was tied back in a tight bun, making a very avian face appear sharper still; the leather jerkin, pale tabard, and rapier all marked her as a soldier or duelist of some sort.

She raised an eyebrow, now, even as she gestured for the guard at the table to fetch her the keys. "Welcome to leave? No longer under arrest? Seems fairly clear to me."

"But . . . But . . ." Widdershins flailed a hand helplessly, feeling strangely cheated. *All that work on this stupid little decoration!*

"Did you particularly want to stay?"

Shins sighed. "No. No, I didn't."

"Well, then."

The guard appeared, handing over a ring of keys. The older woman began flipping through them, occasionally glancing back at the lock.

"Why am I being released?" the soon-to-be ex-prisoner inquired. "Isn't this going to get you in trouble? Who are you? What about Lady Delacroix? When—?"

"Gods, girl! Do you ever stop talking?"

"I don't make a habit of it, no."

Keys clattered. "My name is Rosselin Veroche. I serve as reeve for Aubier."

"Reeve?" Shins had heard the term earlier but wasn't familiar with it.

"Ah . . ." Veroche chose one key, held it up to the light, then inserted it into the latch. "Mayor, speaker, chief constable . . . To an extent. All the duties, precious little of the authority."

The lock *thunked*, and the door of bars opened on screeching hinges.

The thief rose from her cot, stretched, and stepped from the cell. "I think you got the raw end of that deal, yes?"

The reeve smiled faintly, then called over her shoulder. "Fetch the young woman's possessions, would you?" She tossed the keys back to the other constable, who began sorting through them as she had done. "Look, Mademoiselle . . . Ah, 'Widdershins'? Truly?"

"It's a name."

"Very well. Widdershins, I've spoken at length to m'Lady Delacroix—and to her guard captain, well beyond his mistress's hearing. As I understand it, her objections to you are largely personal. There is no evidence against you of any of her accusations—beyond trespassing—and her own son is likely to make a statement supporting your version of events?"

"Um . . . I guess?"

"I trust Jourdain. We've served together." The lid of one wooden chest clattered open, revealing Widdershins's belongings. "I don't know what in the names of the Pact is happening in Galice, but nobody's keeping the Houses in check. They used to at least be subtle; now they just throw their weight around without a care. Frankly, I have more important things to do with my time and resources than hold you and try you in pursuit of some blue blood's vendetta."

"Why are you telling me this?"

The guardsman across the room snorted softly. "She tells everyone."

Veroche tossed him a glare she clearly didn't mean. "It's not a secret how I feel. I expect I'll no longer hold this post after the next House gathering. Until then . . ."

Shins nodded, gathering her stuff. She noted that her rapier had been peacebonded—tied in its scabbard—with a thin leather cord. It'd be easy enough to unravel, but it meant she couldn't immediately draw the blade or turn on her former jailers.

"Guess not every guest is as satisfied with their stay as we are," she murmured to Olgun. More loudly, she continued, "Well, I certainly appreciate it. Thanks so much, I'll just be—"

"Leaving Aubier," the reeve interjected.

"Um, that's not precisely what I was about to—"

"Yes, it is. I've enough trouble in my city, Widdershins, and you are very clearly a magnet for it."

"Oh, sure, blame the victim!"

Veroche was clearly unwilling to be sidetracked. She leaned one shoulder against the bars, though Shins couldn't imagine how that was a comfortable posture. "You've seriously angered one of our most powerful noble Houses and put me in a position to irritate them in the process. You have at least one of the thief gangs after you, do you not?"

"Thousand Crows," Shins muttered.

"Figures. They've been everywhere, past few months. That sort of trouble, neither of us needs. So, for both our sakes—and because your other option is back in that cell—you are to head straight from here to the road. You may stop to purchase supplies, if you require. Other than that, get out of Aubier, and kindly take as many of your troubles as you can with you."

"All right, all right, fine!" The younger woman finished strapping on her sword belt and whirled her cloak over her shoulders. "Anything else? Am I allowed to breathe your air on the way? Should I check my boots, make sure I'm not stealing any of Aubier's dirt or snow?"

This time, she was fairly sure that Veroche meant every bit of the glare crinkling her face. "Go with her," she ordered the guardsman, who had slunk back to the table in an apparent bid to be forgotten. "Escort her to the edge of town and make sure she keeps going."

He nodded glumly, rose again from his chair, and moved to stand beside Widdershins. "Sorry."

"Eh. Not your fault." Shins pushed the door open, stepped out into the bright but blustery winter day. "What's your name?" she asked, more out of habit than real interest.

"Alexandre."

"Of course it is." Widdershins threw her hands over her head in exasperated surrender to the whims of a cruel world and started walking.

CHAPTER TEN

"Would ya quit bein' such a ponce, already?!"

"I'm telling you, Treves, I saw something move!"

"Sure. It's called shadows, what with all them clouds in front of the moon."

"But—"

"Shut up and get a move on! Wanna be back before supper's gone *completely* cold."

"As if the others left any for us anyway . . ."

They were of different builds, these two men skulking across a property that wasn't theirs. Different heights, different hair, different complexions. Both were wrapped in loose clothes of blacks and grays, however, and both wore the cruel, sneering expression that made people the world over immediately think "thug."

Which, given that they were both members in good standing of the Thousand Crows, was hardly an inaccurate assessment.

Treves's doubt in his companion's observations was understandable. Other than the tree line but a few dozen yards in front of them, and the manor house so far behind them it was barely a glimmer in the moonlight, the field was broad, open, and empty. Shadows did indeed glide overhead, the last surviving tufts of grass bowed to one another as they danced in the breeze, frost glinted on the dusky soil. Flickers and shades were everywhere, genuine movement utterly absent. Nobody was out here besides the two of them; that was the whole point.

Except, between one step and the next, they became three. The newcomer, so far as either Crow could tell in that split second before thought caught up with vision, simply materialized from within those shifting puddles of light and dark. He—she? it?—almost seemed to *consist* of those dappled patterns, light gray competing with dark gray on a gray that was somewhere in between.

Something nudged Treves's shoulder; not hard, just enough, when combined with his gasp of shock, to throw him off-balance. Before he could so much as begin to recover, to straighten or draw his blade or both, the figure dropped. Crouching, spinning, cloak flaring, it once again became a blur in the gloom. Something—a leg?— smashed hard into the back of the brigand's ankle. Already unsteady, Treves felt his feet fly out from under him, felt the ground reach up and punch him in the back. Very much as if it were getting even for the damage he and his partner had so recently inflicted upon it.

What he took at first to be a ringing in his ears resolved itself into a pained scream. Bleary, dazed, Treves turned his head, and only then realized that the same spin that had driven the stranger's leg against his own had also plunged the tip of a rapier into the other man's thigh.

Still she spun, never slowing—and it *was* a she, the Crow could just barely make that out, now—and all Treves could think was, *Doesn't she ever get dizzy?*

He saw her foot rise, knew he needed to roll aside and couldn't do it fast enough. The heel of her boot dropped like an executioner's axe, not into his throat but his gut. Agony roared through him, yanking him into a fetal curl as he vomited all over the hardened dirt.

He had just enough presence of mind to watch her sword whip around again, slapping against his partner's throat—with the flat of the blade, not the edge. The man's wail of pain disintegrated into ragged gasps, his eyes bulged, and he fell to his knees, clutching at his neck.

A few more steps, almost a pirouette, and then the woman was *behind* him. Treves watched as her arms snaked around the man's head and neck, and squeezed. He flopped and struggled for only a moment before his body went limp.

The stranger let him fall—the faint *whump* of breath when he toppled was Treves's only sign that he was still alive—and then slowly bent to retrieve the sword she'd dropped to perform the choke. She swished it through the air before her, almost idly; two times, then three. Then, with equal nonchalance, she strode his way. . . .

Widdershins, as anyone who'd known her for over an hour would have anticipated, had wandered down the road precisely as far as it took to leave Alexandre's sight before cutting cross-country—traversing acres of barren, rolling hills—to approach Aubier from the other side. Once there, it'd been easy enough to wait until dark before setting out to once again trespass on Delacroix property.

Well, no, it'd been *simple*. Given Widdershins lack of patience—and Olgun's constant delighted poking at said impatience—"easy" was perhaps an inaccurate description.

Nor had she found it particularly enjoyable to slowly creep her way across the fields, crouching behind this hillock or slipping into that patch of shadow, relying on her divine partner's augmentation of hearing and night vision to ensure that she detected any approaching patrols before they detected her.

And there were a *lot* of those patrols. Whatever else one might say about her, Calanthe Delacroix was taking the protection of her House and family *very* seriously.

So when she'd spotted a pair of not-so-gentlemen sneaking their own way across the grounds, it had more than piqued her interest.

And when she recognized them for the criminals they were—and thus, almost certainly, Crows—it had piqued her, well, pique.

All of which, after a burst of violent exercise that might have proved greatly cathartic had it lasted longer, led her here.

Widdershins dropped into a squat beside the one man who

remained conscious, her rapier balanced jauntily across her knees. "So, Thousand Crows, right?"

He flinched, then glowered at her—or tried to around the occasional dry heave.

"I'd really like to know," she said, idly tapping her cheek, "how you made it this far onto the property, given that the guards are sprouting up like it was growing season."

"Same way you did, bitch."

"Hmm. No, it's taken me a *while* to get this far. It wasn't easy, and there's only one of me, yes? Also, I'm better than you." Then, at his attempted scoff, "I'm sorry, did I misremember who snuck up on who?"

Another sneer. "I'm not tellin' you anything."

Shins dropped her hand, switching from tapping her cheek to tapping her blade.

"Naw, see . . . It's a bluff. You're not a killer, girl."

"No?"

Treves, or so she thought she'd heard him called, jerked his head to indicate the other man.

"Maybe I just wanted to make sure he was alive to chat with if you turned out to be rude," she suggested.

"Ha! You didn't kill the boys came after you at the smithy, either!"

Widdershins's grin sparkled in the moonlight. "So you *are* one of the Crows!"

After an unintelligible mutter, "Fine. Not saying another word."

"I don't have to be a killer, you know. I *could* just hurt you. Done a pretty good job of that so far, yes?"

Treves, however, seemed determined to keep his tongue, and Shins couldn't honestly blame him. She wasn't the most intimidating figure to begin with, she knew, and it wasn't a stretch to imagine that Ivon Maline would scare his men a lot more than she did.

Instead, with a faint sigh and an even fainter request to Olgun to help ensure she got this just right, she leaned in and took hold of him just as she had his partner. He was out just as quickly—with, if she and Olgun had managed it properly, no real damage.

At least until one of the wandering Delacroix patrols stumbled across them, anyway.

"So what now, Olgun?" Shins frowned, nudging the unconscious thug with a toe. "How *did* they sneak in here? Blind luck? Their own pet god? It's another god, isn't it? You'd tell me if there was another god, yes?"

As Olgun was too busy doing his best impression of an outraged sputter at the term *pet*, he offered no comprehensible answer. That, though, was answer enough.

"Yeah, figured. Blind luck, maybe?" Then, "No, they *aren't* good enough to have just 'managed it'! Did you see them? They weren't really even trying! I . . . What? Oh. Well, of *course* I was going to search them before we left! It's the obvious thing to do, right? What kind of idiot do you take me for? Also, don't answer that."

Rather desperately hoping that the god couldn't sense the flush in her cheeks, Shins bent down to check the pockets and pouches of first Treves, then the other thug whose name she'd never heard.

Both, oddly enough, were carrying small wineskins hanging from their belts—skins that were, to judge by a quick prod, empty of wine, water, or any other beverage. Out of idle curiosity more than anything, she brought the first of the vessels up to her nose for a quick sniff.

"*Gghuuuurrljchkl!*"

The wineskin hurtled over yards of field to land in a small clump of frost-stiffened dead grass. Widdershins staggered, hunched, hands on her knees, breathing deeply and struggling not to vomit hard enough to turn completely inside out. Her nostrils, tongue, and throat felt slick with undercooked fat, tasted as though she'd just taken a swig of "tea" brewed by steeping the disembodied finger of a week-old corpse.

"Oh, *gods*! What is . . . ? Why . . . ? What . . . ? How . . . ? What . . . ? Why . . . ?"

A faint warming touch of Olgun's power cleared the worst of the fume from her nose and throat, the extremes of queasiness from her gut. It was followed rapidly by a strong mental image of dying farmland.

"Well, yes, I *know* it's the source of the blight!" she groused at him. "Or I'd have figured it out, anyway, once my brain stopped flinging itself against the inside of my skull and trying to escape through my ears."

After a few more minutes of panting, once Widdershins could make herself believe that the whole world didn't consist *entirely* of regurgitation, she straightened and shuffled over to the other Crow. Lifting his wineskin—keeping her arms rigidly straight and her face turned away—she carefully folded the leather, then slipped the skin inside one of her own pouches. Evidence, should she ever need it, and excuse to either buy or steal a new pouch, as she was *never* going to use this one for anything else, ever again.

Beyond that, her examination didn't turn up much, really. A few coins, which she pocketed. A few additional blades and other weapons, which she hurled as far as she could into the dark night. A tiny lantern with a bit of oil remaining.

And, just as she was about to quit in disgust, a sheet of folded paper in a pocket sewn into the lining of Treves's tunic.

"Oh, ha, ha," she snorted in response to her partner's unspoken suggestion. "Why don't *you* sniff it, if you're curious?"

It briefly appeared, however, that smelling it might be her only option. Unfolding the paper revealed only that she lacked sufficient light, even with Olgun's assistance, to study whatever might be on it. Fortunately, the brigand's own lantern solved that little problem.

Hunching over it, to minimize the chances of anyone seeing the glimmer from across the field, she glanced at her prize once more.

It took a moment, and several turns of the paper, before she recognized the patterns as a crude map of the Delacroix property. Yes, this was the main road here, *that* was the manor house there, which would put her roughly *here* . . .

Another minute, then, before she realized that the seemingly random hash marks scattered across the image were, in fact, a sequence of numbers written for the illiterate. Not a one of them repeated itself.

"What do you make of this?" she asked Olgun. "And if you say 'a map,' you're walking home."

"A map" was, however, all he had. Neither thief nor god doubted that this diagram was at least partly how the two Crows had been able to cross the property undetected, but they still couldn't determine *how* it had helped them. It wasn't as though the patrol routes— assuming they weren't utterly random—were marked.

Ultimately, all she could do was fold it back up and store it away for later consideration. She'd come here for a reason, after all, and still had a great deal to do before dawn.

❀

"Hey, Cyrille."

The resulting sound wasn't quite a squawk, wasn't quite a yelp, wasn't quite a gasp. As best she could describe it, it sounded like an angry chicken slapping a puppy with a fish.

"Could you repeat that?" Widdershins asked. "Define it? Possibly spell it for me?"

The boy, who had been lying atop his quilts, fully dressed, brooding so intently at the ceiling that it had almost certainly begun to feel irritable, wore an expression very similar to the aforementioned hypothetical fish. "Widdershins?! How . . . How did you get in here?"

From her current seat on the corner of a writing desk—a large thing of cherrywood, carved with various designs to perfectly match the bed, the chair, the wardrobe, and even the wainscoting, silly aristocrats—Shins gestured over one shoulder with a quick jerk of the head. "Came in the window."

"Came in the . . . I've been in this room all night!"

"So?"

"I didn't hear a thing!"

"So?"

"How . . . ? What . . . ? How . . . ?"

"You know, I was just having a very similar conversation earlier this evening."

Since Cyrille's expression, though highly amusing, didn't seem likely to change any time soon, Shins took the opportunity to look around. Other than the aforementioned furniture, any single piece of which was worth more than every apartment Widdershins had ever owned or stayed in back in Davillon, the room was . . . well, as equally ostentatious as the furniture. The carpet was thick enough to serve as armor, the water basin and toiletries on the bureau were genuine silver, the quilt was ermine, and the chamber was completely bare of the discarded clothes that were, in Widdershins's experience, common to all adolescent boys' living spaces. (Thanks, she was certain, to the efforts of the servants, not Cyrille himself.)

"Sorry to see the family's doing so poorly," she scoffed.

"I'm sorry, what?"

Widdershins swallowed a sigh. "Nothing. Never mind."

The exchange, brief as it was, snapped Cyrille out of his shock. "How did you know which room was mine?"

"Um, I kept looking until I found you. Did you know that nobody in your family seems to actually *sleep*?"

Cyrille chuckled. "Oh, we do. Just not until morning. Sleeping at night is just so '*common*.' So what's everyone up to, then?"

"Remarkably boring stuff, for the most part," she said with a shrug. "At least, the ones with rooms on this side of the house. The twins seem to be practicing card tricks."

"They do that," Cyrille said with a nod. "Card tricks, coin flips, all that. I think they think it's creepier, or at least more impressive, if they perform all their little quirks and tricks in unison."

"Fifi," Shins continued, "whose room is a mess, by the way, is experimenting with hairstyles in the mirror and, believe it or not, *not* playing with that silly glass lantern of hers."

"The miracles of the gods are many and strange."

"And the one girl who wasn't at your family meeting the other night . . ." Widdershins trailed off abruptly, blushing.

"Marjolaine," Cyrille offered with a half smile. "And yes, she does that. Frequently. Mostly because of how much it upsets Mother. You'd be surprised how many servants have been dismissed—or been beaten by Malgier—because of her. Why are you looking at me that way?"

"This is a really frog-hoppingly awful family you have, Cyrille."

"'Frog-hoppingly'?"

"Don't change the subject."

"Shins . . ." Cyrille rose from the bed, then glanced back at it as if only just now realizing what it was. His gaze flickered to meet hers, and his face reddened, but he kept speaking. "They're not all that bad. Well, I mean, Malgier, maybe, and a few of the others. But mostly we bring out the worst in each other. House politics, status. There aren't a lot of Delacroix bloodlines left in any positions of wealth."

Fewer than you think. But even Widdershins, to whom *tact* meant little more than the past tense of *tack*, knew better than to say that just now.

"We've given a lot to Aubier," he continued. "Provided for many of its poorer citizens. We're just . . ." His hands twitched as though literally groping for words.

"Rude and bad-tempered as badgers in the process," she finished for him.

"Um . . ."

"Badgers with hemorrhoids," she clarified.

"Shins . . ."

"Badgers with hemorrhoids and ingrown toenails."

"Were you going to tell me why you sneaked in here?"

"Oh! Right. I need an extra set of eyes, and someone to tell me who's from Aubier and who's a stranger. You're elected. Let's go."

"Wait, what? Go? I don't—"

"You believe I'm trying to help you and your family, yes?"

"Yes," Cyrille answered without hesitation.

"Then trust me. I need your help to help me help." And then, much more softly, "What? It made perfect sense, and he followed it just fine!"

Indeed, Cyrille didn't appear at all confused. If anything, the expression on his face suggested . . .

Disappointment? Hurt? *Why the figs would he be hurt?*

He stood, tense, arm rising as though he wanted to reach out to her. "Is that . . . the only reason you're here?" He sounded almost plaintive.

"I don't . . . Why else would I be here?"

Cyrille's hand fell back to his side. "Never mind. Wait just a minute, let me get my boots and my sword. Then you can explain to me how you plan to get us both off the property."

Shins leaned back, watching him gather his belongings, well and truly befuddled.

Nor could she quite figure out why Olgun was projecting the very distinct impression of rolling his eyes at her.

CHAPTER ELEVEN

Getting off Delacroix lands hadn't ultimately proved that difficult. Cyrille might have lacked either Widdershins's skill or her god-given advantages, but he still had her to guide him, to watch and listen for any sign of the household guards. Furthermore, she'd gone briefly ahead to see if the two unconscious Crows had been discovered yet; when she realized they were gone, clearly having recovered and limped away, she left their lantern where they had lain, burning merrily away. That should attract attention, swiftly enough and in sufficient quantities, to make escape in an alternate direction that much easier.

Once off the House grounds, it was, perhaps ironically, the young Delacroix who took over as guide. This was, primarily, because he knew Aubier's streets and Shins didn't—but also because, even though they went nowhere near the gang's territory, the thief was nearly paranoid about watching for the appearance of the Thousand Crows.

Several hours before dawn, they had made their way to the Carnot property, scrambled atop a nearby house—or rather, Widdershins scrambled and Cyrille struggled—and firmly planted themselves.

And then they waited.

And waited.

"It's a natural phenomenon," she explained the fifth or sixth time her companion expressed his boredom. "The hours between midnight and dawn pass three times slower for me than anyone else. You're just near enough to be caught in it, I'm afraid."

More waiting.

"Let me get this straight." Cyrille glanced at the palm of his glove, wet from the melted frost coating the roof, then idly wiped it dry on his cloak. "We're here to spy on the Carnot household. To see if anyone suspicious, or anyone I recognize as a foreigner to Aubier, enters or leaves."

"Unless we changed the plan when I wasn't listening," she confirmed.

"And we're doing this here, even though we both agree they're not going to be open or obvious about such things, and you aren't even certain the local Carnots are involved, because you don't know where the Thousand Crows are holed up, so we can't spy on *them*."

"We've been through this already, yes? I'm positive we have. I think I remember actually being there for it."

"You know there are multiple inns and hostels in Aubier that cater to outsiders, right? If you're correct about the Carnots coming here from Lourveaux, we know about when they'd have arrived. It'd take a bit of digging, but at least you'd be watching people you *know* are part of what's going on." Cyrille sounded smug as a king's cat, presumably at having come up with a course of action Widdershins had missed.

"Mm-hmm. Cyrille?"

"Um, yes?"

"I'm an outsider to Aubier."

"Yes."

"The Thousand Crows, and possibly your mother's people, are looking for me."

"Yes . . ."

"Where do you imagine, first and foremost, they'll be looking?"

Had his face fallen any harder, it might have cracked not only the frost, but a shingle or two beneath it. "Oh."

Widdershins reached over, gently patting his hand. "If the Carnot house proves a dead end, that'll have to be our next step, yes.

But first I'd rather exhaust the options that *don't* involve putting us in undue proximity to people who want to stick pointy things into me, all right?"

Cyrille cast the strangest look her way, but nodded.

And so, more waiting.

The dawn began to break, casting the shadow of Castle Pauvril over Aubier like a giant (and mildly arthritic) sundial. The streets began to bustle with first a trickle, then a flow of humanity. And the pair of youths on the rooftop watched as that trickle and flow continued to have absolutely nothing to do with the Carnot household.

"Hey, Cyrille?"

The boy glanced up from where he'd been tracing idle patterns in the frost. "Hmm?"

"You're an aristocrat," Shins observed.

"Um, yes?"

"Formal education? Tutors and classes and books you didn't want to read to learn facts you couldn't have cared about less?"

"Yeah . . ."

"How come nobody uses alchemy anymore?"

Cyrille blinked, shifted around to sit with his legs crossed, wincing only slightly—at the cold of the roof on his rear, Shins assumed.

"I mean," she continued, "if it actually *works* . . ."

Her companion nodded slowly, squinting a bit as he worked at dredging up the memories of old history lessons that—as she'd theorized—he hadn't really given a damn about.

"Alchemists worked for generations before they started getting results," he began slowly. "Once they did, the formulas and recipes and all that proved maddeningly complicated. Something like one person out of ten could make them work with any regularity, and that's just drawing from the people who got through their years of apprenticeship.

"It also proved ludicrously expensive. The different reagents—uh, alchemical ingredients—needed to make the more interesting procedures work . . . Yes, a few alchemists even managed to turn lead into gold, but it was so costly, the profit margin was surprisingly low. And when it came to more basic stuff—poisons, medicines, solvents—there were just far easier sciences. Ultimately, alchemy became a curiosity, a hobby practiced by the occasional rich or half-crazy eccentric, nothing more."

Widdershins, of course, had honed in at least partly on the gold. "Low margins," she said, "but still profitable, yes? So why would it vanish so completely?"

Cyrille's gaze grew unfocused. "I'm not entirely sure I'm recalling this right," he admitted. "I only half understood it back then. Near as I can explain, though, objects and elements resist transformation through the alchemical sciences. Which means, it's difficult and expensive to create a solution that'll turn lead into gold, or nickel into iron. It's much easier, and much *cheaper*, to create a substance that'll *undo* the process."

"Ah. So even if you pulled it off, odds were the law or your enemies or whoever would catch you in it."

"Precisely. There was a brief period where the reagents to reverse the changes had a wider market than the ones to cause them. In the end, it just wasn't really worth it to anyone."

"Except lunatics like Fingerbone," she muttered.

"Uh . . ."

"Seriously, who goes by 'Fingerbone'? Who masters something like alchemy and then devotes its use to a gang of thieves? And who the happy hopping horses is *that*?"

"Uh," Cyrille reiterated. Then, following Widdershins's insistent scowl and pointing finger, "Oh!"

The "Oh" in question was a balding, broad-shouldered fellow in brocades and fabrics at the absolute lowest end of what could be called "fine." He moved casually, just another man on the street, going about his early-morning business, worthy of Widdershins's attentions *only* . . .

Because he'd stepped onto said street from within the Carnot property.

"Name's . . ." Again Cyrille's face screwed into odd shapes as he struggled to remember. "Josce Something. I've seen him around at a few shops and events. Highly trusted Carnot manservant. I think he might even be head of the household staff, which is curious."

Shins, who'd just been starting to relax, tensed up. "Why curious?"

"Well, he's only been in their employ about half a year. That's remarkably swift advancement, so we just figured he'd come to them from a different branch of the . . . Oh, come on! Don't give me that look! That was well before the Lourveaux Carnot bloodline left!"

"Which doesn't mean they couldn't have sent someone ahead to get their little scheme rolling," she snarled. "Come on. Let's get moving before we lose him."

"He could just be running an errand!" Cyrille protested.

"Fine. Feel free to stay here. There's important frost to be melted."

Grumbling, the aristocrat followed.

As it turned out, "get moving before we lose him" had been unduly optimistic. They very nearly lost him multiple times *after* they were moving.

Widdershins recognized the techniques the moment Josce began employing them. Innocent stops to examine this shop or chat with that person, very slight twists of the head to study the street reflected in a window. This "servant" was ever alert, ever watching for anyone tailing him.

And he was subtle. He was *good*. Certainly not what one would expect in a model majordomo.

Shins found herself with the same problems she'd had earlier, and then some. Wide streets, routes and twists she didn't remotely know, long swathes where rooftop pursuit was out of the question—plus a very perceptive mark and a companion who was about as unobtrusive as a collection plate.

It took every trick she knew, splitting up multiple times, and every bit of extra help Olgun could provide. Thanks to the tiny god, she spotted a faint twitch just before Josce turned, giving her the opportunity to duck aside; or someone in the crowd stumbled slightly, passing between Cyrille and the Carnot servant, briefly blocking the latter's view.

Still, they fell constantly farther behind, and by the time they'd reached the southeast edge of town—not one of the several directions through which Shins had yet either entered or exited—even Olgun had to admit they'd lost the man completely.

"Well," Cyrille offered, "there's nothing out here but a few farms and the like. Can't be *that* hard to find him again, can it?"

Widdershins couldn't tell which of his struggles was the more obvious, the one to sound chipper or the one to hide his fatigued gasping from the long, brisk walk. She decided to glare at him with equal vehemence for both.

"Yes, I *know*," she hiss-snapped at Olgun. "We *don't* have any better options! Stop ruining a perfectly good glare!"

By then, however, she'd lost the moment. With ill-concealed poor grace and a childish urge to kick something in the roadway, she turned to seek likely prospects among the farms and barns.

In less than an hour—or so Olgun informed her; with the overcast rapidly building between her and the sun, Shins couldn't have been sure—they proved Cyrille right. As they'd seen no trace of Josce on the road ahead, nor moving across the largely barren fields, only a handful of buildings stood near enough to have hidden him. They found him at the third: an old grain mill, wind-driven, at the very edge of a property.

"Not sure which House owns this field," the aristocrat admitted in a whisper. "Mother would lecture."

"Let her." Shins crept nearer, feet silent over the dry and pebbly soil. Cyrille was rather less quiet, but thankfully, it shouldn't matter. Even before they got close, Widdershins could hear the grumble of rolling, grinding stone from within. She looked up at the tattered blades, idly rotating in the wind, and nodded.

"They've engaged the millstone."

Cyrille snorted. "You think Josce sneaked out here to make grain out of season?"

"I think a man constantly watching to see if he's being followed is probably going to worry about eavesdroppers, too, yes? You turkey. Come on, let's see if we can find somewhere we can hear them over that racket."

The mill itself was old, worn, surrounded by flakes of stone and shreds of sailcloth. Footing was uneven, the air redolent of powders both grain and rock. What slight noise could be heard over the grinding from within was lost in the creaking and squeaking of the sails above. Widdershins still moved softly, silently, if only out of habit, and Cyrille did his best to mimic her efforts.

The front door was a no-go, not even to be considered. Unfortunately, that didn't leave a great many options, since the designers—for some reason—hadn't felt the need to include a wide variety of windows in the structure.

Given that even Widdershins, city girl to her soul, had heard of the dangers of stirring up too much dust in a mill, she couldn't say she blamed them. Still, it was grossly inconvenient, bordering on rude.

It was Cyrille (and when had *he* gotten ahead of her, in their gradual circumnavigation?) who spotted the one exception. A small, horizontal rectangle with thick, wooden shutters that currently hung wide open, it faced onto an expanse of empty field: Perhaps it was intended to air out the place if the powders and dusts *did* accumulate to a choking or explosive degree? Shins could only guess and could barely bring herself to care. At the moment, she was more concerned over the fact that the boy was *standing right in front of it* as he waved her over!

"I'm just wondering, Olgun. Is there a *reason* the gods put more souls than brains in the world? Is it supposed to be funny? Or was there just a shortage?"

Cyrille continued to beam at her as she approached, right up to the point she grabbed him by the collar and yanked him away from the window so fast she was surprised the wind didn't whistle between his teeth.

"Are you *crazy?*" she hissed at him. "Or just dumb? I suppose 'both' is an option. You *are* a blue blood."

"I . . . Widdershins, I looked! There's nobody in the room, and they weren't going to *hear* me over—"

"It has a door, this room?"

"Well, yes, of course it—"

"Then someone could have walked *into* it while you were standing there waving like a monkey in an anthill, yes?"

Cyrille looked as though someone had just eaten his kitten. "I'm sorry, Shins. I didn't think."

He looked so miserable, she couldn't even bring herself to scold any further. (The fact that she'd done more than her share of equally foolish things in her time, and Olgun was currently parading images of every single one of them past her in a cavalcade of humiliation, might also have had something to do with it.) "Look, just . . . learn from it. Don't do it again, all right?"

"I will. I mean, I won't. I mean—"

"Good." Widdershins took a single running step and dove through the open window, rolling to a stop beside the door that the room did indeed have. A quick peep underneath revealed nothing at all, and pressing her ear to the wood merely gave her a clearer perspective on the grinding.

A quick glance around told her nothing about the chamber, save that it wasn't used much. A few old tools and a chair lying in one corner, coated in dust, made up the entirety of its contents. Idly she waved Cyrille to follow her, but her attentions remained focused on that door.

"Olgun?"

Doubt, but a willingness to give it a shot. She felt the whole side of her face begin to tingle, focused on her ear, which she again pressed to the door.

For a moment, the millstone was painful, almost deafening, but it swiftly faded back to normal levels. It reverberated in her head, however, a peculiar blurring effect, as though the *echoes* of the grinding were now louder than the sound that birthed them.

Still Olgun's power flowed, the god almost seeming to juggle sounds, drawing some nearer and hurling some away, until finally, *finally* what might just have been a voice leaked through.

Unfortunately, that proved to be the limit of the god's ability. She could tell that there *were* voices, but could understand only the occasional word.

Something about a schedule? Not a voice she knew, or at least not one she could identify under the circumstances, but definitely worried.

A second voice, also a stranger, too low for her to pick up anything at all.

When the third man spoke, however, she recognized the phrase "damn girl" readily enough, had no doubt to whom the speaker referred. Perhaps more importantly, she recognized the voice itself.

Ivon Maline's wasn't a voice one would soon forget. She'd felt the need to take an extra bath to scrub it off of her the last time.

And *that* meant . . .

"We found it!" The soft hiss was intended for Olgun alone. In her excitement, however, Widdershins had been loud enough that Cyrille, currently hauling himself awkwardly through the tiny window, might have heard if not for the constant rumble.

Ivon and Josce, collaborating. Solid evidence, finally, of House Carnot's involvement with the Thousand Crows. She even had a witness with her that Calanthe Delacroix and the Aubier authorities couldn't readily dismiss.

Except, as Olgun pointed out, they still *hadn't* witnessed any-thing. They only assumed one of the two unknown voices had been Josce's; only assumed he'd come here when he'd disappeared from their sight.

Widdershins grumbled something about horses and figs, then grumbled a second time at the clumsy *fwump* of Cyrille sliding from the window to the floor behind her. She stood, examined the hinges of the door—old and slightly corroded metal, as she'd anticipated—and then reached for the ubiquitous tools she kept in various pouches and pockets on her belt. A few dabs of oil, a pause to let the stuff soak in, a few dabs more, and that should do it.

She checked to make certain Olgun was ready, decided there was very little point in making certain Cyrille was ready, and then laid a hand on the latch. Slowly, carefully, every nerve prickling, she eased the door open a couple of inches.

What she saw, after allowing her vision to adjust to the dimness beyond, was—the inside of a mill. An open chamber, shelves for storage, a screen to sift the grain and a basin to catch it. She couldn't see the millwheel itself, though its presence resounded everywhere, nor could she see any sign of the three speakers.

Open it farther for a better look? If Ivon and the others were anywhere within sight of the door, any wider could well draw their attention, no matter how silent, but if she couldn't see the bulk of the room . . .

Ah.

Shins stepped to one side, pressing her face against the narrow crack between the door and the wall to which it was hinged. Not much of a vantage, but it proved enough.

There they were, closer to the doorway than the young woman was entirely comfortable with. Ivon she couldn't see at all, but that was fine. She didn't have to. Her clearest view was of a man she didn't recognize, a pinched-faced, mouse-haired fellow who wore the clothes of a merchant but the sycophantic simper of a lifelong errand boy.

The third had his back to her, stood so she could only glimpse him through the aperture, but that was sufficient. She'd seen the balding head and brocaded tunic recently enough to identify them now.

"Cyrille!" Then, just a bit louder, "Cyrille! C'mere!"

He crept up behind her, idly rubbing an elbow; probably banged it on the way in. "What?" he whispered.

Shins moved away from the door. "Tell me if you recognize anyone."

Cyrille nodded, leaned in, placed one palm on the wall to steady himself—and the other on the door.

Simple habit, reflex. He caught himself almost immediately, yanked his hand back, but that brief moment of contact was enough. The door drifted open a few inches farther, and what few snippets and blurs of conversation Widdershins could hear ceased completely.

Gods, save me from turtle-brained, hoof-fingered blue bloods! "Go! Get out!"

"Shins, I'm so sorry—"

"Running comes *before* apologizing! *Go!*"

Shins pulled the door shut, searched frantically for any means of locking or holding it, and ultimately had to settle for grabbing an old spade from the heap of tools and shoving it hard under the door. It wouldn't hold long, especially as the thing opened outward, but it might stay wedged between wood and stone long enough to buy some extra seconds.

Seconds they'd need.

A grunt grabbed her attention, and Widdershins wanted to stamp her foot in exasperation. Cyrille was struggling to haul himself back through the window, but the aperture's small dimensions and the stone of the wall—smoother inside than it had been out—conspired to slow him. He had only just now wormed his way about halfway through, legs kicking as he sought a bit of extra purchase.

Widdershins dashed up behind him, grabbed one of his feet, and shoved. Cyrille popped through the window, a thrashing, yelping cork, and vanished from view. Shins retreated a few steps, called on Olgun as she darted forward, and jumped. She felt the stone whip past her on all sides, felt the rocky earth beyond come up to meet her waiting hands, and was tumbling back to her feet when she heard the wooden door disintegrate behind her.

Without stopping to look behind her, trusting Olgun to warn her if she was about to be shot in the back, she hauled the whimpering aristocrat bodily to his feet and ran, dragging him, stumbling and panting, behind.

INTERLUDE: DAVILLON

He was a big man, the kind of big that just seemed clumsy, no matter how carefully he moved. Broad shoulders and long arms, a thick, bald head on a squat stump of neck. He looked dangerous; he looked strong; he looked mean. He did *not* look graceful or sneaky. Or, for that matter, especially smart.

He was just fine with all of that. In his profession, in his world, deception was more than a way of life. It was the *only* way of life.

Specifically because those who didn't learn to deceive, didn't tend to live.

Laremy "Remy" Privott, taskmaster of the Finders' Guild, second-in-command over Davillon's thieves beneath the mysterious Shrouded Lord himself, would normally have been inside at this hour, rather than tolerating the frigid humidity that couldn't decide if it wanted to be fog, rain, sleet, or some ungodly spawn of all three. He would have been—*should* have been—deep in the bowels of the complex that was the guild's headquarters, either ensconced in his office or settling into his own personal chambers. Possibly with one of the pretty younger thieves who mistakenly believed that the taskmaster's bed was the shortcut to advancement. There were *always* a few who thought that way; it was a rumor Remy himself encouraged.

Normally. Not tonight.

Tonight, for the first time in a few years, the taskmaster himself was in the field. Wrapped in cheap, tattered clothes that just "happened" to provide perfect camouflage against the night's shadows, accompanied by three of his most trusted Finders, he slipped in

ghostly silence through Davillon's streets. His destination loomed
ahead, or rather the fence surrounding his destination did.

Locked, guarded, and watched, obviously. It wouldn't matter,
also obviously.

A few loose boards in the fence—boards that *remained* loose,
thanks to a few well-placed coins in the hands of the carpenters hired
to maintain them—provided Remy and his men with easy access.
Within was an entire lot filled with wagons, from tiny carts that
were barely more than old-style chariots to multiwheeled contrap-
tions capable of carrying several families, or whole heaps of cargo, in
comfort.

Davillon boasted a number of such lots, in which traveling mer-
chants could load, unload, or store their vehicles. Perhaps unsurpris-
ingly, the better the location and security of a given lot, the more it
cost to use.

This one was cheap. Very.

It was *also*, of the cheap lots, the nearest to any of the main gates.
Thus, it wasn't entirely uncommon for successful but parsimonious
traders to use this lot, make a big show of how poor their business had
been this season, and then attempt to sneak away with much greater
profits than they were believed to have. Security through secrecy.

The Finders had enough eyes on the lot that such "secrets" were
anything but.

They struck here only occasionally, only if a score seemed particularly worthwhile. Too often, and people would catch on; they *wanted*
vendors and travelers to believe that their hidden treasures were
secure. Tonight, however, the Guild had moved against a spice-and-
perfume merchant whom they knew had made some ten or twelve
times the coin he'd sadly reported to his compatriots. (And, for that
matter, to Davillon's tax collectors.)

It should have been simple. Straightforward. In-and-out, easy.

It should also have been over with hours ago.

When the team he'd assigned failed to return, Remy had followed all the procedures that, as taskmaster, he was supposed to follow. He had dispatched runners, each assigned to acquire very specific information.

When they returned, their reports were all negative. No, the Finders hadn't been pinched; the Guard had undertaken no operations in the area, and none of the gaols had seen a sudden influx.

No, none of the other (and far smaller) criminal gangs had interfered. All of those were keeping their heads down, still reeling from the last time the Finders had made an example of one of their number.

No, none of the missing thieves were at any of their favorite drinking holes, hideouts, or homes.

All the runners gave the same answer, all save the one assigned to dash by the target and see if the team, for some reason, remained there.

That runner had not returned at all.

And it had been then that Laremy, taskmaster and lieutenant to the Shrouded Lord, had decided *not* to follow one particular procedure.

When he chose to head out in person with his own trusted seconds, he *should* have reported it. He should have sought permission from the Shrouded Lord, or at least left detailed word of where he was going.

It was a risk; even if nothing went wrong, he could face some unpleasant discipline if the Shrouded Lord found out. But there was one other detail of the plan for tonight's job, one tiny factor that made Remy bound and determined to solve any problems before his guildmaster learned of them.

The plan had been his.

"All right, gents," he rumbled, his voice startlingly deep even in a whisper. "Spread out, eyes open. You see something, you bloody well speak up! I don't need anyone else disappearing tonight."

"Oh, Remy. Nobody's disappeared. Your boys are just a bit indisposed."

He knew the voice. It rang every bell in his head, tugged on his memories like a ravenous dog, but he couldn't *quite* place it, not in this context. He *could* tell that it was feminine, and that it drifted down to him from atop one of the covered wagons.

The taskmaster glanced up casually, hand drifting slowly and obviously to his belt. He knew, at that moment, that three small but brutal crossbows—less powerful than flintlocks, yes, but also *much* quieter—were trained on the stranger from multiple directions. He'd chosen his companions tonight carefully, for just this—

The canvas atop the wagon billowed as the figure, all but invisible in the darkness, slid down one side. Remy heard a brief yelp, a snap that sounded sort of, but not exactly, like the twang of a bowstring, and then a limp *thump*.

The big man drew his blade and sprinted around the vehicle, skidding to a halt when he saw one of his own people charging from the other direction. Another of his men lay on the earth between them, unmoving, but of the stranger, there was no sign.

No sign except another dull thump from the side of the wagon he'd just vacated.

"That's two of your people down, Taskmaster. They're still breathing. So's your team from earlier. A gesture of goodwill."

"Oh, *thank* you. I'll just kill you a little bit, then."

Something flashed from above, a dark raptor plunging from the night sky. By the time Remy registered that he'd just seen a nigh-impossible leap, that what he'd mistaken for wings was in fact a billowing cloak, his third companion was down, bleeding from a nasty gash in his arm.

"You could attack me," the stranger observed. "But I think we both know how that'd work out for you, don't we? Put the steel away, Remy. I only lured you out to talk. No need for you to hurt yourself."

She moved forward, then, walking with a faint limp that seemed utterly incongruous with the acrobatic prowess she'd just displayed.

Hands reached up to lower her hood, revealing jagged features and a cascade of fiery hair.

But by then, she needn't have bothered, for Laremy had finally placed her voice.

"Gods . . . Lisette . . ."

Lisette Suvagne, taskmaster prior to Remy and now hunted exile from the Finders' Guild, grinned wide enough to give a serpent nightmares. "How do you like the office?"

"I should . . . I'm supposed to take you in. We all are. Dead or alive."

She nodded thoughtfully. "It would be hard to take me in if you're dead, though."

Remy glanced at the two men lying nearby, and nodded. "My team's all right?"

"Some of them won't work for a while, but they'll live. You want to do the same?"

"Uh . . . Given the option, I'd prefer it, yes."

"Oh, good!" Lisette actually clapped once. "Self-preservation is a wonderful motivator, don't you think?" Then, before he could answer, "I have a proposition for you, Remy."

"You're about to ask me to betray the Shrouded Lord." It wasn't a question.

"Only temporarily," she protested.

Remy cocked his head, puzzled. "The betrayal's only temporary?"

Somehow, Lisette's smile widened farther still. Remy would have sworn unnaturally so. "The Shrouded Lord's only temporary."

The taskmaster knew he said *something* in response to that. He just wasn't certain what it was, or that it was even a word.

"Are you going to hear me out?" Lisette asked, the first traces of impatience creeping into her tone. "And if not, could you tell me who's your most likely successor, so I needn't waste too much of my time?"

She could, and she would, kill him. Somehow, even if he hadn't seen her drop his people so easily, he'd have known that to be true. No harm in listening, then, and quite a bit of harm in refusing. He could always turn her in to the Shrouded Lord later on.

Or make whatever other decisions seemed appropriate at the time.

"Let's hear what you have to say."

Lisette's disturbing smile finally faded, but it truly appeared as though her eyes began to burn.

CHAPTER TWELVE

A small and winding depression, carved through the dirt and lined with occasional flattened stones, was probably a stream in wetter months. Now it was a makeshift hiding place, where Cyrille and Widdershins lay flat in the cold dirt, peering through barely visible flurries of light snow, watching to see who might come after them.

Or rather, Widdershins peered over the tiny lip, watching. Cyrille—whom she'd dragged to the ground and now lay atop of to make sure he didn't move, hand clasped over his mouth to make sure he didn't speak—probably couldn't see much of anything.

He also, despite a position that couldn't possibly have been comfortable for anything with an interior skeletal structure, wasn't putting up much of a struggle to *change* that position.

The brutish, oily leader of the Thousand Crows had appeared first, leaning through the window, brandishing a heavy flintlock. Moments after he'd pulled back inside—rather like a snail retracting into its shell, Widdershins had thought—he and Josce both appeared from around the side of the mill. Ivon now had his grotesque cleaver in one meaty fist, pistol in the other. The Carnot servant carried a double-barreled flintlock, both hammers cocked. Some distance behind them followed the third, carrying nothing in his hand except his *other* hand; he wrung them both together, whining nervously. (Shins couldn't begin to make out the words, but the tone said "nervous" and "whining," thank you very much, and she'd dealt with enough of both in the Finders' Guild to know.)

A brief but animated argument, or discussion, or arguscussion followed. Again, Widdershins couldn't hear much other than tone

163

from that distance, but judging by the broad gesticulations in their general direction, Ivon wanted the trio to spread out and scour the property for whomever might have been there, while Josce was more inclined toward returning to town.

The third man obviously favored Josce's preference, and eventually, perhaps because Ivon didn't care to do his searching alone, they turned and headed away from the mill, in the direction of Aubier proper.

Shins rose, taking a moment to brush the powdery soil from her gloves and her knees.

"Widdershins," Cyrille began hesitantly, also standing, "I'm—"

"I *did* say you could apologize after the running," she admitted, "but I have to tell you, if you do, I'm very seriously inclined to break your nose. This isn't a game, Cyrille, and your birthright won't protect you! You mess up doing what I do, you get hurt, or you get dead! Or hurt, *then* dead. And it's hard to apologize when you're dead, yes? At least, that's the rumor.

"So don't apologize. Just *stop messing up!*"

"I understand," he said softly, scuffing the toe of one boot in the dirt.

"Good. Now, they're far enough along not to spot us easily. Let's move before we lose him entirely."

"Him," as Widdershins explained—quietly but impatiently, the third or fourth time Cyrille asked—was the third and currently unknown member of the trio. Much as she wanted to know where the Crows were holed up, following Ivon into their territory— especially given that she didn't yet have a solid grasp on how skilled the man actually might be—was a risk she preferred not to take with the youngest Delacroix son in tow. Josce was too good at spotting tails, and besides, they already knew whom *he* worked for. But the last? Widdershins very much wanted to learn who he represented, and while he nervously checked behind himself on a regular basis, he clearly lacked the knowledge and experience of the other two.

Indeed, Widdershins swiftly grew certain that Cyrille could have followed the man, utterly undetected, without her help at all. When she commented as much, the boy's face beamed so proudly that she decided not to tell him it hadn't really been meant as a compliment.

As they drew deeper into Aubier and the streets grew more crowded, Widdershins began to get nervous. Not that they might lose their quarry, no; that still proved simple enough, and her skills were more than sufficient to prevent them from being detected, even without Olgun's assistance. No, she worried that someone *else*—one of the Thousand Crows, or perhaps a Delacroix servant—might recognize either her or her companion.

"Trade cloaks with me," she said abruptly.

"Um . . ." Cyrille glanced at her shabby gray garment, then at his own fine cloak of blues, deepest navy outside, sky-bright within. "What?"

"Trade!" she insisted. It wasn't *much* of a disguise, certainly, but if anyone was looking for her—or him—by description alone, their eyes might just flit on over without stopping.

Of course, her cloak only came down to his knees, while his hung nearly to her heels, but one couldn't have everything.

The man they were following finally turned down one last street and stepped inside a large wooden structure, old but still in good repair and freshly whitewashed. A placard above the door identified the place, both in art and in letters, as the Second Home. It was, as Cyrille explained even though Shins already knew, one of the many hostels catering to visitors staying in Aubier long-term.

After which, he asked, or began to, "Was this one of the handful of—"

"Two hundred ninety-one," Widdershins interrupted.

Twelve, Olgun corrected her.

"—places you checked earlier?" Cyrille concluded.

"Yes," the young woman admitted. "But I was looking for the

Crows, specifically. And it's not as though I saw or spoke to everyone here."

"Just asking. No need to be defensive."

"I'm not defensive! *You're* defensive!"

"Um . . ."

"You're also," she added more calmly, "going to wait out here while I poke around."

If Cyrille had huffed up any further, Shins was convinced he'd actually have burst a button. "Not a chance! I—"

"Of the two of us, Cyrille, who's the actual outsider?"

"You, but—"

"Of the two of us, who's the one who won't draw inordinate amounts of attention if a server or some other citizen inside happens to be familiar with the local nobility?"

"You," he repeated, growing sullen.

"Of the two of us, who's actually had some fair idea so far of what the figs she was doing?"

Cyrille merely glared this time, rather than answer. Just as well, as Widdershins might not have heard him over the sudden sound, or rather sound-like sensation, of Olgun's hysterical laughter.

"Oh, I have, too!" she murmured. "Most of the time, anyway. Shut up. I could just rent a room and leave you here, you know. You wouldn't be able to leave. You have no hands. I . . . No, you *couldn't* just walk through the walls! They . . . Because it's not fair, that's why! Didn't I say shut up?"

She turned her attention back to her flesh-and-blood companion, who was looking at her funny. "Cyrille, I'm not just trying to keep you out of the way. We have no idea who that man is, or why he came here. He *probably* works for someone inside, but if he's just ducking in for a few minutes, for whatever reason, I need someone on the street to see it. Someone who can follow him to wherever he's *really* going? It's important."

The boy's face twisted in blatant disbelief, but he nodded. "All right. Whatever you need."

"Thank you." She started to move away.

"Shins? What's the signal if you need help?"

"Screaming," she said over her shoulder. "Lots of screaming. Probably breaking things. Sometimes, there's fire."

With that, she slipped into the small knot of people gathered aimlessly before the Second Home and vanished through the open doorway.

❀

Cyrille watched until she was gone, and for several minutes more. People came and went, the throng in the street shifted and flowed, the wind grew chill, and the snow began drifting downward in flurries large enough to stick. Only a few of Aubier's citizens or visitors seemed inclined to let the weather drive them indoors; the rest merely pulled up hoods or tightened collars, and otherwise went about their conversations.

The young Delacroix chose the latter, and then nearly lost himself in the scents of Widdershins's hood. The dirt and perspiration of a garment not washed as frequently as he himself was accustomed to, yes—but also the soft tang of her hair. He swore he could feel her breath on his cheek, and his fingers twitched of their own accord, seeking the touch of her skin.

He would have berated himself, severely, for becoming so distracted, for failing to keep up the careful watch that was the job she'd asked of him, had he been given the time to think of it. As it was, he was still all but blind to the world, reveling in imagined intimacies, when a pair of hands closed on his shoulders from behind and yanked him back off the street.

✺

Shins went straight for the hearth, and the fire roaring within, pulling up a chair and joining several others who sat with hands outstretched, warming themselves. A few surreptitious glances as she crossed the room were enough to offer the gist of the place, and the fireplace itself provided an excuse to sit, study, and scheme.

The common room of the Second Home was not so much tavern-like, as with the case in most hostels with which she was familiar, as it was a communal social area. Multiple tables were set up for games, including cards, dice, and a complex board game of unique tokens and tactical maneuvers representing two of the pre-Galicien tribal states attempting to "civilize" one another. The normal tavernish odors were at least partly cloaked by some combination of floral herbs thrown on the fire, though where they'd gotten such things at this time of year was a mystery unto itself.

Food and drink were available, of course, but they were selected from a menu and provided by servers who came and went from a kitchen off to one side. The concept of the restaurant was only a few generations old in Davillon; she was a bit surprised to see that it'd taken root in a community as small as Aubier. Then again, the place *did* have to cater to a wide variety of travelers and . . .

And she was getting way, *way* off track. "Quit distracting me!" she hissed at Olgun, then ignored his emotional double take in response. All this was well and good, but it wasn't getting her any closer to finding the man she'd followed—or, for that matter, identifying anyone, Crow or otherwise, who might actually be here looking for *her*.

"Shouldn't be too hard getting upstairs," she noted to her incorporeal companion. Indeed, people were tromping up and down the wide, wooden steps all the time, heading to or departing from the various rented chambers. "Problem is, then what? Going to attract a *little* attention if we just start knocking on random doors, yes? If we—"

The serving girl didn't actually look all *that* much like Robin. This young woman was taller, not quite as thin. Her hair was darker, longer, curlier; her carriage somehow, in a paradox Widdershins couldn't begin to resolve, both more graceful and clumsier all at once. Put the two of them in a room together and nobody, from close friends to utter strangers, would ever mistake one for the other.

Still, the general waifish resemblance was just enough to send an icicle of homesickness through Widdershins's heart, hotly pursued by an angry, despairing clench in her gut. She only realized she was staring when the serving girl tossed her a nervous glance and then skittishly headed for the kitchen, just shy of a run.

It was only then, struggling to rein in her wildly disparate emotions, that it occurred to Shins: That girl, and all the other servers of the Second Home, were differentiated from the patrons only by the simple aprons they wore over whatever clothes they'd happened to don that morning.

"Olgun," she said, a smile breaking through the mask of tension, "I bet you've always wanted to be a bar wench, yes?"

❈

Since Not-Robin had already noticed her, and Shins felt disinclined to make herself stand out to any more people than she must, it was the waifish girl she eventually spoke to. (Once she'd finally emerged from the kitchen and gone back about her duties, of course.) She'd been more than a bit frightened when Shins approached her, and seemed ready to break into a run when the thief offered her a handful of coin, but calmed a bit when Shins explained she wanted only to borrow the woman's apron. That, in turn, had led to a number of suspicious but predictable questions, which Widdershins had deflected with some yarn about sneaking up to see a lover who didn't visit Aubier that often, and whose staff would only let her pass if she appeared to have legitimate business.

It took a bit more convincing after that—but given that the coin Shins offered was more than the server would make in a week, *only* a bit. Not-Robin "got sick and had to go lie down," while Widdershins carelessly stuffed Cyrille's cloak in a corner, donned the apron, and proceeded upstairs.

Where she discovered doors, and hallways, and more stairs, and more hallways, and more doors.

Guests came and went, servers came and went, tromping down what might once, long ago, have been fine carpeting into a solid, if fuzzy, slab. The place had absorbed the odor of so many people through the years, it could have driven a bloodhound to hard liquor. Voices rose and fell as doors opened on conversations or groups of people chattered their way along the halls.

It wasn't truly as packed and bustling as Shins felt it was—the Second Home was still only a single establishment, after all, in the midst of what was not precisely the busiest trading and traveling season—but it was more than busy enough to complicate things. She *still* couldn't just start knocking on doors, nor could she loiter indefinitely in hopes of recognizing one man. She'd be spotted by one of the other servers, who would almost certainly recognize her as an imposter, even if she didn't start to make the guests suspicious.

She absently slipped aside, clearing room for a rotund little man with an armful of boxes to stagger past. She watched him go, not really seeing him at all, until he almost dropped the whole stack while maneuvering himself onto the stairwell. Then, smiling again, she dashed downstairs to recover Cyrille's cloak.

After that, it was just a matter of finding a guest who—due to dress or (if she could sneak a peek) the general state of his room— gave the impression of having been staying here for some time.

"Begging your pardon for disturbing you, sir, but could you help me out? Someone left this"—and here she held up the cloak that was *clearly* too fine to belong to some mere servant—"in the common room downstairs. I didn't get a very good look at the fellow while he was sitting there, but I *did* spot one of his companions." Then, after as detailed a description of the third man from the mill as she could produce, "It would look very bad for me if I had to go to my employer and admit I couldn't find the owner. Do you have any idea, maybe, where he might be?"

The first two guests she approached had no idea who she was speaking of. The third rudely dismissed her two sentences into her speech, demanding she get out of his way. The fourth directed her to someone who vaguely resembled, but clearly was not, the man she sought, and the fifth, once more, expressed ignorance.

Number six, however (which was two beyond the point where Olgun had been forced to talk Shins out of giving up on the whole idea), directed her to the third floor, a full half of which was occupied by a single large party in adjoining chambers. A moment with Olgun boosting her hearing, allowing her to absorb the tone, if not the meaning, of the conversations within various rooms—along with a guess that whoever was in charge would want the most possible privacy—inspired her to begin with the room farthest from the stairs.

The door opened to her timid tapping, revealing a younger servant who was clearly not the man she sought, though he was dressed somewhat similarly. It didn't matter, though, for what drew her attention wasn't him at all, but someone else in the room, seated on a plush settee, a silver goblet in his hand.

It was all she could do not to stare, to keep focused on the servant as she apologized for the interruption and demurely asked if any of them had lost a cloak. The younger man glanced back, several voices spoke up in denial, the old man with the goblet merely shook his head, and Widdershins went on her way. It wasn't until she heard the door latch firmly that she broke into a mad dash for the stairs.

She'd seen the man only once before, and even then it hadn't been the fellow himself but a large portrait, hanging within a large manor in the city of Lourveaux. Still, she'd looked closely enough then to know him now. Despite the artist's liberties, despite the fact that he'd changed to far less ostentatious garb, she recognized Lazare Carnot, patriarch of House Carnot, when she saw him.

Finally it made sense to her. Once the Carnots had obliterated their rival's businesses in Lourveaux, they had indeed turned toward Aubier, last stronghold of House Delacroix. But they'd come in secret, anonymous and hidden. Only servants carried word from Lazare to the Thousand Crows, only Josce to the *native* Carnot branch. Hens and horses, how much did the local Carnots even really know of what was happening?!

"Cyrille will believe me," she told Olgun between breaths, taking the steps three at a time, dropping her rented apron unnoticed behind her. "Matron Lemon-Face will grumble like a constipated cat, but she'll have to at least look into it, yes?" She dodged around a pair of startled customers and a server at the base of the steps, ignored the attention she drew in her sprint across the common room. "Once they know Lazare Carnot's here, they'll *have* to—"

Widdershins hit the front door like it had insulted her family, stepped out into the street . . .

And found it swarming with House Delacroix armsmen. A few Aubier constables stood in the throng as well, but none appeared to be officers, and they were very clearly subservient to the house guards.

No sign of Cyrille. Was he all right? Had the family taken him, or had something happened to him before they arrived?

No sign of Jourdain. Either the man had other duties, or he'd been held back from this outing for other reasons.

The only one Widdershins recognized, in fact, was the man leading them. One of Cyrille's older brothers; the fist-happy one.

Malgier.

"It's painfully apparent," he said loudly, facing her but clearly addressing his men, "that Veroche cannot be trusted to perform her duties." His smile was wide, cruel; his eyes colder than the slowly accumulating snow. "So I don't think there's any need to further disturb her with this. Trials are long and expensive, anyway.

"Make sure there's no need for one."

CHAPTER THIRTEEN

"What in the name of gods and gophers is *wrong* with you people?! Your enemy's here! He's *right here*, right inside!"

The first rank of House Delacroix's soldiers advanced, blades sliding free of sheaths, a bristling thornbush of razor-sharp steel. To either side of the Second Home, the street emptied like an unstoppered tub, most of the civilians taking shelter in this building or that, a few hunkering in windows or doorways to watch.

This was a statement, then, as much as a move against her personally. Calanthe was flexing the family muscle for the edification of the Thousand Crows, and anyone else watching.

Not that ulterior motives would make Shins any less dead.

"You don't even have to believe me!" she tried once more, growing desperate. The sounds filtering through the door behind her faded as the people inside began to realize something big was occurring only yards away. "Just come with me and I'll show you! If I'm lying, you can kill me then, yes?"

A couple of the guards did falter at that, glancing back to their commander for guidance, but it lasted only briefly. When Malgier gave no order to stand down, they fell back into step with their more stony-faced comrades.

And Widdershins, who'd struggled hard thus far to keep her newly inflammable temper in check, had finally bloody had it. She actually felt her pulse pounding in her temples as the whole world took on the faint tinge of red.

Fine! If that's how they want it . . . "Olgun?"

She swore she felt him nod.

They approached with care, those first guards, clearly having been warned of Shins's unnatural prowess. Perhaps they hadn't fully believed those stories, or maybe it was simply the best they could muster; whatever the case, "with care" wasn't careful *enough*.

The first man lunged, rapier extended in perfect form. Widdershins spun aside, unslowed by the thin skin of snow beneath her. She snagged the guard's wrist and yanked him forward, off balance. His blade sank into the wood of the door, stuck fast. The man himself flew back as Widdershins reversed her spin with impossible speed and planted a kick in the soldier's chest. He collided hard with a second guard, tangling them, if only momentarily, in a web of flailing limbs.

Another charge, and this time, the young thief leapt, fingertips snagging the top of the doorframe. She kicked both feet, so she hung nearly horizontal from her precarious grip. Nose broken and lip split against her heels, another man struck the frigid dust of the roadway.

When Widdershins's boots hit the ground once more, she held her own rapier in one tight fist.

"Stop dancing with her!" Malgier hollered.

Guards closed, steel chimed, snow crunched, blood flew. Here, the flesh of an arm opened up; there, a calf muscle utterly collapsed, punctured and torn. Shins was everywhere, a whirling dust devil of blacks and grays and browns. Olgun warned her of fists and blades from behind, quickened her limbs, held fatigue at bay.

Four soldiers down. Five. Seven. Had she wished them dead, they would, to the last, be dead.

They weren't. Even in her fury, Shins wouldn't cross that line, not unless they left her no other choice.

She came close, though, a time or two. A few of these men might *never* run or wield a sword with quite the same facility they once had.

Widdershins stood alone in the doorway, breathing heavily, blood sliding in rivulets along her blade. Armsmen groaned, sobbed, bled in a carpet of suffering all around her. Malgier and the remaining guards stared at her in an appalled mixture of anger and an almost superstitious fear.

Then the cruel Delacroix's hand dropped to the flintlock at his side.

"He wouldn't!" she gasped at Olgun. "Not when a miss could punch through the door or a wind—"

"Pistols!" Malgier shouted.

"Oh, *figs!*"

To their credit, most of the guards did no such thing, a few even daring to point out to their employer that a room full of civilians stood just beyond their target. A smattering of the armsmen *did* obey, however, firearms rising, and when Malgier snarled an abrupt, "Then don't miss!" Widdershins knew Cyrille's older brother really was genuinely mad enough to do it.

"Olgun!"

As familiar as he was with the little trick, the god couldn't cause every weapon swinging their way to misfire. Thankfully, he required only one. A pistol spat near the rear of the group, sending a lead ball deep into the snow and dirt, causing everyone to flinch, to twist about to see from where the shot had come.

In that snippet of distraction, Shins yanked open the door to the Second Home—setting the rapier embedded in the wood to wobbling obscenely—and dashed inside.

Patrons scrambled to clear her path, due perhaps to the blood-stained sword she brandished, perhaps to the stampede of armed soldiers who pursued only a few seconds behind her. She didn't *think* any of them, not even Malgier, would be insane enough to open fire in the room itself, but she ran an uneven line just in case. A leap to a table, a few running steps through various squishy meals, back to the floor, a jog to the left, spinning back as she sheathed her blade (which would require a *thorough* cleaning when she had a moment to herself).

Nobody shot at her, but her crooked course had kept her from building any distance between her and the armsmen.

"That's all right," she explained to Olgun between breaths. "We *want* them close!"

The tiny god did not, for some reason, seem greatly comforted by that.

Widdershins pounded up the stairs, again taking three at a time. A quick glance told her that only a portion of the Delacroix guards chased her; the others, she assumed, must be waiting outside, in case she tried to escape from some alternate exit.

No matter. Once she'd led them to Lazare Carnot's suite, that ought to be the end of it. Even if the patriarch denied his identity, *someone* on his staff would be intimidated enough to corroborate it. Once they had their hands on the patriarch, the guards would have to—

That the hallway was empty was no surprise; she'd expected most of the guests to be hiding in their rooms until the chaos had passed. When Lazare's room—which she entered via a swift, Olgun-powered kick to the latch—proved equally empty, that was a bit more of a shock.

She wanted to break things, to lie down and weep, to curse as abhorrently as she ever had during her days on the streets. Furniture, clothes, the various comforts and decorations of a long sojourn, these all remained. Even the scent of expensive cologne lingered in the air, and while a small brazier had been doused, it was so recent that the ashes and charcoal still radiated a comforting warmth. No people, though; and Widdershins didn't need to search to be certain they'd taken anything incriminating or identifying with them.

"They must have fled the moment the soldiers appeared in the street," she muttered bitterly. "Of all the lousy, rotten . . ."

She moved as she groused, having scarcely stopped to look around before going straight to the window. She had only heartbeats before the room began to fill with pointy metal things, as well as men who wanted to stick her with them. A look outside and, yep, as she'd figured: Delacroix soldiers in the street. Not a *lot*—they had to be pretty spread out if they were surrounding the place—but enough to slow her down until the others arrived, should she attempt to challenge them.

All right. She'd give them a different sort of challenge.

Shins threw herself through the window, three limbs and head tucked into a ball, left hand outstretched. She grabbed the edge of the pane as she passed, swinging herself around rather than straight through it. Her legs and her other hand shot out, fingers and toes striking the wall *just* before her face would have.

Even for her, even with divine aid, it was tricky. The outer walls of the Second Home weren't especially smooth, but neither did they display many obvious flaws. Her fingers and toes scrabbled a bit before she found enough purchase. A quick, slapdash climb—she could only imagine how it looked from the ground, but she assumed it bore some resemblance to a drunken beetle trying to scale an icicle—and she vaulted onto the roof.

She'd definitely been spotted; several of the soldiers below were indeed pointing her way and shouting. Well, good. She'd have hated to pull a stunt like that and have had her audience miss it.

So where to . . . ? Ah.

The nearest building to the Second Home was off to her right. The distance between the two structures, factoring in height, represented a jump Shins wouldn't have wanted to try by herself on her best day, and only marginally more with Olgun's help on *his* best day.

"Trusting you not to let me slip or otherwise go splat," she said to him. "If I go, you go with me, and I'm pretty sure nobody around here wants to spend hours scraping god off the roadway."

Widdershins knelt, swept Cyrille's cloak from her shoulders, scooped up some snow, and held the garment closed like a large sack. She ran, then, pushing up one side of the peaked roof to stand at the very pinnacle. From here, she could see much of Aubier, poking up through thin sheets of white. Shins couldn't help but remember the last building from which she'd had such a view, and wished bitterly that this roof had been as flat as the earlier. Would've made this a *lot* simpler. And safer.

And saner.

"Ready? Too bad."

Taking enormous strides, each one a stretch, she started down the slope toward the eaves. Each step was taunting fate, a veritable death wish. With each one, her foot began to slide, her balance to fail, her body to topple forward where she would doubtless slide like a greased eel and shoot off the roof to her squishy doom.

Widdershins had lived by her agility for much of her life. Olgun could perform a great many unnatural feats. Still, the two of them together found it a struggle; by the time she reached the edge, the young thief was sweating despite the chill.

It had worked, though. Looking back, she saw a trail in the snow that very strongly suggested someone had *run* down the peaked roof, clearly in a desperate jump for freedom. Sure, any skilled tracker, or even a sharp-eyed guard, could probably tell the tracks weren't made by a runner, but Shins was counting on her pursuers being in a hurry. She just had to help them along a bit.

She spun the cloak-turned-sack over her head once, twice, and let fly. Carried by the extra weight of the snow packed within, it sailed over the gap and flattened out atop the opposite roof. A dozen signs revealed she *hadn't* actually made the leap and lost the cloak—the lack of other marks or tracks on that roof, the snow scattered atop the cloak—but with luck, they'd be on that roof (and off this one) before noticing any of them.

A few deep breaths, the chill air searing her lungs. They were exhausted, she and Olgun both, but they had one more impossible feat ahead.

Widdershins tensed and jumped. She felt the god's invisible

touch under her heels, propelling her, bringing the impossible within reach.

She almost didn't make it. Had they both been stronger, fresher, she'd have landed cleanly atop the edge of the chimney, feet planted to either side for balance. As it was, she fell a bit short. Her thighs slammed into the edge of the stone with brutal force, and the resulting topple sent a sharp shock, and probably a deep bruise, across her upper ribs. For a moment she lay there, sprawled over the flue, ragged breaths and muffled sobs racking her body. The smoke—a thin tendril, thankfully, as the innkeepers would burn only so much firewood at a time—leaked past her to either side.

No time, no time . . . She didn't know if the hostel had stairs to the roof, or where they might be; or whether the soldiers would have to find a ladder. She knew only they couldn't be far, now. *Need to get up. Move, you turkey!*

Groaning despite every effort not to, she levered herself around and slid feetfirst into the chimney. Back pressed against one wall, feet against the other, knees tight against her chest, she waited. Her muscles, already fatigued, began to cramp. The heat of the fire three stories below would soon cross over from nicely warm to a slow broil, and even the fairly light flow of smoke would begin to choke her, as well as back up into the common room, if she remained too long.

Now that her slapdash escape plan was no longer in danger of being interrupted, Widdershins found herself wishing, hoping, even praying that the Delacroix soldiers would kindly hurry up—before said escape plan did the job of killing her *for* them.

Night descended. The waning moon hauled itself into the sky, frequently stopping to rest on the backs of passing clouds. Traffic throughout Aubier grew sparse as lanterns and hearths began to gleam through shuttered windows across the city. The snow let up, replaced by biting winds and the occasional finger of sleet.

And Widdershins, for the third time since she'd come to this godsforsaken place, crept carefully through the Delacroix fields, drawing ever nearer the main house.

She was scarcely recognizable as the same person she'd been the last time. She shivered in the cold, lacking any sort of cloak, warmed only by her leathers, her constant motion, and her searing, resentful fury. She was covered in chimney ash, her face and hands and clothes caked with the stuff. It had taken everything Olgun could do to keep her from leaving a trail when she'd crept off the Second Home's rooftop. (The soldiers might have left enough tracks, in their search, that her own prints wouldn't show, but regular clumps of flaking ash would have been another story altogether.) Her ribs and legs throbbed where they'd bruised; her chest ached and her throat burned from both the cold air and the choking smoke she'd had to endure for long minutes on end. She stank of sweat, wood smoke, and desperation.

Twice she'd dropped flat, hiding in the shadows and the rolling divots in the plain as Delacroix guards passed nearby on patrol. Both times, she'd had to squelch an urge to stand and draw their attention, just as an excuse to vent some frustration.

This place was poison to her. This *family* was poison. How could they possibly be related to the man she'd known, so long ago?

She knew the window she wanted this time and headed straight for it. Sure enough, there he was, asleep in his bed. She could see, from the redness in his cheeks and puffy eyes, that he'd been crying before he fell asleep. No doubt the matriarch's discipline had been harsh, perhaps even physical. But the point was, Cyrille was safe, or relatively so. He had, indeed, been grabbed by his own family, not by the enemy. He didn't need saving—at least not of any sort she could provide.

Which meant there was nothing left holding her here.

"Come on, Olgun. We're leaving."

They were a few dozen yards from the house before Olgun realized she didn't just mean leaving the *property*. Multiple visions of Alexandre Delacroix, striking and intense, flickered across her vision.

"I don't *care!*" she snapped back. "I've tried as hard as he could ever have asked, even harder! They tried to *kill* me, for pastries' sake!"

More imagery, more emotion.

"And do you know for sure it *was* just Malgier being a raving idiot? That it wasn't on Mommy's orders? Because *I* don't! No. Leaving. Now."

Then, "No. No! I *don't care!* Alexandre would understand. And even if he *would* be disappointed, *I don't care!* I don't!"

A final surge of emotion, sharp, stabbing.

"No, I . . . don't care if you're disappointed, either." But she'd have had to be both unconscious and deaf to miss the quiver of doubt in her own protest.

She had, by then, gotten some slight distance from the house—and apparently at least a few yards beyond the boundaries of good fortune. Arguing too loudly with Olgun? Failure to pay attention, to drop into hiding at the first sound? Whatever the case, even the combined abilities of god and thief weren't infallible.

"Hold where you are, hands on your head!"

"Oh, figs."

A trio of them, household guards, faintly glowing specters in the diluted moonlight. Shins couldn't tell in the gloom if these were men she'd run into before—though she couldn't imagine the Delacroix employed *too* many more armsmen than she'd already encountered—but she *could* make out the muskets pointed her way.

"I'm tired of this," she growled, not bothering to keep her voice down.

"Then perhaps," the first of the guards began as he neared, "you shouldn't go places you're not—"

Widdershins sidestepped and jumped, hurling herself at him while clearing his line of fire. The soldier, with an abortive sound that might have been distantly related to a yelp, swung his weapon around, struggling to bring it back on target.

Her hands closed on the barrel, yanked the musket from his grip, and then drove it back again, slamming the stock into his face. The guard screamed through split lips and missing teeth, gurgling horribly as he folded. Widdershins crouched, hurling the musket like a javelin and then catching the semiconscious soldier, interposing him between herself and the other two guns.

Or one gun, rather, as her makeshift projectile knocked one of the remaining guards reeling.

Recognizing that opening fire was a poor option, the nearer man charged, throwing his musket aside and pulling his rapier. Shins dropped the wounded man and met her attacker halfway, parrying a single thrust, pirouetting past him, and—as she'd done with the Thousand Crows in the foundry—focused instead on the more distant foe, the one clearly unprepared for her attack.

Her sword took him deep in the shoulder before his own blade had fully cleared its scabbard.

She heard a noise in the air, a vicious tremor, and realized she was literally snarling as she flung herself back at the middle guard. Steel kissed and sang, and the third man fell, crying out and clutching at a knee that had just been broken by an inhumanly powerful kick.

They'd live, all three of them. Shins sniffed, knelt to wipe her blade clean on one of their cloaks, thought about taking one to warm herself, began to reach for the clasp . . .

The guard spasmed, clutching, clawing at his mutilated knee. It seemed, in the faint light and against the uneven earth, to flex at angles no human limb should bend.

Three men who would live—but who would not soon, perhaps would not *ever*, live as they had. Whose bodies might never fully recover.

Widdershins felt her stomach lurch, her gorge rise. She doubled over, and only Olgun's calming touch in her gut, her mind, her soul kept her from dropping fully to her knees, vomiting profusely over the grass.

"What's happened to me?" She couldn't even cry; wanted to, felt as though she *needed* to, but the tears wouldn't come.

And Olgun had no answer she could comprehend.

It took a moment, but she finally brought herself under control and stood. "All right, we can't just leave them here. I could fire a shot from one of their muskets. That should bring someone running, yes? Another patrol, or maybe somebody from the house?"

She glanced that way even as she had the thought, watched the faint twinkle of firelight in many of the windows . . .

Something slipped into place in her mind, so abruptly it made her jump and dragged a startled squeak from Olgun.

I know how they did it. I know how the Crows and the Carnots pulled it all off.

Shins absently patted the pouch on her belt that still held the map she'd acquired from the unconscious thug some nights past. A map that showed the Delacroix properties, broken into numbered sections. She tapped, and she peered across the field at the house, a dull hulking shape with glinting windows, and tapped some more.

"I'm done with this," she insisted.

Olgun said nothing.

"They'll figure it out for themselves. Or maybe they won't. I don't care."

Nothing.

"I'm just going to draw some attention so these men get help, and then we are *leaving*."

Still nothing—an emotional void, bereft of the slightest sensation or response.

"Oh, *figs!*"

Widdershins broke into a jog back toward the Delacroix house.

And Olgun smiled.

CHAPTER FOURTEEN

"All right, Cyrille." The matriarch's voice was cold, flat, a thin sheet of ice over a bottomless, sunless lake. "We're here, as you requested. You do, of course, have something of *such* tremendous import that it absolutely could not wait for a more reasonable hour?" Her lack of expression, lack of tone, promised very unpleasant results if he did not.

Cyrille nodded, only half-listening. "As he requested" indeed! It had taken close to an hour of arguing, insisting, pleading, even shouting—and it had been, it seemed, the last that had convinced Calanthe, if only because it was so greatly out of character for her youngest son.

So here they were, gathered in the library as they had been the night Shins had come into his life. Or almost as they had been. Mother took the same central chair, a queen ruling her tiny domain from her tiny throne. Arluin stood nearby, his attentions on the bookshelves while waiting for someone to speak. Anouska, opposite her mother like a younger reflection; Josephine with her lantern, the twins with their coins. Marjolaine was absent, as always, but this time, so was Malgier. Apparently he was confined to his chambers until the matriarch decided on a fitting discipline. Cyrille had known Malgier was in serious trouble, but not for what. Not until—

"Did you drag us down here to spend what's left of the night gawping?" Anouska demanded of him.

A quick blink, and he was back in the moment. "No. First, though . . . Mother, would you permit me to dismiss the servants, please?"

Multiple scoffs, then, from his siblings. Chandler and Helaine asked, in unison, "Don't want to embarrass yourself in front of the help?" Several of the others rolled their eyes, and even Arluin looked skeptical. Hell, the servants by the door were, themselves, only scarcely managing to hide their entitled smirks.

"Don't be tiresome, Cyrille," Calanthe scolded. "Nothing you could possibly have to say, no family business involving you in any way, is so sensitive as all that."

"You might be surprised. Mother . . . Please."

Calanthe studied him, much as though she were attempting to discern what strange species of being he was, and then waved a pair of fingers behind her without looking back. The two servants started a bit, as did several of the Delacroix, but they knew better than to argue. The heavy doors clacked together behind the departing attendants.

Cyrille earned himself even more scoffing and muttering from his siblings as he moved to the door and threw the heavy bolt, ensuring nobody could open it from the outside. He wandered to the other, smaller door, locked that one as well.

"If you're quite finished," the matriarch began, no longer even pretending to conceal her impatience, "perhaps you could tell us what this is about before dawn begins to—"

She was staring at him, suddenly alert, and Cyrille had no doubt why. He'd seen his reflection in the window as he moved to the second door. His face was ghastly pale, his lip trembling despite his efforts to bite it still.

"What have you done?" she hissed at him. The rest of her children went still, their attentions snagged by her tone.

"I—"

"He hasn't done anything." He didn't know precisely where she'd been hiding; in a chamber such as this, *how* she'd been hiding. He knew only that she seemed to appear from nowhere as she spoke. "All he did was arrange an opportunity for us to talk. So let's talk, yes?"

✳

Shins had no idea how many blades or other weapons to expect. It was one of the details Cyrille hadn't been able to guess at, when she'd snuck into his room to plan. Thankfully, it appeared only two, as the two eldest children drew steel—Arluin a heavy dueling dagger; Anouska a wicked, fat-bladed stiletto. With Olgun's aid and aim, a quick crescent kick sent the latter weapon spinning across the library to land in the corner, while a series of quick thrusts and twists with her rapier yanked the larger blade from Arluin's hand. Shins stepped in, caught it, hurled it, in one smooth motion, her fingers alive with a touch of the divine.

It sank deep into the wood of the smaller door, just beside the latch, blocking the bolt from sliding back. A few quick sidesteps and she stood before the larger door, blocking the only other easy exit from the library.

"You could try shouting," she said to the Delacroix, who thus far hadn't gotten much past the wide-eyed, slack-jawed gasping stage. "But even if your people heard you, they're not getting in anytime soon. If I *wanted* to hurt you, I'd have plenty of time to do it. Hopping hens, I could have done it just *now*." She waved her sword idly at Anouska and Arluin. "Can we *please*, for just a moment, accept that I'm here for reasons that *don't* involve blood, pain, and the ruining of such fine outfits?"

Calanthe turned her head, not toward Widdershins but toward Cyrille. Her youngest son visibly quailed before whatever it was he saw, shrinking back, his lips trembling. Only then did the matriarch focus on Widdershins again.

The thief knew she wasn't exactly at her most presentable. Despite quick efforts to clean up in Cyrille's room, much of her face and neck were smeared with ash. Her clothes were spotted with it, her hair thickly dusted. Trails ran through the darker splotches, where her sweat had sluiced bits of it away before threatening to freeze in the cold. She didn't even want to know what she smelled like to other people, but was fairly certain she could turn wine to vinegar at thirty paces.

"Why should we believe a single word you have to say?" Calanthe demanded. If she was at all afraid of Shins, it certainly didn't show.

"Better question," she replied, sheathing her sword, "is why shouldn't you? Or at least hear me out?"

"Mother?" Josephine clutched her lantern to her chest, trembling like a child. "Make her go away!"

Arluin's expression went cold at his sister's plea, and he took a single step toward the intruder, fists clenched.

Oh, crepe. Time to cut straight to the point, then; she couldn't afford to build to it if things were about to go violent again.

"There's a traitor in House Delacroix."

That, at least, rooted everyone to the spot.

Calanthe cast a quick glance at Cyrille, who flushed and looked like he wanted to climb into his own pockets.

"Not what I meant," Shins snapped.

"Nonsense," Calanthe spat, even as several of the others protested, often with more intensity and vulgarity both. "We're family. Nobody here would turn on us."

"Did you send Malgier to kill me?"

For the first time, the matriarch blanched, her fingers tightening on the arms of her chair. "No," she admitted. "I wouldn't send my people to commit cold-blooded murder unless I had no choice. I *certainly* would not have had them open fire outside a bloody hostel! Malgier thought he would ingratiate himself; he will learn otherwise."

"Don't have quite the leash on your family you believe, then, do you?"

Anouska and the twins growled. Calanthe's lip curled.

"Malgier can be overzealous, but he is protective of the family, and he is *loyal*!"

"Like a guard hound," Widdershins suggested.

"If you like."

"If he's a hound," the thief asked sweetly, "what does that make his mother?"

Cyrille slapped both palms against his face as if he were trying to wipe it off his head.

Before the half a dozen indrawn breaths could transform into furious shouting, Widdershins stepped forward and slapped something down on one of the small library tables. Several of the Delacroix offspring were too far back to see what it was, but the nearer, and Calanthe herself, could make it out just fine.

"I took this," Shins told them, "from two of the Thousand Crows. Whom I found on your property. They also had these." She tossed the gruesome-smelling wineskin to the floor beside the table. "I think you'll find it's the source of the blight."

"How do we know these aren't yours?" Calanthe asked, but it was a reflex, a protest without heart. Clearly, she was running out of reasons to suspect that this was some elaborate ruse.

"So, it's a map of our properties," Helaine scoffed. "So what? Anyone could make such a thing."

"Anyone could," Widdershins agreed. "See, I'd wondered for a while how the Crows were doing it. Just sort of poking at it, while I thought mostly about other stuff. I mean, your grounds are extensive, yes, but your patrols are pretty thorough. *I* had trouble getting past them . . ."

She glanced sideways at Cyrille, who nodded subtly. The boy *had* sent servants to collect the injured men, then. Good. The iceberg of guilt in her gut melted just a bit.

". . . and trust me, I'm better at this sort of thing than the Crows are. They might've gotten through once, *maybe* twice, but not as often as they have."

"Except they clearly did," Calanthe observed.

"Clearly. How did they know which of your fields were related to your textile interests, as opposed to food crops? They *did* only try to poison your textiles, yes? It's not as though the fields are labeled or look all that different during winter."

"There *are* people who know," Arluin muttered, "hired hands and the like." But he, too, sounded uncertain.

"The Thousand Crows," Shins continued relentlessly, hammering each point home, "have no magic. Their 'sorcerer' practices alchemy. No mystical scouting of your properties.

"They needed someone inside who could tell them where the patrols were assigned, when to strike, *where* to strike. With that." She pointed at the map.

"This doesn't show our guard patrols," the eldest son protested. "It *can't*. We determine them nightly."

"But it *is* divided into sections. It'd be easy to communicate a few numbers, even at a great distance. You just need the right tool, something that could be seen from clear across the fields. Something like, say, a blinking light. In unusual colors, maybe, so it's easily picked out from among the other lights in the house?"

Dead, utter silence, like the corpse of a mime. Every eye in the room fixed on Fifi; her expression was blank, her hands clenched on her favorite toy.

Then Calanthe began to laugh.

It started with a tremor in her shoulders, scarcely visible beneath her gown, then grew to a soft, dignified chuckle. The old woman raised a hand to her lips, but they did nothing to muffle the tittering, and then the open, full-throated guffaw. Most of the others were close behind, a variety of chortles, snickers, and outright cackles. Of all the Delacroix, only Arluin, Josephine, and, of course, Cyrille, refrained.

Well, that could maybe have gone better. Not that Shins had expected a credulous response, but still, the open mockery was vaguely disturbing.

Just as abruptly, the matriarch went silent, her jaw tense as hardwood. It took a minute, but the others slowly followed her lead, the cacophony fading.

"If you're not dishonest," Calanthe snarled, "you're insane. Of every member of my family you could have pointed to, it wouldn't be less believable if you'd chosen *me*! Josephine is *harmless*."

"I'm not even sure she knows how to count as high as that map goes," Chandler muttered.

"Hey!" Fifi protested, at the same time Arluin snapped, "Don't speak of your sister that way!"

Calanthe silenced the lot of them with a raised hand. "I'm going to offer you one last opportunity to leave," she began, "under the assumption that you're a fool, not an enemy. Would you care to take it?"

Widdershins smiled, in part to cover the grinding of her teeth. *Anytime now . . .*

"There's an easy way to prove it."

Finally!

Cyrille stepped away from the smaller door, moving to stand beside Widdershins. "A quick search of Fifi's room."

Again the library filled with angry and indignant protests. Arluin looked ready to start swinging, and Calanthe appeared as cold as Widdershins had ever seen.

"Mother?" Josephine asked, quivering.

"It's not going to happen, Josephine. Cyrille, I don't know *what* this girl has told you, but—"

"There would have to be a copy of the map." Calanthe seemed taken aback as much by the interruption as the words, but either way, she permitted Cyrille to speak. "A means of matching the numbers, section to section, to be certain of no miscommunication. We do a quick search for a map like this one. If it's not there, I'll help deliver Widdershins to the reeve myself."

This was it, then. Everything she and Cyrille had discussed hinged on these next moments. Would they go along with it, if only to assuage any tiny flicker of doubt? *Would* the traitor have such a map? It wasn't *probable* she would try to memorize it—the divisions were many, the odds of error high—but neither was it impossible. Would they—?

Calanthe gazed, unblinking, first at Widdershins and then her youngest son. Widdershins thought she saw the barest quirk of the matriarch's lips. And it was all the thief could do to keep from bursting out in laughter herself.

She's going to go for it just so Cyrille can see for himself that I'm wrong! To "break my spell."

"Very well," Calanthe said. "But I will hold you to this, Cyrille. Josephine, dearest, wait here with the others. Anouska and I are just going to poke around your room a bit, all right?"

"I don't like her!" Fifi wailed, pointing at Widdershins.

"I know. As soon as we're done, she'll be gone. For good. Anouska, shall we—?"

"No!" Fifi actually stamped her foot, scowling. "I don't want you looking through my room. It's not nice."

Anouska shook her head. "We'll put everything back—"

"Don't want it!" She hugged the lantern to her chest, squeezing it as though it were a stuffed animal. "I'm allowed my privacy, too. Just like all of you."

"Josephine, you stop this!" Calanthe ordered. "What's gotten into you? You have the staff in your room on a regular basis!"

"Um . . ." Arluin practically chewed his beard, clearly not certain he wanted to speak. "The staff haven't been permitted in Fifi's room for weeks. She's been doing her own straightening. Hugh mentioned it to me, once, while collecting my laundry. We dismissed it as just another of her whims."

Nearly everyone was standing at this point, save the matriarch herself, and the attentions they'd turned on Josephine were perhaps a touch less certain, a touch less sympathetic, than they'd been.

"I don't understand!" Tears ran freely down Josephine's face, now. "Mother, don't do this!"

"I'm afraid I have to, Josephine."

The face behind those tears and curled locks of hair *twisted* in sudden rage. The hatred and resentment seemed almost to push at her flesh from within, angry snakes behind a mask of skin. Not since the inhuman Iruoch had Widdershins seen an expression so horrid; she wasn't certain she'd *ever* seen it on a human being before.

"Fine!" It was a banshee shriek, raw and ragged. Widdershins throat hurt just *thinking* about it. "Fuck you all!"

Josephine spun and hurled her lantern against one of the looming bookcases. Glass shattered. Burning oil, such a tiny amount, sprayed out from the wreckage.

The books ignited instantly.

Widdershins was moving almost as instantly, springing across the room, vaulting over any furniture in her path. "Move that sofa! Get the carpet out of the way!"

The bookcase itself was hardwood, heavy; maybe enough to smother the flame before the burning tomes ignited the wood itself. But only if half a dozen things went right.

"Olgun, I can't move this thing! I need every—"

Except, she realized, she wasn't working alone. Arluin appeared only a step behind her, arm raised to shield his face from the sparks and embers. He saw her scrabbling for a handhold, away from the flames, nodded once, and dashed to the other side of the bookcase. "On three!" He called, then coughed as a puff of smoke drifted his way.

Shins glanced back, saw Anouska, Chandler, and Calanthe herself dragging the sofa that would otherwise have interrupted the bookcase's fall, as well as the carpet beneath it. This was as good as it was going to get.

"One!"

"Olgun, I need you to try to make sure any of the books that slip out . . ."

"Two!"

". . . fall straight, so they're still beneath the wood, don't go scattering across the—"

"*Three!*"

Face turned away, eyes squinting against the heat, Widdershins heaved, even as she felt Arluin do the same. Her arms quivered, muscles protesting; Olgun's power surged through her, but not so much as she might have hoped, not with the god also focusing on the burning books. The bookcase teetered, rocked back, settled itself straight, teetered forward once more . . .

And finally tumbled with a resounding, ember-spouting crash.

Olgun came close. Only a few bits of burning paper or showers of sparks escaped from beneath the massive weight, and those were easily smothered by the curtains Shins and Arluin tore from the window. By the time they were done, even the tiniest tendrils of smoke had ceased to trickle from beneath the fallen furniture, and the wood itself remained blissfully not on fire.

Widdershins only then realized she was hearing a sound unrelated to the fire, a shrill howl that only vaguely shaped itself into vile obscenities and gruesome curses.

Her hair fallen loose, all semblance of childish innocence gone, Fifi struggled and screamed. Cyrille and Helaine held her arms pinned behind her, slowly marching her away from the main doors at which she'd apparently made a final dash. Judging by their expressions and the emotional tremor of their limbs, Widdershins was pretty certain that, had the fire caught and spread, Josephine might well have found herself flung into its embrace.

She halted her tirade as Widdershins approached, her glare hotter than her lantern had ever been. She spit, once, but Shins sidestepped the splatter without breaking stride. The thief stopped just beyond arm's reach, finger held to her lips in thought.

"Middle children," she observed. "Always under the most scrutiny, yes? Doesn't do the younger ones any good to scheme and play politics, but you guys? Only have to discredit a few siblings to become top dog of the heap." Then, softly, "Hush, Olgun. They're my metaphors, and I'll mix them as I choose."

She spoke aloud once more. "Playing dumb was clever. Keeps that scrutiny off you. Don't know if I could've done that for years on end, but I guess the role came naturally." She smiled sweetly. "Please, tell me I'm wrong. Tell me that your part in all this wasn't just the spoiled brat who's not inheriting as much as she thinks she's due and"—she stepped back a few paces, scooped up the evidentiary wineskin, and held it up as emphasis—"wants to punish her family for it."

"Stupid bitch." It was Fifi's only overt reply, but the slow flush in her cheeks and grinding of her teeth were all the answer Shins needed.

"So, here's what you're going to do—" Widdershins began.

"Go to hell! I'm not doing anything for you!"

"Oh, yes, you are."

Shins and Josephine both turned to watch as the matriarch of House Delacroix approached. Her cheeks were puffy, her eyes rimmed in red; whether from the face full of smoke or a show of humanity Shins would never have dreamed her capable of, the thief wouldn't dare guess. Whatever it was, whatever she *had* been feeling, showing, she was granite now.

"You are going to do *precisely* what you are told. Without argument, without hesitation, without deception. Am I clearly understood?"

"Mother, you can go to hell, too. Am *I* understood?"

From the sequence of gasps, one might've thought that talking to

Calanthe that way was a more shocking sin than Fifi's initial betrayal, or trying to burn them all alive.

"You stupid, idiot girl!" For all her defiance, Josephine recoiled from the sudden venom in her mother's voice. "You were smarter when you were playing dumb! What are you expecting out of this? Grounding? Chores? Maybe even exile to one of our other properties?

"You are going to *prison*, Josephine! I will hand you over to the reeve and testify against you at your hearing myself!"

The girl's face went pale, as did several of her siblings'. "Mother? I—"

"Don't call me that. How would you care to be treated by the constabulary and the courts? As noble blood, or a nameless peasant? Shall I disown you before or after your sentence is passed?"

Josephine literally stopped breathing for a moment before breaking down in racking, heaving sobs. "Mother," Arluin said tentatively, "perhaps we should—" He flinched, his speech smothered beneath the matriarch's disapproval.

"Your cooperation," she continued, hammering her daughter with every word, "determines at what point of the process you cease to be my child. Do you understand *now*?"

The girl's frantic nods splattered the toes of Widdershins's boots with tears. Contemptuous of Fifi's petty, selfish treason, she couldn't help but feel a bit of pity for the weeping aristocrat.

"So," Widdershins repeated, "here's what you're going to do. . . ."

INTERLUDE: DAVILLON

When the wagon trundled to a halt, when the bouncing and juddering over uneven cobblestones ceased to rattle his bones like dice in a gambler's hand, it still took him some time to realize that they had truly stopped; that this was not some pause mandated by late-night traffic or the driver taking the time to reorient himself, but a final destination.

Emphasis, quite possibly, on *final*.

His disorientation wasn't just from the discomfort of the ride itself, though that was severe enough; Major Archibeque of the Davillon Guard wasn't nearly so young as he used to be, nor were his joints so resilient. Still, had it been *only* wooden wheels clattering on uneven roadway, he'd have been a tad sore at worst. Archibeque, however, rode not on the bench at the wagon's front, but stretched out in back, buried under foul-smelling heaps of old fabric and scraps. And the beating it had taken to get him there made the everyday aches of aging absolutely pale in comparison.

His memories of how it had happened were jagged, broken, and sporadic at best. He'd been walking home, tired, after his shift. He was, it seemed, *always* tired after his shift, these days; ever since the Guard had lost several of its best people around the so-called Iruoch affair. No, Archibeque wasn't fool enough to believe the rumors that the actual fairy-tale creature had appeared in Davillon, but whatever the truth, the repercussions had been real enough.

So he'd already been at rather less than his best when the first of the thugs had jumped him just outside his house.

He recalled a brief tussle; lashing out, connecting with a fist here, an elbow there. Cost someone teeth with that one, he hoped. In the end, however, he'd had no chance even to draw rapier or pistol, let alone for victory.

Archibeque *did* have the presence of mind, however, to note that his attackers wielded saps and small clubs, and that even during the worst of the beating that followed, they took special care to avoid his face, head, or neck.

Someone badly wants me alive.

Not a comforting thought, that, but also their mistake. He'd been a fighter all his life, and if they thought age had robbed him of that spirit, they were sorely—

"Up and out, geezer!"

He felt the weight atop him shift, hands close around his wrists and collar, before he was manhandled from the wagon. Archibeque blinked, studying his surroundings.

They stood before an old house in middling condition, not all that different than his own, save for its larger size. A vegetable garden, barren for the winter, was the only concession to aesthetics he could see. The other homes nearby looked much the same, and the street was, at this hour, largely empty.

The old guardsman knew he must look a fright: disheveled, filthy, limping faintly, and—despite the care his assailants had taken—he could taste a bit of matted blood in his mustache. He wasn't even certain if it was his or not.

Shout for assistance, or even just attention? This wasn't the most upstanding of neighborhoods, but neither did it appear a bad one. It would take only the right person to peer from a window at his cry. . . .

Either something in his face or his posture gave him away, or—more likely—the brigands were simply taking no chances. A fist sank into the flesh of his gut, forcing the breath and very nearly the most recent meal from his body. Doubled over, wheezing, Archibeque felt hands lifting him by the arms, hauling him like a sack of meal. Drunken meal, in fact.

It was the piercing and all-too-familiar tang of gore, no longer fresh but not too aged, that snapped him out of it. As he glanced around, equilibrium gradually returning, he saw a fairly simple dining chamber, a plain but sturdy table, and a pair of corpses. Man and woman—*married couple*, the major's guard training suggested, based on a dozen tiny signs—shy of, or having just crossed into, middle age. He lay flat on the floor, facedown, pointed away from his chair; she was slumped on the table, chest in what, a day or two ago, had been dinner. Both had died violently, but at least, from appearances, swiftly.

Unfortunately, while Archibeque was no stranger to carnage, the gut punch already had him on the verge of vomiting. He felt his shoulders spasm, the sweat form on his forehead; tasted bile in his suddenly burning throat. The guardsman successfully choked back his surging gorge—no chance would he show any such weakness in front of these bastards!—but it was a long and difficult struggle.

By the time he'd recovered from *that*, several more people had entered the room. One or two he recognized from past experience—members of the bloody Finders' Guild. The woman between them, however—slender, sharp-featured, hair like searing flame—he didn't know.

"If you're having difficulty with this," the woman told him, gesturing vaguely at the bodies, "I strongly suggest you not take a look in the grandfather's bedchamber. Or the children's." Then, at his expression, she merely shrugged. "We do what we need to."

"Your Shrouded Lord is growing sloppy and stupid," Archibeque snarled, determined to take charge of the conversation. "If you think the Guard is just going to ignore the slaughter of a family, let alone the abduction of an officer—"

"Relax, Commandant. We don't represent the Guild."

Archibeque stiffened. Was this all a bizarre case of mistaken identity? "You've been given bad information. I am not Commandant Trivette."

"Oh, we know who you are. Archibeque, Major, Trivette's most probable successor. My name is Lisette.

"And as for Trivette himself . . ." The woman's grin was positively unholy. "Who do you think the dearly departed grandpa I mentioned might be?"

The guardsman choked, staring once more at the corpses, only now seeing the family resemblance between the woman and Archibeque's superior officer. Or former superior, apparently. He found himself struggling, thrashing, and accomplishing nothing at all. The men held him too tightly, were still too strong.

"Whatever you thought to gain from Commandant Trivette," Archibeque announced, back stiff once more, "you'll not have from me, either."

Lisette laughed, a rather twisted chuckle. "So easy to say, old man. Perhaps you should wait until I've explained."

"Explain all you like. You'll have no cooperation from me."

A second, softer chuckle. "I've been flitting around Davillon for a little while, now, Major. I've offered a proposition to a great many important people. Some accepted. Some are dead. Strangely, there is no overlap between those two groups. I can't imagine why that is."

She stepped nearer, grinning, and delivered a light, almost playful slap to Archibeque's cheek. "Can *you* guess why that is?"

"Of course Trivette declined. As, to my last breath—"

"Oh, shut it." A second slap, harder, made his ears ring. "I'm tired of hearing it.

"Listen well, Major. I didn't *ask* your commandant a thing. My plans hinge on a few particular people, people I can't *afford* to have reject my generous offer. For them, I've had to resort to . . . other methods. Trivette, unfortunately, was too old. The process killed him. I do believe, though, that his successor is a stronger man. Let's find out, shall we?"

Other methods? "What are you—?"

The words turned into a scream, high, piercing, like a child trapped in a nightmare. It tore his throat ragged, strained his lungs, and kept coming.

And at first, he didn't even know why. He felt no pain, saw no horrors. Nothing had changed, save for a sudden alien scent, vaguely herbal and sickly sweet, and the involuntary shriek that he could not, no matter how he tried, make himself stop.

Lisette's thugs released his arms and stepped back. Archibeque felt his body slump, every one of his muscles slacken, and yet he remained upright, if slouched. The room blurred as his eyes grew unfocused. He tried to clear them, and realized he couldn't even blink. Felt a wet warmth down his leg, as his final grip on control was wrenched away.

Finally, as his face purpled and he felt ready to pass out, the scream pouring from between his lips finally ceased.

"See? This one survived." Lisette took a step back, studying the guardsman as though he were a work of art. "Now, shall we discuss our next step?"

This time, his scream was purely internal, resounding through his thoughts without the slightest audible sound, as something *else* began to answer Lisette's questions through Archibeque's own lips and breath.

CHAPTER FIFTEEN

"Can you explain to me," Widdershins begged of Olgun, "why, after traveling across more than half of Galice and over the span of three separate identities, I still can't seem to get away from the *stupid parties*?!"

Olgun's only answer was one of his metaphysical shrugs.

"Fat lot of use you are! Go back to eyeing all the hors d'oeuvres you can't eat or whatever it is you do at these things. I need you sober, though, so don't 'not drink' too much of the wine."

Indeed, the banquet hall of Castle Pauvril had been bedecked and festooned—after, Widdershins imagined, a frantic but thorough dusting, sweeping, and de-cobwebbing—for as grand a gala as any she'd attended in Davillon, as either Adrienne Satti or Madeleine Valois. What the noble houses of Aubier lacked in terms of Davillon's rich excesses, they more than made up for in quantity and exuberance.

Banners displaying the icons of a dozen Pact gods hung from the rafters, along with the occasional Galicien flag. Widdershins *still* flinched each time she glimpsed Cevora's leonine symbol fluttering among the others. And flutter they did; the halls of Pauvril might have been built with defense in mind, but they were utter garbage where invading armies of breezes needed challenging.

Tables staggered and groaned beneath the weight of enough food—smoked meats, fresh pastries, and out-of-season candied fruits—to feed an army. The only army present within the walls, of course, was one of servants, dashing back and fro and to and forth, clad in clashing house colors, and permitted not a bite of the repast. That was for the aristocrats, who picked or nibbled or politely gorged (a talent Shins had never mastered), as their individual attitude and appetites demanded.

The odors of lingering dust and age tainted the aroma of food sufficiently that Shins, rarely one to turn down a free meal, had lost most of her appetite. She wasn't sure how the blue bloods managed it. Maybe they *didn't* manage it; maybe they forced themselves, at the risk of being sick, all for the sake of propriety and appearance. She wouldn't have been at all surprised.

Only two details separated this particular fete from its spiritual brethren that she'd attended in the past. One was the utter lack of an orchestra or even a single mingling minstrel. That, apparently, had been deemed *too* festive for a gathering that wasn't really a party at all.

The other was a cluster of people off to one side, huddled under a heavy arch. All of them were clad in the formal colors of a single House, and they stood hemmed in by a small but grim-looking circle of city constables.

House Carnot, Aubier branch.

The Carnot outsiders, those who had come to Aubier alongside Lazare, languished, or so Shins understood, in the city's gaol. With the exception of the servant Josce Tremont, who had thus far eluded all efforts to locate him, the local members of the family were in a rather more nebulous state. They had been gathered together, their coin and any liquid assets confiscated, until the nobles of Aubier could determine how involved they had been in Lazare's plot, and to what extent—if any— they owed reparations to House Delacroix, or fines and penalties to the rest of the city. It was to make just those decisions that the nobles were here today, in the most neutral spot in Aubier—assuming they ever tore themselves away from the food and the chatter to discuss the issue.

Knowing the aristocracy as she did, the visitor from Davillon was fairly certain that, even if they were found largely innocent of any direct wrongdoing, the Carnots weren't likely to see much of that wealth again.

Said wealth, currently stored in one of the castle's lower chambers, was one of the reasons—the other being the paranoia of the nobles themselves—that, while the only army *within* the castle was made up of servants, a small army of constables and armsmen from every local House were currently standing guard *outside* the walls.

Not long ago, the situation would have had Widdershins drooling over the opportunity, looking for any means to liberate a portion of the riches from the room below. Now, however, it just made her edgy.

"Ah! There she is!"

Or maybe the edgy has something to do with them.

Calanthe Delacroix and Aubier's reeve approached, drifting easily through the throng as people readily, even eagerly, cleared them a path. Widdershins offered the latter a shallow nod, the former a shallow curtsy—which looked rather peculiar, given that she had refused the offer of formal clothing and wore the same leathers (although thoroughly washed) in which she'd arrived. Compared to Veroche's outfit, which was tailor fitted and loose shouldered, perfect for dancing or dueling, and the matriarch's, which was full and flowing and worth more than some villages, she looked like a crow among peacocks.

"I wanted to thank you again for staying," Rosselin Veroche began.

Widdershins grinned, lips tight. "You wanted me to leave when I wanted to stay. Only follows you want me to stay when I want to leave, yes?"

The reeve returned a polite smile. "I realize this has taken a little longer than you'd hoped to remain . . ."

A little?! It's been over two weeks!

". . . but your testimony is rather essential to offer the nobles a clear picture of what happened."

Yes, so you've said a million and a half times. It's why you've had me go over the story until I'm sick of my own voice, and bring that stinky, nauseating thing as evidence.

But as none of that seemed worth saying aloud, Widdershins instead asked, "Any word from the observers?" As soon as they'd arrested Lazare Carnot, Rosselin had sent couriers requesting representatives both royal and ecclesiastical. One simply didn't try a House patriarch without such oversight.

"No. And given the political chaos you've described out there, I doubt it'll be any time soon. But once you've given your statement to the nobles here tonight, they can swear to your testimony on record. You won't need to remain for the trial itself."

Thank the Pact for small favors!

"Veroche," Calanthe said, "I wonder if you would give me a moment with the young lady."

Oh, figs.

"Of course. I'll check on the status of the guards. Trying to organize the soldiers of every house? It's like herding cats."

"Really, really dizzy cats?" Shins asked. The reeve blinked, gave her the sort of look she really ought to be accustomed to by now, and left.

"Walk with me," the matriarch invited-slash-commanded.

Shins actually found herself casting about for an escape route. There were plenty, of course; even discounting the main doors, which currently hung open to the outside, the banquet hall boasted any number of archways leading to various halls and several sets of sweeping stairs. She could even climb the walls, if necessary; the brick was rough enough she could do it blindfolded. Some of the banners might even support her weight, if only briefly. . . .

She suppressed a sigh and answered the only way she truly could. "Certainly."

The matriarch began to stroll, Widdershins keeping up. The thief had attended enough formal events to recognize that Calanthe was idly circling the edges of the room, offering them some privacy for speech while remaining seemingly sociable.

"Any news?" Widdershins asked, abruptly disturbed by the woman's continued silence.

"No. Veroche believes there was at least one hideout unknown to the men who Josephi—who we caught in our trap."

Widdershins nodded. Once Josephine had been well and truly cowed, getting her to send false signals to the next trespassing Crows had been easy, a matter of ordering her to do so and acquiring her a bit of colored glass to replace her lantern. They, in turn, had led the Delacroix guards and the constables to most of the Thousand Crow bolt-holes—including the ones in which Lazare and his Carnot had taken refuge. (It had been Calanthe herself who convinced the tight-lipped criminals to talk. Widdershins neither knew how, nor wanted to.)

Unfortunately, perhaps thanks to their spies in the Houses and constabulary, the Crows had seen them coming. A significant minority of the gang had escaped, and while several had been apprehended in the subsequent days, a handful—Fingerbone and Ivon Maline chief among them—remained uncaught.

"Is Aubier big enough for someone to hide this long?" Widdershins joked nervously.

They drifted past knots of conversation, a few of which the matriarch even deigned to join, if only to exchange pleasantries. Shins was beginning to grow irritated, and was contemplating asking Olgun to arrange some embarrassing mishap with Calanthe and the next bottle of wine they drew near, when the old woman finally spoke.

"Why did you help us, Widdershins? Honestly."

"An old debt." She shrugged. "One of your distant relatives saved my life—*changed* my life. He's gone, now." She was surprised to find herself choking up, however slightly. Usually she could speak of Alexandre without *too* much pain. "This was my only way of repaying him."

Calanthe nodded and continued walking, her gaze fixed straight ahead, seeming unwilling even to glance in Widdershins's direction.

"I want you to understand," she began, distant and stiff. "The Delacroix have always had political enemies, here in the Outer Hespelene. A House doesn't dominate local textiles as we have without upsetting rivals. I've seen any number of plots against us, even before the recent upheavals. I've had allies turn on me. Try to turn my children against me." Her voice grew brittle there, but briefly. "Seek political gain using us as a stepping stone. Even an attempted assassination, now and again. Every sort of sordid aristocratic scheme you can envision, we've repulsed."

You'd be surprised what I can envision, you old—

"And now we appear to be the *last* surviving branch of our house. So, if I was . . . excessive in my distrust, my zeal to keep you away from us, and from my son in particular, I hope you'll understand. It's my family."

The graceful, dexterous, almost inhumanly agile Widdershins stumbled briefly over her own feet. "I . . . Was that an apology, Lady Delacroix?"

"Of course not! Don't be silly. It would never do for someone in my position to be seen apologizing to someone in yours. Just isn't done."

At which point the elderly, iron-spined and ironfisted matriarch of House Delacroix threw Widdershins a vaguely mischievous wink.

Before Shins could recover from *that* shock, Calanthe concluded with, "You are going to have to have some stern words with my son, however."

"Wait, what? What are you talking—?"

But the matriarch had already stepped away, smoothly interjecting herself into a conversation of high-ranking aristocrats, where she began explaining how Josce Tremont had been funneling local Carnot resources to their newly arrived brethren.

"Olgun? What's she talking about? What words with Cyrille? Hey! You may not have eyes, but I can still feel it when you roll them at me!"

It was, however, all the god would offer—though Widdershins
did somehow get the impression he was stifling the urge to chortle.

She made several more confused rounds of the room, occasionally stopping to answer this question or that about her experiences,
growing ever more irritated, until the boy himself appeared at her
side. The softest hint of wine wafted from his lips; a tiny spot of pink
blossomed in his cheeks.

"Widdershins, um . . . Can we talk a minute?"

"If it gets me away from all these questions, we can talk for two.
What's going on?"

"Uh . . . Could . . . ? Maybe somewhere a bit more private?"

"It's kind of a crowded room, Cyrille." She thought about following Calanthe's example, circling the edges of the chamber, but she
wasn't entirely confident in Cyrille's ability to be discreet, or her own
to flow in and out of conversations as smoothly as the matriarch had.
"And I'm pretty sure the kitchen and coatrooms are swarming with
servants. Maybe upstairs?"

"Yes! I mean, yes, that'd be fine."

"Are you drunk?"

The red in his cheeks darkened. "No. I just had . . . no."

"Right. Make sure you keep a tight hold on the banister, yes?"

The nearest stairwell, which seemed as viable a choice as any of
the others, was a curved thing of stone, sweeping its way upward in
an utterly unnecessary arc. Bits of dust, dirt, and the occasional insect
carapace lay in a few of the more awkward corners, suggesting that
the cleaning job here had been rather desultory.

And why not? Everything of import was occurring on the ground
floor, after all.

Cyrille and Shins reached the top of the flight, then made their
way along the balcony overlooking the banquet hall. The Delacroix
scion stopped and gestured at the first door they came to; Shins
shrugged and nodded.

The room itself might once have been almost anything: storage, guest bedchamber, gods knew what. Today, like most of Pauvril, it was stone walls, a stubborn wooden door swollen slightly in its frame, and musty emptiness.

"If I have to answer one more question," Shins burst out before the door was even shut behind them, "I just might scream. Or hit someone. Or hit someone while screaming."

"Widdershins—"

"We haven't even gotten to the hearing yet! I'm going to be testifying to all this! Why can't they all just shut up and leave me alone and *wait*?"

"Shins—"

"I swear most of them are going to make up their minds based on three words they heard strung together, secondhand, by a drunk whose half-deaf cousin thought he heard me from across the room!"

"If you could just—"

She realized she was actually waving her hands in the air like a lunatic but couldn't bring herself to stop. "Did you know that Lazare Carnot has already confessed? To targeting the Delacroix, hiring the Crows, all of it! But oh, no, he's a *patriarch*, still needs a full-on formal trial, and we can't tie in the *local* Carnots without finding Josce first, and I'm just so sick and tired of this whole—"

Cyrille sighed, threw his own hands briefly over his head in exasperation, then stepped in, took Widdershins firmly by the shoulders, and pressed his lips to hers in a passionate, if clumsy, kiss.

For an instant, she utterly froze; it took a hundred years for the following few seconds to pass. She couldn't breathe, couldn't think. And for that instant, a part of her wanted to respond in kind. Olgun notwithstanding, she'd been so alone for so long, since Davillon . . .

Renard. Robin. *Julien.*

She planted a palm on Cyrille's chest and pushed him away. Not hard, really, but he staggered as though he'd been shoved by an ox.

"Shins?" A single syllable, it sounded like rippling water.

Oh, gods. He looks like I just told him the family dog has leprosy.

But at least she knew, now, finally knew, what Calanthe had meant; what Olgun had found so funny; why Cyrille had done, well, pretty much all of what he'd done.

Also, I am an idiot. I mean, even for an idiot, I'm an idiot. I have the brain of a parsnip.

A parsnip *who is* also *an idiot.*

"Cyrille, I don't . . . I think you've misunderstood. I—"

"*Misunderstood?* Shins . . . Everything we've done together, everything we . . . You came to my room, you came to *me*! For help!"

"Because I could trust you. And I'm glad I could, but—"

"Oh, you can trust me. Bloody fucking fantastic. I'm trusted."

Widdershins felt her fist clench, her jaw tighten. "There aren't a lot of people I *do* trust, Cyrille. You have no idea how hard it was to make *that* leap, but I did. And I was right. We saved your family together."

"And that's all? We were, what, partners? Coworkers?"

"And friends."

In a fit of adolescent melodrama of the sort that bridges all castes and all cultures, he spun and pounded the base of his fist against the wall, abrading the skin and leaving a void in the dust. "That's not enough."

"It's what we are. I'm sorry."

"You're sorry. Well, praise Cevora."

"Cyrille—"

"Gods dammit, Shins, please, couldn't you at least *try*—?"

"Cyrille, please don't make this more awkward than it—"

Only Widdershins heard Olgun's cry of warning, but she and Cyrille both *clearly* heard the abrupt chaos from the floor below.

The screams.

The guns.

And the deafening, echoing slam of the castle doors.

CHAPTER SIXTEEN

"My lords and ladies, your attentions, if you would."

Ivon Maline, looking even larger and oiler and generally meaner than Widdershins remembered him, strode across the room to stand beside one of the food-laden tables. Around him, a dozen of the Thousand Crows held flintlocks and gape-barreled blunderbusses on the various clusters of suddenly horrified guests and on the surviving guards who had been watching the Carnots. A number of those guards were already dead, cut down in the fusillade that had announced the Crows' presence. A few more of Ivon's thugs were placing heavy bars across the doors they had slammed shut.

"Where the hell did they come from?" Cyrille hissed in Widdershins's ear. The pair of them lay on their bellies at the edge of the second-floor balcony, peering at the havoc below.

Widdershins just shook her head, equally bewildered. "Not through the front door, that's for hopping sure. Not with a small forest of guards and constables outside."

"Shins, Mother's down there."

All she could do, for the moment, was lay a hand on his arm and squeeze.

"As I'm sure most of you have already figured out," Ivon continued, voice not so much booming through the room as oozing, "you have all just volunteered to help me and my friends out with a little problem. Or, in plain terms, you're hostages.

"Do not misunderstand me. Every damn one of you is expendable; I have plenty of spares." He drew a flintlock from his belt, waved it at the bleeding corpses of the armsmen. "Now, these men were soldiers. They expect to die—and you hoity-toity bastards *expect* them to die."

Without pause, without so much as a change of expression, he raised the weapon and put a ball through the skull of a young noble-woman, barely older than Shins herself, who had been huddled, weeping, against a table.

The cries of horror and choked sobs were an almost-physical presence, pressing against the chamber walls and everyone within. They were also, thankfully, loud enough to drown out Cyrille's own outcry and Widdershins's ragged gasp. Her fingers tightened on Cyrille's arm, even as his other hand reached over to clutch hers.

"I trust," Ivon said, studying the crowd as though he were thinking of buying them, "my message was not lost in translation?"

"I think we understand you just fine."

Shins couldn't help but grin. It figured she'd be the first in the crowd to speak out.

"Why don't you tell us," Calanthe Delacroix continued, each word an icicle, "what it is you want from us? So nobody else here has to die."

"Lady Delacroix, human nature being what it is, I think we all know that other people are going to have to die before this is all over." Mutters and whimpers from the crowd, then. "I—"

Someone appeared from one of the archways—Shins couldn't see which, from her angle—and approached Ivon, whispering something in his ear. Widdershins's brow furrowed; she wasn't *entirely* positive, as she'd seen the man only twice, but . . .

"Is that Josce Tremont?" she whispered.

Cyrille leaned a bit farther out, then nodded.

"Olgun? Any chance we can hear what he's saying?"

Whether the god could have managed that level of enhancement or not proved a moot point, however, as Josce finished whatever report he was making and stepped away. The leader of the Thousand Crows turned his attention back to the gathered hostages.

"To answer your question, for now, I just want you all to gather in small groups. You'll be told where to wait, either in this hall or one of the adjoining rooms. If you run, if you protest, if you move too slowly, if you talk to one another out of turn, if I decide I don't care for your bloody fashion sense, you'll be shot. Any more questions?"

One of the surviving guards raised a hand in the air. "Can we—?"

Ivon drew a second, smaller flintlock and pulled the trigger. Again the crowd gasped, and several aristocrats screamed as the armsman's blood, and worse, spattered over them.

"I don't like questions, either." His gaze fixed not on the man he'd just murdered, but on Calanthe, as he said it. "Get a move on."

Shins took a breath, preparing to make some suggestion or other, when Olgun shouted in her head once more. She saw one of the Crows happen to glance their way, grabbed Cyrille by the collar, and rolled back from the edge of the balcony, her other hand over his mouth to stifle his startled yelp.

"Olgun? Did he see us?"

Uncertainty, tinged with deep fretting and the same simmering anger she felt in her own gut.

"Don't move!" she whispered to Cyrille, then scurried along on knees and elbows so she might peek over the edge from a different vantage. Her crawl kicked up substantial amounts of dust—again, the cleaning staff had been far less thorough here than downstairs—but a quick word with Olgun, and a tiny tingle of power, prevented a sneeze that might have given her away.

Sliding *just* near enough to see over, she spotted the man who'd looked up, standing beside Maline and talking low. After a moment, as his boss turned back to the hostages, the Crow tapped one of his companions on the shoulder, and the two of them headed for the stairs.

"All right," she breathed. "He thinks he *might* have seen something, but he's nowhere near sure. Probably figured it was just some stray servant, even if he did. He and his bird of a feather are coming to check, just to make certain."

Then, at a questioning surge from Olgun, "Because of how they're moving. Their guns are drawn, but they're walking casually, yes? They don't look worried. Ready for trouble, but not expecting it."

She twisted around on her belly, started crawling her way back, then halted once more as an idea settled on her like dislodged cobweb. She scuttled sideways, a particularly stealthy and oddly brunette crab, and pressed herself against the wall. In the feeble lighting up here, she knew the shadows provided more than sufficient camouflage.

"Yeah, it's mean," she told Olgun, once she'd explained her plan and he'd protested in no uncertain imagery. "But it's also the best way to make sure the wrong people don't get all full of holes and dead and all that. You know . . . How can something actually be 'full of holes'? Isn't a hole an *absence*? Wouldn't it be 'empty with holes,' or maybe—

"Yes, I hear them coming! You don't have to sound so relieved about it!"

It happened fast, and roughly as she'd anticipated. The two Crows appeared at the top of the stairs, began their search, and immediately discovered Cyrille. The boy'd been wise enough to try to hide, presumably when he'd heard them climbing the stairs, but Widdershins he wasn't.

Eyes widened. Flintlocks rose. Lungs filled, ready to shout challenges or threats.

The first of the Crows was toppling backward, feet knocked from under him by Widdershins's leg sweep before he had the slightest hint she was there. She came out of her spin, straightening up and lashing out with her rapier, guided by her own keen eye and Olgun's divine influence. The flat of the blade sent the gun hurtling from the man's fist and away down the hall. She knew that the powder would spill from the flashpan so the weapon wouldn't discharge when it hit; her unseen partner would see to it.

The fallen thug's partner, however, proved a bit trickier. He'd shuffled a quick step back even as the first Crow fell, putting himself beyond easy reach. His flintlock was already almost in line, ready to fire. Even if it wasn't too late for Shins and Olgun to pull their early-discharge trick, the noise would certainly summon more Crows from below.

All of which meant, even with her Olgun-boosted reactions, she had only one way to stop him before the weapon fired.

Inwardly she winced, felt her stomach roil. Externally, she displayed no sign of her distress save for a brief quivering at the corner of her eyes and lips, as she launched herself into a textbook-perfect lunge and slid the tip of her blade between the man's ribs and into his heart.

It couldn't actually have been minutes, couldn't really have been *seconds*—but it felt to Shins as though it were at *least* that long before he tore his stunned and accusing stare away and slid from her rapier in a limb, bleeding heap.

"Yes," she snipped at Olgun's tentative caress of comfort. "I've killed before, when we had to. It's not a big deal."

Which was, of course, a lie almost too big to have fit within the banquet hall downstairs, let alone the hallway overlook. It was a lie she clung to with brutal stubbornness, though she'd have been pressed to say why. Was it because killing the Crow *did* bother her, as such things always had?

Or because it *didn't* bother her quite as much as she'd expected it would?

She turned back to the man she'd first taken down. He gasped like a fish—a surprised fish who'd just run a footrace—only now recovering the wind that she had knocked out of him. Widdershins studied, then almost casually stomped on his crotch.

Something that might have been a sound—she'd have needed the hearing of a dog to be certain—passed through his abruptly pallid lips.

"Where were you?!"

She jumped at the sudden rasp, and only then remembered Cyrille, who was now standing beside her. "What if you hadn't been in time?"

"I was." She knelt, biting her lip long enough to clean the streaks from her blade on the fallen man's pants, then stood once more. "So what's the problem?"

"What if you *hadn't*? It took you a lot longer than I'd expected—"

"I had to make sure they were fully distracted, yes?"

Cyrille's lips kept moving, but his store of sounds and syllables seemed to have run low. "You used me as *bait*?!" he finally squeaked out.

"If it helps, you did a marvelous job at it. Now," she continued over his unintelligible sputtering, "help me drag these men somewhere not quite so much in the middle of everything."

"I . . . You . . . *Gah!* Fine."

Manhandling the two bodies, living and dead, into the room from which Shins and Cyrille had just come wasn't terribly difficult. They could do precious little about the bloodstains, but hopefully the poor illumination up here would cloak that, at least for a while.

"Help me find something to tie this guy with," Shins instructed, casting futilely about the empty room.

"We should kill him."

Shins froze, so sudden and stiff her neck began to ache. "What? No!"

"Why?" Cyrille sounded genuinely puzzled. "You already killed one of them."

"That's different! I was defending myself! Defending you!"

"We still are." Cyrille thrust an arm out, pointing toward the door and the balcony. "Look what's going on down there, what they've already done! If he recovers, if he's able to slip his bonds, or cry for attention? We're dead before we can stop these people!"

We? Stop? But that was for later; at the moment . . .

"Cyrille . . ." A part of her, a large part, wondered if he was right, if she was being foolish. It *would* be easier, now. Now that she'd seen what the Crows were capable of, now that killing the first man hadn't twisted her up as she'd expected.

Now that she and Olgun were so *angry* all the time.

"I can't. Cyrille, I just can't."

"You're being a fool!"

I was just wondering about that.

Shins stepped toward him, paused, then turned. The Crow was staring widely at both of them, for which Widdershins couldn't blame him. She stepped over him, to the corner where they'd temporarily tossed the fallen men's weapons.

"Here." One of the Crow's sword belts sailed through the air, sheathed rapier included, to land perfectly in the boy's clumsy catch. "You want him dead? You do it."

He nodded, drew the rapier, and swung through a few practice slashes. Cyrille crossed the room in three paces, lay the tip of the blade against the man's throat. The crow gurgled something, squeezed his eyes shut.

A long minute passed. A minute more.

Cyrille sighed, sheathed the weapon once more, and stepped back. He grinned shyly at Shin's bright, genuine smile and began fiddling with the buckles on the belt.

Of course, Cyrille wasn't entirely wrong, either.

"Olgun?"

He responded with an emotional nod.

Widdershins stepped around the wounded man, dropped to her knees, and wrapped an arm around his throat. He barely had the strength or energy to thrash before he was completely out cold—hopefully, thanks to Olgun's aid and guidance, without much in the way of long-term damage.

Then, just to be sure, and again being careful not to overdo it, she rammed a backhanded fist into the Crow's throat.

She shrugged in answer to her companion's startled gasp. "Even if he wakes up sooner than I expect, he won't be calling out any time soon. Might not be able to speak clearly at all for a day or three.

"Would you bring me that belt back so I can tie . . . Why are you wearing that?"

Cyrille adjusted the last of the buckles so the belt hung comfortably but securely across his waist. "Um, so I have somewhere to carry this?" He tapped the hilt of the thug's rapier. "And this," he added, moving across the chamber to collect one of the flintlocks and powder bags.

"You don't *need* to carry those, Cyrille, because you're not going anywhere."

"Uh, no. I'm going with you."

"Uh, also no. You're going to find a place to hide, you're going to lock the door behind you, and—"

She winced as Cyrille shoved the flintlock hard through a loop in his "borrowed" belt. "That's my family down there. And friends. My odds of success—and survival—are a *lot* higher with you than alone, but I'll go it alone if you make me. I *am* going."

"This isn't a game, you turkey!"

"I'm aware."

Widdershins's teeth were clenched so tightly, she could probably have bitten *Olgun* and made it hurt. *Is this what I was like to deal with for Alexandre or Julien? I might've died to get away from me, too.*

She and Olgun jolted in unison. *Where in the wide and wiggly world had* that *thought come from?!*

No time to worry about it now, though. Not when she had a stubborn young aristocrat to talk out of suicide.

"People are going to get hurt, Cyrille. Killed."

"I'm aware," he said again. "I'm going to help make sure it's the right people."

Widdershins's fists clenched around an imaginary neck, but no amount of wishing seemed to incline the boy to suddenly appear in them. "I *could* just knock you out," she said, pointing her chin toward the surviving Crow.

"Then come do it. It's the only way I'm staying behind."

Gaaaaah! "You'd also be completely helpless if—when—they found you," she pointed out.

"Yes. I would."

"Oh, shut up," she hissed at Olgun. "I *know* I'm beaten, don't rub it in!" Then, so Cyrille could hear, "Fine! Whatever. But if you get spotted or heard, or slow me down, you're on your own!"

"Of course." She couldn't tell if he believed her threat, or cared even if he did. "So what's first?"

"First, I finish this." She quickly tied the slumbering Crow, using the remaining sword belt and the man's own trousers.

"Then," she said, dusting her hands off, "we see if we can tell what the happy hopping horses Maline's up to, so we know what exactly we're trying to ruin."

After dropping to their stomachs and sidling up to the edge of the balcony once more, however, it became very clear that whatever Maline was "up to" had already begun. One of the huddled groups of hostages—guards and servants, if Shins recalled correctly—was now absent from the banquet hall. So were a handful of the Thousand Crows and Ivon Maline himself.

"Still way too many of them down there," Shins muttered.

"So what do we do? Trying to find the missing would be . . . There's about five hundred possible exits from that room!"

"Eleven," the thief replied with a faint grin. Olgun cackled.

In fact, it was closer to half a dozen, not counting the main door, but even that was a lot of random searching to do. Except . . .

"Olgun?"

It took a few moments of pacing the hall, trying to make the echoes of the old gaping passageways work for her, her ears tingling until they itched. Eventually, however, her god-enhanced hearing picked up the staccato percussion of shoes on stone. Several walls stood between her and the source—but of far greater importance was that the sound came from progressively *higher* as she listened.

"They're climbing," she whispered. "The ramparts, or maybe one of the towers."

"What are they doing up *there?*"

"I have an idea," Widdershins told him, casting about for the nearest stairs. "Let's go find out before they manage to actually do it!"

CHAPTER SEVENTEEN

No snow had fallen in almost a week, but winter hadn't remotely relinquished its grip on Galice, or the Outer Hespelene in particular. The winds flowed over the parapet and through the merlons, so that anyone standing atop the wall felt a constant barrage of biting cold.

Standing or, as Widdershins and Cyrille had uncomfortably discovered, even crouching.

Finding their way up to the ramparts had been simple enough, as Castle Pauvril had multiple sets of stairs leading to almost every level. Once there, although they'd stepped out into the open via an exit far from where Maline and his people would have appeared, they heard enough of a commotion to know that their quarry was indeed on the wall, as opposed to climbing one of the towers.

Since striding openly into sight of the Thousand Crows would have been so foolish that even Cyrille knew better, the only remaining option had been for the two sneaks to press themselves against the inside wall and work their way forward at a slow crouch. Bits of old leaves and feathers jutted from between the bricks and from various widening cracks. Guano, old enough to crunch underfoot but not so old it had lost its oh-so-pleasant aroma, speckled the walkway. To Widdershins, who had spent whole nights traversing the roofs of Davillon, it felt like home.

Or it did until the sounds ahead grew clearer, and she was forced to remember who and what she was dealing with. As one of the Finders, as an enemy of religious fanatics, she'd encountered men and women of extreme violence, harsh brutality. But she had never seen anyone kill so callously as she'd seen Maline do below—or no one human, anyway.

She heard other sounds as well, beneath the shuffling and muttering and occasional frightened sob, beyond the low wail of the wind. It took her a moment to place it as the amalgamated symphony of speech and movement from scores, if not hundreds, of people on the ground below.

Of course. The armsmen and constables—probably more now even than there had been. At least the Crows had no easy means of escaping the keep.

Then again, that might just make them more desperate. *And how the happy horses had they gotten* into *the stupid keep, anyway?*

A few more feet, a few more degrees of the ramparts' curve, and Shins could just see the group ahead: Ivon and a gaggle of his thugs, along with over a dozen servants and household soldiers. The former carried firearms—at least two per person—and Shins saw a few of them wearing bandoliers that held several more. The latter had hands bound behind their backs and were lined up at the parapet, ensuring that any incoming fire would strike them first. Most of the armsmen stood rigid, defiant; most of the servants shuffled or sobbed. Maline seemed equally contemptuous of both.

"I'm waiting!" he shouted, voice booming over the wall, making Widdershins jump. "I don't enjoy waiting! Don't make me show you how much!"

Clearly, at least some amount of discussion had already occurred before the two young eavesdroppers arrived.

"All right, all right!" This second voice came from below; distant, tinny, muddled by the breeze. Still, Shins was fairly certain she recognized the authoritative tones of Reeve Rosselin Veroche. "I'm here, now, Maline! Anything you want to say or negotiate, you say it to me!"

The master of the Thousand Crows snorted. *"You're* in charge? The Houses actually deigned to let you lead something more important than a barn raising? They *must* be desperate!"

"Just say your piece!"

"Right." He stopped a moment, took a wineskin from one of the Crows, and drank.

All the yelling must be hard on his throat, yes?

"It's simple enough! All the Thousand Crows and all the members of House Carnot currently in custody are to be brought here *immediately*. Once they've arrived, and I've determined they're all present and largely intact, you will permit us to leave with some of the hostages, who will be released when we're on the road!"

"Isn't it kind of stupid," Cyrille whispered in Widdershins's ear, "to bring them all here? Wouldn't gathering someplace easier to get away from make more sense?"

Shins waved him off, but in truth, she'd been wondering the same.

". . . could take some time," Veroche was calling back. "You'll need to be patient!"

This time, when Maline snorted, it wasn't with humor. "Let me explain my idea of patience!"

A flintlock spoke, heard clearly across the castle and the surrounding fields. One of the servants dropped. At a gesture from their leader, two of the Crows lifted the body and dumped it over the parapet. Widdershins couldn't hear the reaction of the soldiers below over the cries of the remaining servants—or Cyrille's choked gasp.

"Until my people are here, I am going to keep killing hostages on a steady basis! I'll *start* with guards and servants, but I have *no* compunctions about moving on to the nobles if you test me!"

One of the Crows, glancing over the wall, aimed his own weapon downward and fired.

"Don't even think of approaching the castle!" Maline continued. "That includes any effort to reach the bodies! You can collect them after we're done, not until then!"

"How long are you giving us?" Even from this distance, the frustration and burning anger in the reeve's words rang clear.

Maline's answering smile made Widdershins shiver. "Until I feel I need to reiterate my point."

Every one of the gathered Crows opened fire. And every one of the hostages atop the wall died screaming.

Widdershins wept openly as she and Cyrille staggered back to the stairwell from which they'd emerged, each of them unsteady, each leaning heavily on the other. Her shoulders shook, she struggled to breathe, and the whole world had gone blurry behind her tears.

Cyrille, it appeared, couldn't manage even that, through his shock. His eyes—wide, glazed, and bloodshot—focused on nothing in particular, and were redder, in fact, than his face, so paper-pale had he become. He took each step by rote, keeping up with his companion but always turning where she led, moving at her chosen pace.

When the door finally closed behind them, it mercifully silenced the last of the lingering sounds: the occasional shot, if one of the Crows decided someone wasn't dead enough; the coarse jests and occasional laughter of the heartless bastards; the grunts of exertion as body after body was hefted over the parapet to tumble down to the growing heap of torn flesh and splintered bone below.

It also finally cut the bite of the wind, but Shins hardly noticed. She wasn't certain she'd ever feel warm again. Even Olgun couldn't comfort her, as she sank down to sprawl on the steps beside her companion; he seemed far too horrified, and far too enraged, himself.

"Widdershins . . ." Cyrille could have been some unreal spirit, for all he seemed to be fully present. "They just . . . He . . ."

"I know." She sniffled, dragged the back of her hand across her cheek.

"I've never . . ." He cleared his throat. "Never seen anything that . . . that . . ."

Shins clasped her hand over his, thinking back to the veritable sea of gore on the day Olgun's other worshippers had been slaughtered. "I'm sorry you had to."

"We need to kill him."

Shins scowled, though in all honesty, she could probably have driven her blade into Maline's gut or throat in that moment without any of the remorse she'd felt earlier. "That's part of what we're trying to figure—"

"No, I mean *now*." When all she did was stare, puzzled, he continued, "They weren't rushing to be done with . . . with everything. We could go down a floor or two, cut across, ambush them on the other stairway."

"Cyrille—"

"They'd never see it coming. And I know you've taken on more people than that at once! We—"

"No!"

The young Delacroix recoiled as if slapped.

"Yes," she said more softly, "I've fought that many people before. But only when I've had to. It's *always* a risk, especially in such tight quarters. Odds are pretty good *we'd* end up dead.

"And even if not, what sort of orders do his people have? What happens to everyone downstairs if Maline dies?"

"I don't know," he grudgingly admitted.

"Right. We don't know enough yet, Cyrille. When we do, *then* we do something about it, yes?"

"All right," he grumbled. He began dragging himself to his feet, one hand on the banister, and then paused, his expression quizzical.

"Hmm?" Shins inquired, standing smoothly.

"Just . . . Isn't it weird? For a man that bloody heartless?"

"What's weird?"

"That he wants his people brought to him. That even a right bastard like Maline won't run off and leave his friends behind."

Widdershins's whole world compressed itself into a razor-edged dagger, thrust up through her stomach and into her heart. She felt every pulse of blood through her body, felt it pounding in her head. She couldn't breathe; would have literally doubled over, perhaps collapsed entirely, had not Olgun stepped in, catching her, holding her muscles upright with a sharp surge of power.

She wanted to scream. Cry. Curse, as she hadn't even in her youth, let alone recently. Lash out, break her fist against a wall—or break Cyrille's jaw against a fist. She wanted every last one of the Thousand Crows before her, a blade in her hand, and damn the consequences.

None of it, however, could mask the overwhelming shame blossoming like an unwanted weed in the depths of her soul.

Even a right bastard like Maline won't run off and leave his friends behind. But I did.

"Olgun?" She said nothing more, but he *had* to know what she was thinking. She felt his touch, his genuine efforts to soothe; to reassure that it wasn't the same thing at all. She felt, but she couldn't absorb, like listening to mumbled words through a heavy curtain. She couldn't understand most of his reassurance, let alone believe, and most of what she *did* comprehend she felt certain had to be a lie.

"Shins? What's wrong?"

How long had she been standing there, marinating in horror and self-loathing? She had no idea, couldn't even begin to guess. All she could do was raise her head to meet Cyrille's worried gaze, and shrug.

"Fine. Sorry. Let's move."

She turned and bounded down the first flight of steps before he could even begin to ask a question.

❀

Thankfully, Olgun remained sufficiently together to warn her before she bounded right into the midst of a milling handful of Crows.

"So now what?" Cyrille whispered. The two of them were huddled on the steps, roughly halfway between the second floor and the next-highest landing. The balcony and connected halls, empty when they'd made their way to the ramparts, were now quite thoroughly occupied. Shins didn't know if the Crows had yet found their two missing companions, stashed away in one of the rooms, but clearly they'd at least noticed the pair's absence.

"I'm not sure," she confessed, sucking at her lip between her teeth. "We can't do anything if we can't see what's going on downstairs, but the balcony looks kind of crowded just now. They're scrambling around like ants out there. Really big, person-shaped ants."

"With guns."

"I seem to remember . . . Hmm." Cyrille traced a finger through the air, seemingly drawing random patterns.

"What the figs are you doing?"

"Trying to re-create the layout of the castle in my head," he answered. "So we would be over . . . right." He dropped his hand and smiled. "There's a small gallery that overlooks the banquet hall from the end opposite the main doors. Several of the banners are hung really close to it, so we should be able to peek through without anyone seeing us from below.

"We *could* get hemmed in by the Crows searching this floor," he acknowledged. "There's no door to close off the gallery. But it's accessed through a fairly obscure hall, and it's got two separate, open arches leading into it; they'd have to come at us through both to pen us in."

"How in pastries' name do you know this?"

"Grew up a noble in Aubier. I told you, we've held occasional functions here before. I was so curious, before I was old enough to attend, I listened to and read everything I could on Castle Pauvril."

"Fantastic!" Shins clapped him on the back, hard enough to make him wince. "So how do we get there?"

"Uh . . ." Was he blushing? It was hard to tell, but she was pretty sure he was blushing. "About a third of the way around the hall. To the left."

"Past the room we left the first two Crows."

"Right," he said through a sickly grin.

"And the bulk of the *other* Crows currently on the second floor. Whom, I would like to point out, are currently failing *spectacularly* at being either unconscious or dead."

"Right."

Widdershins sighed, crept back down the stairs to the second-story landing, and dropped once more to her stomach. From there, she wormed forward and took two quick looks through the doorway, one in each direction.

"That one guy to the right," she breathed. "The one in that monstrous green tunic that looks as though it's made of lime pelts."

A brief tingle of acknowledgment; Olgun knew who she meant.

Again a quick look, then another, as the Crows checked various doorways. Until, "Now!"

They were all armed, the thugs and brigands scouring the second floor. Two of their own had vanished; of course they were prepared for trouble. They also, however, were men who—though accustomed to violence—had never been formally trained.

Thus, while many of them were disciplined enough to keep the flintlocks in their hands aimed upward when not actually preparing to shoot someone, not all of them did.

The man in the aforementioned tunic—which really did make him appear to have some personal grudge against citrus—stepped back, allowing one of his companions to pass down the hall.

Olgun reached out, and the man-in-green's pistol fired.

He'd held it casually, only half-extended, so it wasn't a particularly good shot. The ball punched a hole through the other Crow's arm, but it wasn't a lethal or, depending on how well it was treated, even necessarily crippling wound.

It was, however, sufficient.

Drawn by the screams and the thunder of the shot, the Crows on the second floor—and, indeed, a few from the first—converged on their brethren, one huddled against the wall, bleeding and wailing, the other staring at him with shocked incomprehension. Whether they would believe his tale of a misfire or assume he'd turned on one of their own and treat him accordingly, Widdershins neither knew nor cared.

She knew only that for a few precious moments, the path between them and the gallery was clear.

She could make it fine. At this distance, in this light, she could make herself all but invisible. Cyrille, however . . .

Cyrille could only run and pray that their distraction was distracting *enough*.

"Run," she hissed at him. "And pray."

He ran. She sneaked, watching over her shoulder until her neck ached. Olgun waited, poised, ready to attempt another trick if someone *did* glance their way before Cyrille had made the bend in the corridor.

None of them did, and Widdershins breathed a sigh of relief so intense she nearly deflated as she followed him around the corner.

Where she almost ran into him, standing with his arms crossed in the center of the hall. "What are you—?"

"How did you do that?" he demanded.

"Do what?"

"That thing with the pistol. I've seen you do some amazing things, but *that* was unnatural!"

The thief shrugged. "Flintlocks misfire. It happens."

"Not that conveniently, it doesn't."

"Guess we'll never know." She started to walk past him; he stepped over to block her way.

"You put me off once before," he said. "This time, I'm not moving until you explain."

Shins nodded slowly. "Very well." A quick leap to the side and a single step, and she was past him. "That's probably wise. You stay and guard the hall. I'll go hunt for the gallery."

She'd gotten perhaps five paces when he caught up with her and took the lead, muttering all manner of ignoble imprecations.

Cyrille had been entirely correct. The corridor to which he led her, branching off the main hallway, was absolutely unobtrusive. The entrance was a narrow archway, smack dab in the midst of a number of arch-shaped niches; not hidden in any real sense, just readily overlooked.

Which makes sense, since it leads to an overlook. Shins actually had to catch herself before she giggled. *Get a hold of yourself, you gibbering gosling.*

The "gallery," as Cyrille had called it, was really just a tongue of balcony, jutting farther out than the rest of it. Streaks and footprints in the dust, from the two entryways to the rim and back, had probably been left by the workman who'd come through here to hang the banners.

Banners that did, indeed, hang remarkably close to the balcony itself. Shins could easily creep to the edge and look between the nearest two.

One of which displayed the leonine visage of Cevora.

Of course.

She also realized, studying the handrail that ran around the gallery and the banners hanging a few feet away, that there was only a single vantage point from which they could see the hall below. If they were both to have a clear view, one of them would have to lie atop the other.

Also of course.

"On your stomach," she said, finger jutting imperiously at the spot. "All the way to the railing, so you can look through."

"Um, all right . . ." He dropped, scowling at the dust that now caked his outfit, and scooted until his face nearly protruded over the edge. "I can see the hall," he confirmed.

Widdershins sighed. "If you even *think* an inappropriate comment about this, I'll kick you over the side."

"Um, about what, exactl*llrrrrrk* . . . ?!"

"I can hear you thinking," she warned as she grudgingly climbed onto and flopped down atop him.

"No, I'm . . . really not thinking at all right now. . . ."

"Hush, now. Spying."

At some point while she and Cyrille had been getting settled, Maline and the others had returned to the banquet hall. Only a few of the groups of hostages were currently visible from Widdershins's angle, but those she could see looked absolutely terrified, their faces pale and twisted.

And no wonder. They must assuredly have heard the shots from above; the fusillade had been a veritable man-made storm. For the Crows to then return without any of the servants and guards with whom they'd departed—well, it required precious little imagination to picture what must have happened.

Maline himself was standing beside one of the food tables, munching on a sloppy handful of meat and speaking with Josce. She wished she could hear as well as see, but even Olgun's powers were limited. He probably *could* enhance and focus her hearing enough for her to pick out what was being said, but it would take more of his energies and concentration than she was willing to risk. The absolute last thing she needed was her god running low on fuel before this whole mess was concluded.

Josce eventually nodded to whatever he'd been told, turned, and walked out of sight beneath the balcony from which Widdershins watched. Maline continued stuffing food into his face.

"I've seen raccoons with better table manners," she whispered to Cyrille, who—as best she could tell, given their relative positions—nodded.

Any further commentary on the thug's eating habits would have to wait, however. Josce reappeared some minutes later, this time carrying a wooden box. Maline swept a large platter of fruit and a glass decanter from the table—the resultant sound rather akin to hurling a suit of armor through a stained glass window—and pointed. The balding servant placed his burden there, as directed, tossed open the lid, and stepped back.

"Huh," Cyrille and Shins said in unison.

Maline reached into the box, removed the first of what appeared to be a few dozen lead balls, and began reloading his pistols. One by one, the other Crows came and did the same—some taking handfuls of much smaller pellets for use in their blunderbusses, most sticking to pistol balls. All of which made reasonable sense . . .

Until Shins noticed that several of the Crows were *unloading weapons they hadn't fired*, replacing their old ammunition with the new.

"What the hell?!" Judging by the question, Cyrille had spotted the same thing.

Shins shrugged, a truly awkward motion given where she lay. "I haven't the first hint of an idea of a notion of a clue. I—"

Her throat squeezed itself shut in a horrified choke as Maline and several of the newly rearmed Crows began ordering another group of hostages—servants, again—to their feet.

"Oh, gods." Cyrille's shoulders shook beneath her. "It hasn't . . . He's not giving Veroche any *time*! He can't possibly expect . . . Shins, we have to stop them. We—"

"We can't." It wasn't a whisper so much as a ragged scrap of voice, ripped from her soul.

"What?!"

Cyrille shoved her off and rolled until he could sit facing her, his glare accusing. "How can you *say* that? You know what's going to happen to them, we can't—"

She didn't know if it was her expression or her tears of frustrated grief that finally stopped him. "Cyrille . . ." She cleared her throat, tried again. "How would we stop them? We're in the same position we were before. We'd most likely die trying, and that'd still leave most of the Crows with the rest of the hostages. We wouldn't . . . We can't."

"No . . ." He, too, had begun to weep softly. "Shins, there has to be *something* we can do. Please, there has to be!"

"We can end this. We can find out what's happening here—there's definitely something more going on than we know, than he's said—and we end it. Until we do that, nothing we do is going to make a bit of difference."

"If we don't do it fast," he muttered bitterly, "there won't be anyone left to save, anyway."

Shins rolled to her feet, waited for Cyrille to do the same with rather less grace. "We follow Josce," she decided. "Maybe there's something special about those pistol balls, or . . . I don't know. But he's the only one we've seen involved in something beyond the banquet hall and the—the ramparts. So we see where he's been scurrying off to, yes?"

Cyrille's lips parted . . . then hung open, voiceless, at the sound of speech from beyond the archway.

"Hey! Any of you guys check this little hallway over here?"

Once again, the pair spoke in perfect unison. "Oh, figs."

CHAPTER EIGHTEEN

"Subtle! Do you . . . remember *subtle?*!" Cyrille panted, wheezing his words between gasps as he pounded up the winding stairs, struggling to keep pace with his companion. "I'm pretty sure you . . . were the first one to *mention* subtle!"

Widdershins's shrug shouldn't even have been visible in the midst of their mad dash, but somehow it was clear enough. "I *tried* to be subtle!"

"You tried—you stabbed him in the arse!"

"He was about to shoot you! I thought this would be quieter than the gun going off."

"It *wasn't!*"

"Well, I didn't *know* a man could scream like that, did I? Now shut up and run!"

They ran, and a shouting throng of Crows followed.

Getting past the first of Maline's people and escaping the balcony hadn't been difficult; not with both surprise and Olgun on their side. Getting past them *quietly*, however, had very clearly proven untenable.

At the next landing, perhaps three or four floors down from the peak of the tower into which they'd fled, Shins paused. "Keep going!" she hissed. And then, "Don't argue, go!"

Scowling, Cyrille went.

"Olgun . . ." She was already sprinting into the tight circular hall. "We have about fifteen seconds . . ."

A familiar prickling, a surge of strength, and Shins found herself running faster than she ever had, perhaps faster than *anyone*, even with magic, ever had.

She was already exhausted, soaked with sweat, by the fifth or sixth step. But it would be enough.

Several rooms were visible at a cursory examination from the landing, all of which stood with doors wide open, allowing airflow through the largely unused level. She reached one of them, slammed it shut, and zipped back toward the stairs. Just before hitting the first step, she yanked one of the various pouches from her belt—a small one, containing nothing but a few coins and an eating knife—and dropped it against the wall, where it could conceivably have been torn from her in her haste.

She was barely around the bend, out of sight of the landing, when the Crows reached it. Her whole body shook; perspiration dripped into her eyes, stinging and burning. She clenched her jaw so tightly it ached, the only way she could keep herself from gasping loudly enough to be heard below.

Please work, please work, I don't know who the happy horses I'm even praying to, I don't really care, just please work.

It did. She heard a wordless cry from the first of the Crows, and then a barrage of footsteps haring off into the corridor. Shins allowed herself a relieved sigh and resumed her own climb.

The trick itself wouldn't buy them much time. A couple of minutes, if that, for the Crows to risk a presumed ambush, burst through the door to the room, and then do a quick search of the neighboring rooms when they realized the first was empty.

That brief delay, however, would buy them a longer one. They had two or three higher levels in which to hide, and the Crows would have no way of knowing which; they'd have to search them all.

"All right," she panted as she caught up with her companion. "We need to take shelter somewhere, catch our breath. I suggest the top, yes? It'll take them longest to get to; they can't afford to start at the top and work down, would give us too much of an opening to escape."

"That makes sense," Cyrille said dubiously. "But aren't they likely to think of that themselves? Realize the top floor is the best choice and start there after all?"

"Nope. If they *do* figure that the top floor is the best choice, they'll also probably figure that we'd figure they'd figure it, so we *wouldn't* hide on the top floor."

"Um . . . What?"

"Trust me, I've dealt with these sorts of people a lot. You can always count on them to be stupid enough to use it against them, but not *so* stupid that they're *too* stupid to use it against them."

"I . . . You know what? Let's just go."

They had almost reached the top when they heard the salvo of gunfire, reverberating from outside, pounding in through the windows. It was followed, almost immediately, by terrified wails from below; the hostages remaining in the banquet hall had heard the shots, too.

"You're right." Shins once more lay a hand on her friend's shoulder, though whether to comfort him or to steady herself, she couldn't have said. "Let's just go."

※

"What now?"

"Now," Shins said, "we take a few minutes to rest up enough to hopefully not die."

As with the first room they'd occupied—years ago, it seemed, when her most immediate worry was foisting off his advances—this one was brick-walled, empty of furniture, redolent of mildew, and wore dust and insect carapaces like a fashion statement. No telling at all what it might have been used for, back when it presumably *had* a use.

Unlike that earlier room, this one was even more cramped, thanks to the harsh slope of the tower's roof. It was also filthier and boasted a window—a narrow thing with heavy, semirotting shut-ters—to the outside. Outside, and a rather stomach-lurching view, or so Widdershins assumed. She had no interest in checking; it was far more important to sit.

"We need a way out of here," she muttered eventually, glaring with an absentminded resentment at the cracking door and its tar-nished handle.

"Out of the tower or the castle?" Cyrille snipped.

"Uh, the castle? So we can talk to Veroche, see what's going on, tell her what we've learned? Maybe sneak the prisoners out? We *know* the way out of the tower."

"Oh, we certainly do. We just can't use it!"

"You don't have to be grouchy at *me* about it! How is that *my* fault?"

"How is . . . ?" Cyrille's jaw went so slack, Shins was surprised it didn't start to wobble, a flesh-and-bone pendulum. "You led us here! You're the one who ran into a tower when we were being chased! Towers, in general, tend to only *allow* travel in two basic directions!"

"What was I supposed to do?" she demanded.

"Um, maybe run somewhere that *wasn't* a tower?"

"How was I supposed to know? *You're* the one who knows the castle, you turkey!"

"You took the lead! I was just following!"

"Well, that's *your* mistake, isn't it? Why are you blaming me?"

Cyrille made a sound very much as though he'd just sat on a teapot. The hand he threw upward in exasperation might have made a more impressive gesture if the result hadn't been to shower himself with dust, forcing him to muffle a sneeze.

"There's the main door," he rasped when he was finally done. "Obviously not an option. There's a servants' entrance, directly to the kitchen, but that's right off the banquet hall. I think we need to figure Maline's got that one watched, too."

"Probably, yes. Is that it? Nothing else?"

"Windows on some of the upper floors. Think you can climb down the outer wall?"

It was spoken sarcastically, but Shins actually considered it. "Too risky," she said finally. "I'd have to either leave you behind or try carrying you, and I'm not thrilled with my chances in the latter case." Far more quietly, in response to Olgun, "Well, I'm *not* sure we could! Of course it doesn't sound awkward to you; *you're* not the one with *arms*!

"Plus," she continued, speaking for Cyrille once more and ignoring his truly befuddled expression, "if Maline's got people on the wall—and he almost has to, to make sure the reeve isn't trying anything—all it takes is one of them spotting us. A couple of shots or rocks on our heads, and splat. I can't believe there's not *some* other way!"

"There's supposed to be a postern gate somewhere," the young Delacroix said slowly, clearly dredging his memory. "But that's not going to help us, either."

"No? Why not?"

"Have you seen the overgrowth, Shins? I guess not; the city's kept the area near the main door clear. Everywhere else, though, it's pretty damn impressive. If I'm remembering what I read correctly, between that overgrowth, the settling of the foundations, and the rusting of the iron, the gate became impossible to open. I mean literally impossible, even with hammers and prybars. Might as well have been part of the wall. So everyone ignored it, and it's pretty much been forgotten since then."

"We should at least take a look," she insisted. "Where is it?"

"Does *forgotten* have a lot of different meanings where you're from, Shins?"

"You *lost* a *door*?!"

"It's not as though *I* was responsible for the damn thing!"

Shins loosed something between a sigh and a groan, made of sheer exasperation, and stood. "So we still have no idea how to get out of here or what to do next! Fat lot of help your 'inside knowledge' has been!"

"You wouldn't have gotten near this far without me!" Cyrille, too, shot to his feet. "You'd still be wandering around lost on the second floor!"

"Or I'd have already solved this whole thing! And I'll tell you something else!"

"Yeah? What's that?"

"We should probably stop shouting before the Crows hear us!"

Sudden silence. The both of them stared; the both of them blushed just a bit. And then the both of them jumped at the clatter of boots on the nearby stairs.

"We have to get out of here. Now!"

Cyrille nodded, even as he asked the obvious question neither of them wanted asked. "How?"

How, indeed? The stairs were the only way down, and they were swarming with—

Except they're not *the only way down, are they?*

"Olgun? From before . . . How sure are you?"

The flare of emotion that ran through her *said* "very," but it *felt* "iffy." It'd have to do.

Widdershins bounded to the window and hurled open the shutters. Hinges squealed, rotten wood split. Shins now had an unobstructed view of the fields and forests beyond Aubier.

And, as she'd fully assumed, a rather distressing plummet down to a very hard surface.

Ooh, this is going to be fun as a chamber pot full of ants.

"We're going to climb out," she told him.

"Do you really think we have time for jokes right now?!"

"No. I really, really don't."

Apparently, it dawned on Cyrille, then, that she was entirely serious—judging from the tight gurgling sound in his throat.

"What . . . What happened to 'too risky, you aren't happy with your chances'?!"

"Our options have dwindled, yes?"

"And the sentries on the walls?"

"We're not climbing the outer wall. The other towers should hide us from most directions, and if any happen to be near, they'll be looking *outward*, not inward."

Probably.

"So come on, already!" she said, holding a hand out to him.

He put his own hand tightly on the hilt of his borrowed rapier. "I'll face the Crows."

"Don't be stupid! Er."

"It's a narrow doorway. I can hold it a while."

"Cyrille—"

"No!"

Shins smiled softly, stepped over, and placed her hand on his shoulder. "All right."

He began to smile as well—and Shins yanked him around, stood on her toes, and wrapped an arm around his neck.

"Olgun, please don't let me he hurt him."

He was out cold almost before his fingers had even begun scrabbling at her arm.

"Is it horrible," she asked the little god as she removed Cyrille's borrowed sword belt and began looping it around his chest as a harness, "that part of me enjoyed that?"

Then, at his answer, Widdershins said, "Fine, then I'll live with being horrible," and stuck her tongue out at the empty room.

When she finally staggered to the window with her companion roughly and precariously strapped to her back, it was Olgun—despite his earlier confidence—who made the obvious suggestion.

"No." She didn't even take a moment to think about it. "I'm not leaving anyone else behind."

The climb, it turned out, was very nearly a moot point. Shins spent several pulse-pounding moments trying to squeeze through the window. Every time she tried, some part or other of her floppy passenger snagged on the frame, either dragging her to a halt or threatening to yank one or both of them free of the makeshift harness. His knuckles were skinned and bruised from her multiple failed attempts, and she'd accidentally whacked his head once or twice; she was already dripping with sweat despite the cold, her neck and back beginning to ache.

Finally, with an awkward twist that threatened to send her toppling from the window before she was able to find a grip on the wall outside, she managed—barely—to wriggle through, Cyrille squeezed up into the upper right corner, Shins the lower left.

For a moment, she protruded from the wall, a tired and wobbly flagpole, the extra weight on her back threatening to drag her over and down. Way, way down. The wind couldn't possibly have grown so much stronger and so much colder than it had been earlier, but it felt as though the world was attempting to blow her out like a candle.

Crevices between bricks, gaps in the mortar, cracks in the stone. To Widdershins's fingers and toes, these were normally as good as a ladder, or even better. Not only climbing, but scurrying side to side to make a cockroach envious, even hanging upside down, there wasn't much she couldn't do—wasn't much she hadn't done—with Olgun's aid.

Normally, however, she wasn't trying to balance a dead weight, heavier than she was, hanging from her shoulders by a single strap around his own.

Every muscle in her body burned, trembled, partly with strain, partly with the full power Olgun could muster. He couldn't manage it long; already, she felt exhaustion seeping through her, and recognized that not all of it was hers. Then again, she couldn't handle it long, either. *Everything* throbbed.

Tentatively, hesitantly, she let herself hang lower, supporting herself on her fingers and one foot, seeking purchase with the other. She hadn't climbed anything this slowly, this fearfully, since she'd scaled the cracked and dilapidated fountain near her parents' apartment.

That had been only a few weeks before the fire.

Right, because *that* was the most comforting thought to have in her head right now. . . .

The tip of a boot slid into a cranny that few other people would have even seen. Stiff, tense fingers forced themselves free of one brick to clamp tight around the next. Her jaws clenched, the winds whipped her hair across her face. Cyrille groaned and seemed to slip with every move, nearly jerking her from the wall. Her progress was parceled out in increments of pain, rather than distance. Her whole body trembled, hard enough to send bits of old mortar sifting out from beneath raw and cracking fingertips.

All of it on instinct, for after the first yard or so, her mind had room for only a single idea, over and over, repeating like the call of a dying bird.

I'm not going to make it. Oh, gods, I'm not going to make it. . . .

An inch. A foot. The tiniest of footholds, the most precarious of grips. Jaws, fingers, gut clenched tight enough to crush rock. Her ears rang; her vision was swallowed whole by the wall before her. No world, no up or even down. No thought, no memory—even, finally, no fear, perhaps no Widdershins at all. Just rote, instinctive need. Over and over, an endless, desperate repetition, its purpose long forgotten.

An inch. A foot. The tiniest of footholds, the most precarious of grips.

An inch. A foot.

A window.

At first, Shins panicked. She didn't even recognize it for what it was, only that it interrupted the routine that had become the entirety of her existence. The shock almost cost her a handhold, and infinite seconds passed in a mad scramble before she felt even remotely secure, more until she'd gotten Cyrille to cease swaying.

Panic again, when it all came back to her. Given how difficult it'd been to maneuver the two of them out . . . *How the frogs do I get us in through the window?!*

The answer, eventually, proved to be even more awkward than earlier. Shins managed to climb below the window then back up, planting her elbows on the frame and slowly tugging and wriggling until Cyrille slithered off her back into the room. The harness dragged her with him, which proved helpful, and threatened to cut into her arms and shoulders, which was rather less so.

The result, however, was a final desperate skitter, and then Shins followed her companion into the room—and flopped to the floor beside him, equally limp.

She had never, in her life, been so exhausted, so worn. Stars danced across the ceiling, and she was too tired even to try blinking them away. Gods, even seeing or listening sounded exhausting!

It came over her slowly, flowing through her body; she felt warm, almost buoyant. The pain faded, the fatigue dulled, though it still chewed on, a spiritual pack of wolves. For long moments she lay still, giving herself, and Olgun, as long to recover as she could.

She felt better, and she was grateful for it—but not as much better as she'd have hoped.

"How long can we keep this up?" she asked softly.

Olgun's reply was confident, reassuring—and also so deathly tired that she briefly felt his exhaustion overwhelm her own.

"That long, huh?" Widdershins groaned all the way to her feet. A quick look revealed yet *another* empty room (at this point, she more than half assumed the entire tower was decades out of use), and whole constellations of footprints in the dust. The Crows had been here already, searched and moved on. Good.

Widdershins tottered over to Cyrille, knelt beside him, and began lightly slapping his cheeks.

"What the *hell*!"

He all but burst into waking, shoving Shins away from him hard before rolling over to vomit copiously into the corner. Shins herself landed on her rear end a few feet away, wincing at both the sting and the growing acrid miasma.

"What is *wrong* with you?!" His voice was rough, gravelly, but more than intelligible. "I said I didn't want—!"

"Oh, shut it! You're alive! I know you're alive, because you're making way too much noise for a nice, peaceful corpse. You wouldn't be if you'd stayed. You're welcome, by the way. No big deal. It wasn't *the* hardest thing I've ever done, just somewhere in the top one!"

"You had no right!"

"Right?! So I should have just left you—"

From the window, a third fusillade of gunfire sounded from atop the wall.

"Pick this up later?" she asked softly.

"Yeah."

With the Crows scouring the upper levels of the tower—after all, the two fugitives couldn't *possibly* have gotten past them!—Shins and Cyrille had no difficulty in returning once more to the second floor and the balcony overlooking the banquet hall.

The box of flintlock balls still sat on the table—but only the box. Apparently, the multiple reloads had exhausted its contents.

Maline stood beside it, his breathing a bit heavy; apparently he'd only just come from the long staircase himself. Most of the hostages Shins could see were either stone-faced or weeping openly. Surely, by now, none of them had the slightest doubt what fate probably awaited them.

"That food just doesn't smell as appetizing as it did," Cyrille noted. Widdershins turned his way, blinked twice, and went back to studying the room.

Once again, after a few moments, Josce showed up with a box, placing it upon the table and collecting the old one, then conversing briefly with Maline.

"I'm going," Widdershins hissed.

"Going?"

"Staring at Maline until he decides to drag another group upstairs isn't going to tell us anything. So I need to follow Josce, yes?"

"You mean we do," Cyrille corrected.

"No. You don't have the stealth for—"

"I can be sneaky. And I'm not letting you go alone." He crossed his arms, a gesture that was probably intended to convey determination but just made him appear melodramatic.

"We don't have time to argue this!"

"Precisely."

Aaargh! "Fine! You stay at least half a corridor behind me, and you do *not* move up until I signal you to! Understand?"

"Yes."

Grumble.

Pauvril's plethora of stairs made it quick and easy for them to return to the first floor some distance away, then make a quick return to the banquet hall. A side passage, branching off the main corridor that led from the grand chamber back into the depths of the castle, provided a nice, shadowed vantage point. Widdershins had all but vanished in the gloom; she watched a couple of the Crows, along with Josce—carrying his empty box—stroll past without so much as a glance in her direction.

She gave them a slow count of ten and then slipped out to follow, waving for Cyrille to follow her in kind.

The sounds of the banquet hall faded, as did the lingering smell of the kitchen beside it. Josce led them through a major corridor, and then a far smaller one, moving ever farther into the rearmost confines of Pauvril. Shins stopped seeing staircases after a time and realized they must have moved beyond the upper levels, to a portion of the keep with only a single floor.

And then she stopped, whispering bitterly to herself and Olgun both, when she realized this might be as far as she'd get.

Her quarry had entered a room with three unevenly spaced exits, essentially a lowercase "y" with a broad chamber at the intersection. It wasn't that they'd lost her; she could see and hear signs of movement from the rightmost of the two branches. No, it was that almost half a dozen members of the Thousand Crows waited in that room, standing sentry, and showed no sign of planning to leave anytime soon.

"Trouble," Cyrille guessed when she came back to meet him, rather than waving him forward. It clearly wasn't a question.

"Guard Crows," she muttered.

"A lot?"

"Too many for my comfort. Even if we could put them down, it only takes one to sound an alert. Frogs and figs! Let's get back a ways and think about this."

Knowing it to be a reasonable spot to hide, the pair backtracked to the same side passage in which they'd waited just a few moments before. At which point, they stood and looked at one another, constantly starting one suggestion or another, constantly stopping themselves when they spotted this or that flaw in this or that idea.

So wrapped up were they, neither of them noticed the growing commotion in the nearby banquet hall until they heard the resounding *slam* of the castle's main door. Both froze, listening intently—Widdershins far more effectively, thanks to Olgun's aid.

"There's more of them," she whispered.

"More of who?"

"The Crows. The reeve gave in!"

Cyrille shrugged. "Didn't have much choice. Besides, they're still trapped here for—"

"Where's Maline?! Let me speak with Maline!" The shout was loud enough that even Cyrille heard it clearly. It was *certainly* loud enough for Widdershins to recognize the voice.

Not just the Thousand Crows, then. The reeve delivered Lazare Carnot, too.

"Evening, Lazare. Excuse me, Lord Carnot." Shins could practically feel the oil on Maline's words from here.

"Explain to me," the patriarch demanded, "how this mess happened!"

"Oh, that's easy. I made the mistake of trusting the promises of a spineless aristocrat."

Widdershins scarcely even flinched when she heard the shot. She'd practically been expecting it.

"Carry him up and dump him with the next group," Maline ordered his thugs. "No sense wasting a body."

Now what does that mean?

"The rest of you," he continued, "we need to speed this up. Start gathering the next group."

Gods . . .

"They got what they wanted," Cyrille whispered, shaking. "Why don't they *stop*?"

"There's more going on here, I told you that," she replied, her tone distant.

"Shins, we *can't* let this go on!"

No. Gods help me, we can't. "Olgun?"

She almost broke down and wept at the sorrow in his agreement.

"Come on," she said dully, gesturing for Cyrille to follow.

"Where are we going?"

"To stop this," she answered, wondering with an almost despairing calm how much of herself she might have just killed with her decision. "However we have to."

CHAPTER NINETEEN

When Widdershins again approached the chamber with three exits and five Crows, it looked as though nothing whatsoever had changed.

That was untrue. Widdershins had changed.

The young woman was no stranger to bloodshed. She'd taken lives; one of them earlier that same day. She had always regretted it, and it had always, always been her last resort.

When she hurled herself into that room that night, with all the speed Olgun could bestow, Widdershins set out to kill.

They'd been watching for trouble, of course; they stood guard, after all. But they hadn't anticipated it, and certainly not as fast as it appeared. Widdershins leapt, spun, her blade a flickering serpent's tongue of steel. Two of the thugs fell, dead or dying—one pierced through the heart, one with a slit-and-gaping throat—before they could so much as draw a weapon.

Shins didn't even attempt to stop and change direction. Three more steps carried her straight to the wall; a foot planted on it sent her hurtling back the other way. The third collapsed as she slammed into him, the wind knocked from lungs and the flintlock from his hands. Shins thrust herself off him with one leg, dropping—stretching, nearly diving—into an almost inhumanly extended lunge. Barely two inches of her blade punched through flesh and muscle, between ribs, but that was enough to puncture a second heart.

Four of the five sentries were down in less time than it took the Crow with his throat slashed to bleed out.

The last one standing, shaking and pale, had his flintlock out and aimed. Again, Shins couldn't afford to have Olgun trigger it;

the noise itself would ruin everything. So would the shout for help the Crow was even then preparing to utter, inhaling deeply through parted lips.

Shins tossed her rapier—to him, not at him. It sailed in a casual arc, coming at him blade up, handle in easy reach.

Puzzled instinct accomplished the rest.

His eyes flickered to the sword; his flintlock wavered as he reached with his free hand to catch the weapon. In that tiny flicker of distraction, Shins had crossed the distance between them, wrapped both her hands around the one he'd used to catch the sword, and shoved the tip of the weapon up and aside, slashing him just beneath his jaw.

She retrieved her blood-spattered rapier, then turned at the sound of a pained groan. Body rigid, she approached the one man she'd bowled over. He rolled over as she approached, staring at her in undiluted horror.

He was down. He was beaten. Gods, she could smell from paces away that he'd lost control of his bladder.

But he could also still scream, if she let him.

Stiff as rigor mortis and mechanical as clockwork, Widdershins lifted her blade and ran the fallen man through.

For a long while she stood, sword extended, eyes empty. Slowly, even gracefully, she withdrew the blade, knelt to wipe it free of blood on the dead man's sleeve, and rose once more. With great deliberateness, she slid the weapon home in its sheath at her side.

Then, and only then, did she feel the wetness on her cheek. A tear she hadn't known she'd shed? A dribble of dead man's blood? It didn't matter which, really; once her thoughts turned down the path, she couldn't rein them back. She froze. She fought. And then she fell to the stone floor, knees pressed to her chest, bloody hands wrapped around them, and started to sob.

"Shins? Widdershins? You need to get up!" She heard and recognized each individual word, but couldn't seem to put them together into any unified meaning. She felt her cheek grow warmer, wetter; still couldn't tell from blood or tears, still couldn't bring herself to care.

"Shins, please! We need you!"

Along with the words from without came a surge of emotion and imagery from within. The emotions were calm. Comforting. The images were anything but. She saw Brock, lying in an alley with the rest of the trash, herself fully prepared to end him then and there had she not been stopped. The servants of the twisted Apostle of Cevora, dying hideously, cursed by the idol of the Shrouded God—a curse Shins had manipulated them into unleashing. Herself, again, dueling a pair of Finders in the employ of Bishop Sicard, falsifying a supernatural threat that later turned very real; neither of the two had died that night, but Shins had always known that was a near thing.

Street fights in her youth. Duels with rival thieves. Her clash with Lisette Suvagne, which she'd walked away from neither knowing nor caring whether the taskmaster would survive.

None of it mattered. None of it made one iota of difference. Because in every single instance, either trouble had come to her, or she'd stumbled into a situation where she was truly down to her final option.

Never before in her life had she *set out* with murder as her objective—let alone the murder of *five*.

They were the enemy. They would have killed her, given half the chance. It wasn't for them that Widdershins wept.

She felt pressure on her shoulder and was only vaguely cognizant that it was a hand. "You had to, Shins," Cyrille told her softly. "For everyone back there. For my family, for *me*."

It sounded good. She wanted to believe it, even knew on some level it was true. It didn't help. Her heart refused to listen to anything her head had to say. The people she *might* save were abstract, unreal. The corpses around her, *those* were inalterable truth. She was cracked in two, pain bubbling up in an endless fountain. She shook, she cried, and she truly believed it might never, ever stop.

More images, and this time they *did* put an end to her tears—not in comfort, but in shock. As vividly as she'd ever experienced anything he'd shown her, she was back in his underground shrine. Back watching, helpless and terrified, as her fellow worshippers were ripped apart, over a score of people reduced to the scraps in an abattoir. It looked real, sounded real, *smelled* real. For an instant, she was once more the girl who had lost everything *twice*, who didn't understand what she and Olgun were to become for each other. A girl alone, utterly and completely.

"Why?" She didn't even know if she was speaking aloud, or just thinking, until she sensed a reply. "Why would you show me this?"

Olgun's reply, when it came, was a ripple across the image, warping like a melting mirror. When it steadied once more, she stared not at the corpses of friends those years ago, but the bodies slowly piling up at the foot of Castle Pauvril. More bodies began to appear on the heap in her vision, people she knew for a certainty hadn't yet been murdered, with Calanthe Delacroix atop the gruesome knoll.

The vision shifted, not warping this time, but rotating, coming around to show her the gathered citizens of Aubier, gaping helplessly at the growing carnage. By garb they were varied: soldier and servant, blacksmith and baker, craftsman and carpenter.

But their faces were, all of them, Widdershins herself.

Now she understood. Now they were real, as real to her as the men she'd killed. Nobody else would have to feel what she'd felt, not while she still breathed. And sure as *hens* not because she'd fallen apart over what, ultimately, she'd truly *had* to do.

Shins rolled over, clasped Cyrille's hand, and allowed him to pull her to her feet. She ran her own fingers across her cheek; tears only, not blood, thankfully.

She went body to body, collecting flintlocks. Only three remained ready to fire, the others having lost their powder as they were strewn across the room. She handed one to Cyrille, jammed two in her belt, and nodded.

"We're not done," was all she said.

Cyrille, failing utterly to repress a relieved grin, answered with, "We'd better get to it then."

Widdershins matched his smile—and if it didn't *quite* reach her eyes, at least it was a heartfelt attempt—and started down the right-most branch.

✿

Which, in turn, led to no small amount of wandering aimlessly.

Pauvril wasn't huge, as castles went, but it wasn't exactly a house, either. These back sections consisted of far more hallways and small rooms than the front, which was mostly larger chambers. The dust back here wasn't remotely as thick, which would have made tracks hard to discover under even the best of circumstances—and as the two of them were forced to rely on Shins's tiny bull's-eye lantern, lest someone spot the light, these circumstances weren't even in the running for "best." The occasional clank or clatter might have indicated the Crows' location, but the echoing passages made pinpointing those sounds a futile endeavor.

They were on the verge of resuming their mutual recriminations when Widdershins paused, tilting her head and sniffing.

"Do you smell that?"

Cyrille scowled. "I smell musty stone and the oil from that damn lamp."

"No, not those! The *other* smell!"

He, too, sniffed. "Nope. Nothing."

"Oh, come *on*! Are you *blind*?!"

"Um . . ."

It was at this point that Olgun politely, yet smugly, pointed out to Widdershins that perhaps she couldn't take *sole* credit for being able to detect the mild odor, and that—unlike her—Cyrille *didn't* have a god actively assisting.

"Oh." A pause, then, "Well, it's this way."

She set off with more certainty, now, choosing this route and that, until even Cyrille's mere mortal nostrils could detect the scent. "That's plaster," he whispered. "Fresh, but not *too* fresh. Couple of days, maybe."

A peculiar notion began to congeal in Shins's head, but it wasn't *quite* viscous enough yet for her to grasp.

She also had more immediate concerns.

"Noises ahead!" Cyrille hissed.

"I hear them." And indeed, they clearly *were* ahead, now, not mere echoes bouncing around the halls. She doused the lamp, working her way ahead in the dark, her hand on the wall, Cyrille's on her shoulder.

One final fork in the passage, and it was clear they'd reached their destination. The sounds came from the left, now obvious as a mixture of voices and machinery. To the right, a trio of thugs sat around a crate they were using as a makeshift table. Two played some game of dice or other, occasionally bouncing a die off the oil lamp also sitting on the box, while the third watched.

All right, what's wrong with this portrait?

On a tripod beside the crate hung a large gong. The striking mallet leaned against the wall beside it. Obviously, an alarm of some sort, which might have made perfect sense, had the Crows not been guarding the terminus of a dead-end passage.

The notion Shins had been trying to grasp earlier, when her companion identified the scent as plaster, now rose up of its own accord to shake hands and introduce itself.

"A few yards back," she whispered, "I felt a door as we passed. Go back to it, then come back and tell me if you see me silhouetted against their lamp."

"Uh, why?"

"Because the door won't come to us, yes? Go!"

Grumbling, he went, hand trailing on the wall as hers had done. Just a bit later he was back. "I can, but just barely."

"Barely will do." She broke out the stolen flintlocks, making sure they were both still ready to shoot. She raised them, one in each fist, and settled in a runner's crouch.

"Go back to the door again, then watch me. I'm going to mark out a ten count. On ten—not before, not after, *on*—I want you to slam that door as hard as you can."

To his credit, he understood immediately. "Can you make both shots from this distance *and* reach the third before he sounds the alarm?"

"Of course I can!"

"You're sure?"

"Of course I'm sure!"

"Are you lying to me?"

"Of course I am!"

Cyrille's grumble as he went back to the door seemed to be *exactly* the same as he'd grumbled earlier.

Shins braced herself, held one of the pistols out to the side, and began tapping the barrel against an imaginary table.

One . . . Two . . .

"Olgun? I'm not the *best* shot with these things. . . ."

She felt the brush of something incorporeal across her hands.

Seven . . . Eight . . .

On nine, having fully established the interval, she shifted the gun back into position, trusting Cyrille to keep the pattern.

Ten.

The door boomed shut. The flintlocks fired. On the chests of the two Crows nearest the gong, one sitting, one standing, a strange crimson flower seemed to blossom for an instant before they fell.

Shins was sprinting, flintlocks discarded, before the echoes faded. Utterly startled at what had just happened, torn between the instinct to defend himself or reach for the gong, the Crow hesitated for several heartbeats.

It was enough. The race wasn't even close.

Cyrille jogged up beside her as she finished cleaning her blade. "Think it worked?"

"It didn't for me, but I was right next to the stupid things. I assume the inventor of the firearm was a deaf man, yes? Ow."

"Oddly, I don't really care if it worked for *you*."

"Just like a man," she mumbled.

"What?"

"Nothing. I don't hear anyone coming running, or any change in the sounds from the next passage. So yes, between distance and the acoustics, yeah, I think the slam might've hidden it."

"'Think' is good," Cyrille said with a weak grin. "But 'know' would be better."

"When I know, I'll tell you." Shins sheathed her rapier, stepped over the nearest body—with a shudder, but thankfully nothing more—and prodded at the rear wall. "Yep. Plaster."

They looked at one another, spoke in unison. "The postern?"

"But how?" the boy continued on his own. "I told you, it's totally impassable! Even if they'd managed to find it—"

"Then they have an alchemist," Shins told him in sudden comprehension, "who could almost certainly whip up something to eat through the whole thing, overgrowth, bars, whatever."

Cyrille let out a heavy breath. "Then they just throw up a painted wall of plaster so nobody happens to stumble over it."

Shins continued to study it, then pointed out a very simple latch built into the "wall" to keep it shut. "That's got to be how they're planning to get out," she observed. "Pretty clear they were already in the castle before the guests showed up, but maybe they've been coming and going all this time."

"So let's go! We need to tell Veroche and the guards about this."

Shins's nod was blatantly hesitant, would've been even had she *not* been chewing on her lip as though it were her last meal.

"Shins?"

"It's going to take a while for Veroche to get her people mobilized and moving. And we still don't know what they're walking into. I'd really like to find out."

"That means wasting more time!"

"No, it doesn't. You go. I'll stay here and—"

"Forget it, there's no—!"

"Cyrille!" She stepped close, so close, almost touching. "You said it yourself. There's no time! I'm not going. That means you *have* to. They need you to."

"But—"

"*I* need you to."

Cyrille's eyes abruptly glistened in the flickering lantern light, but he nodded. "Shins . . ." He closed the last step, tentatively, and wrapped her in a tight hug—*not*, she gratefully observed, with any effort to kiss her. "Please, please be careful."

"When am I not?" she asked, squeezing back. She *felt* him draw the breath to respond, and spoke before he could. "Of course I will, you turkey. You do, too, all right? You're the closest the Delacroix have to 'decent.' I'd be miffed if I saved the family for nothing."

Again she acted before he could respond, this time disengaging herself from his arms, offering him a parting smile, and vanishing into the shadows.

❀

He watched until she'd utterly faded from sight, and for some time afterward as well. It was, rather unpleasantly, the various growing stenches of the three dead bodies and their various effluvia that snapped him back to the moment.

Right. Time. We have no time. Got to tell Veroche about this.

Cyrille strode back to the door, gripped the latch, pressed, pushed. . . .

Nothing happened. The door refused to budge.

"That's not hopeful," he mumbled, frowning.

He let go, gripped it again, clicked the latch, pushed hard.

Nothing.

Shins was long gone. He wouldn't know how to find her without stumbling into the Crows first. And now, it seemed, he couldn't leave, either.

Cyrille stood before the door, clutching the handle uselessly like an idiot, and all he could think to say was, "Bloody godsdamned fucking . . . hens."

❋

Had it been a larder? Wine cellar? Perhaps even a good old-fashioned dungeon? Widdershins had no real way of knowing. Now, it was merely an enormous section of castle full of broken and jagged interior walls that had once subdivided the whole area into numerous smaller chambers and halls. A few of those walls still met the ceiling; a few were nothing more than lines of brick on the floor; most fell at random intervals between the two. An archway here or a frame with a dangling hinge there was in no way sufficient to tell an observer anything more than "Yes, this was, in fact, a room."

Shins *did* note that these walls appeared thinner, and built of flimsier brick, than most of the castle's interior. Perhaps they'd decided what to do with this place after Pauvril was constructed?

Perhaps, perhaps, perhaps. "Perhaps" didn't matter. What mattered was figuring out what use the place served *now*.

She'd had no difficulty finding it, and a wild boar playing the tambourine could have sneaked up close without effort. Multiple conversations, clicks and thumps and clatters, and a peculiar gloopy bubbling sound that made Shins think of boiling sewage all emanated from within. So, too, did a burning, acidic stench that made her eyes water and probably would have corroded the zills and the fabric off the aforementioned tambourine.

Unfortunately, "close" wasn't good enough, and "in" looked to be a lot harder. While the mechanical sounds came from far in the back, some of the conversation was much nearer the archway Widdershins had approached. A *lot* of Crows occupied this particular nest, and the young thief wasn't particularly eager to try going through them all.

It took some time, but she finally found an alternate way into the man-made cavern of shattered rooms: a smaller door, perhaps for the servants, down at the hallway's far end. For most people, this entrance might have proved useless, as Shins was now separated from her goal by a veritable maze of partial chambers and collapsing walls.

Then again, *most* people would have wanted to make their way via the floor.

Shins scampered up the nearest partial wall and hauled herself atop. The varying heights would prove tricky, and she'd have to make a few jumps to clear the largest gaps, but those didn't worry her. She should even be able to stay hidden; the Crows had lanterns scattered throughout much of the area, shining through the cracks and crevices to where she now stood, but the shadows up here remained thick, and few of the thugs were likely to be looking *up*.

Sometimes on hands and knees—where the footing was particularly precarious or the risk of discovery high—otherwise at a walking crouch the envy of any tightrope performer, Widdershins made her way across the broken chamber.

Her brief journey ended near the rear wall, perched above a scene unlike anything she'd ever seen. A number of Crows ("How hopping big *is* this gang, anyway?" she demanded of Olgun) scurried this way and that around a contraption that appeared to be the offspring of a witch's cauldron and a drunken octopus.

A great basin sat on an iron tripod, a fire burning beneath it with a sickly greenish flame. Numerous spouts and tubes protruded from the thing, most of which were capped. Other tubes—some of various metals, some of glue-sealed leather, a few of glass—led to the cauldron from other, smaller decanters, all standing on tall poles or hanging from the ceiling. These fed various substances into the main basin, a constant admixture of gods-knew-what sorts of ingredients. It was from here that the burning miasma emanated, along with clouds of something that wasn't quite steam, nor quite smoke.

The Crows were moving constantly, gathering various treasures from a massive heap and dumping them into the cauldron. Utensils and dishes, jewelry and picture frames—all of it either gold or silver.

Finally, from a single open spigot near the base of the cauldron, a steady flow of grayish sludge poured into an enormous bowl, carved of stone. As the bowl came near to being full, other Crows would come and drag it away, panting and cursing and straining, while a fresh bowl was put it its place.

And capering about the whole affair like a madman, screeching orders and adjusting tubes, was Fingerbone, alchemist of the Thousand Crows.

"Don't ask me," she whispered, replying to Olgun's unspoken query. "I haven't the first idea." A brief pause, contemplating, and then, "I'm guessing all the gold and stuff is some of what was confiscated from the Carnots, yes? They said the house assets were being kept here until it was decided . . ."

She trailed off, more puzzled than ever, as two of the Crows gathered by the bowl of sludge. Wearing heavy gloves, they gathered some of the stuff in an iron dipper, then poured it carefully into a small mold, also iron.

A spherical mold. A mold of just the right size for . . .

Ammunition.

"Holy gods."

Lead. In a complete reversal of what alchemists had tried to do for centuries on end, Fingerbone was transforming the gold and silver of the Carnot treasury into lead.

And then Maline and the Crows were shooting hostages with it.

Understanding crashed down on Widdershins as though Maline had appeared to explain it to her, so abruptly it made her head swim. This wasn't about the oily bastard getting his people back; this was a theft, one she had to admire just a bit even through her mounting revulsion.

Whatever riches or rewards the Carnots had promised the gang for their cooperation obviously had not been forthcoming, so Maline had decided to take what profit he could. The people of Aubier and the noble houses, however, weren't about to let him and the Crows just walk away. Oh, they'd play along, so long as he had hostages, probably even let him leave the castle, but they wouldn't be planning to let the Crows go far.

Maline and his people were good enough, tough enough, quick enough, that the bulk of them could probably escape any pursuit— but not if they were encumbered with pounds and pounds of gold.

In a few weeks, however, when things in Aubier had returned to normal and the people had let down their guard, it wouldn't be difficult to sneak back in and *dig up the bodies of the murdered hostages.*

Cyrille had told her it was far easier to reverse an alchemical change than to cause it—easier and cheaper. The Crows would still turn a hefty profit, especially if the reagents they were using now to instigate the change had been purchased with Carnot funds rather than their own.

It also, she realized, her stomach lurching, explained why Maline was being so quick with his executions. If the Crows were going to smuggle out enough "lead" for this to be worthwhile, he'd need to shoot each hostage multiple times.

Every hostage multiple times. Maline wasn't planning to leave a single one of them alive.

The whole room spun as Shins tried to take it all in, tried to wrap her mind around the magnitude of the Crow's murderous plan. She felt ready to vomit, actually breaking out in a sweat. It took her a moment, in fact, to realize that part of what she felt wasn't disgust or horror at all, but Olgun screaming a warning in the back of her mind.

Her hands—the only bare skin that had come into contact with the top of the broken walls—and to a much lesser extent, her knees, were slowly beginning to sting.

"Oh, figs."

Shins tried to stand, tried to retreat, but her limbs felt heavier than the lead below. Her vision blurred, the room lurched, and the young woman toppled from the wall, landing with a pained grunt.

When she looked up again, blinking to clear her vision, she found herself surrounded.

❀

"There's a trick to it."

Cyrille froze in the midst of rattling the handle yet again, beetles of ice scurrying down his neck and back. Almost against his will, he turned from the plaster door to face the hall.

Josce Tremont, former servant of Lazare Carnot, now apparently working for Maline directly, watched him from down the corridor, half-obscured in the darkness. Not *so* obscured, however, that Cyrille had any difficulty spotting the rapier in the man's fist.

"The frame's uneven," he continued, casually striding nearer. "You have to lift up on the whole door while you push. It's a nuisance, isn't it? I imagine you wish you'd known that a few minutes ago."

Swallowing hard, hoping that might drown the butterflies in his stomach, Cyrille pulled the last of the three pistols he and Shins had taken from the downed sentries, and fired.

Josce flinched, but he needn't have worried. The ball gouged a divot in the brick over a foot to the servant's left. The only thing to strike him at all were puffs of rock dust.

"Your aim could use some work."

"I haven't had a lot of occasion to practice," Cyrille admitted. He hated the quaver in his voice, and could only hope Josce didn't notice.

The man's grin, reflected in the lantern light, suggested otherwise.

"I have," he told Cyrille, hefting the rapier. "Let me show you."

Josce burst into a run, covering the last few yards instantly, leapt the bodies of his fallen brethren, and swung.

CHAPTER TWENTY

It was purely the length of the corridor that saved him.

Josce's charge took *just* long enough for Cyrille to draw, and then raise, his stolen rapier. Steel screeched against steel, making the nobleman's ears ache and his jaw clench. By rote, more than by intent or even instinct, he launched a quick riposte, sliding his rapier along and then past the other. Josce easily sidestepped, and for a moment, the two faced one another, swords just barely kissing between them, each duelist working to keep eyes on his opponent while not stumbling over the dead or colliding with the makeshift table.

"Nothing personal against your House," Josce sneered, "but I do have to admit, I've wanted to kill an aristocrat for years."

"I've never met you," Cyrille replied, struggling to keep cool, "but I'm sure, for all the aristocrats you *have* met, it's mutual."

The former servant, at that, lunged in the midst of a chuckle.

It was slow, at first, calm and collected. A few thrusts and counterthrusts, parries and ripostes, then another moment of study. Cyrille felt as though every bit of his formal training was draining from his mind in a steady trickle, but thus far, muscle memory had saved his life.

Unfortunately, a swordsman with far less schooling than Cyrille would still have quickly seen that Josce was testing him, probing, perhaps even toying with him. The servant was fast and getting faster; not merely skilled but experienced, his strikes far smoother and less rigidly textbook than Cyrille's. With each exchange of blows, Josce's strikes came nearer to punching past the boy's ever-more-desperate parries, while Cyrille was nowhere near to landing one of his own.

He was going to die here, now, with freedom just out of reach, and both of them knew it.

He was going to die, and quite possibly, so would everyone trapped in Castle Pauvril.

The ring of metal echoed through the corridor; the growing stench of the bodies infused Cyrille's lungs with every desperate gasp. He no longer had any doubt at all; the bastard was playing with him. Even Cyrille was good enough to spot a couple of openings Josce could have taken advantage of.

Now would be a great time for Shins to pop up, to rescue him, as—much as he hated to admit—she'd so often done. Since she wasn't here, though, all he had was this:

What would she do?

He lacked her skill. He lacked her confidence. He lacked her guile. He lacked the magic or witchcraft or whatever it was that enabled her to do all the incredible things she did. He lacked, though again he hated to admit it, her courage.

All he had that Widdershins didn't . . . was family. Several of whom would die today if he failed.

Oh, Cevora, this is going to hurt.

When Josce next struck, Cyrille pivoted on his back foot to take the thrust, not against his blade, but through the flesh of his left arm.

Lightning flashed through him, singeing every nerve. Starbursts filled his vision, his whole body threatened to lock up, and he realized he'd screamed only when his cry began to echo.

Yet he didn't freeze, not utterly. They needed him not to; and *she* wouldn't have.

Josce's shock was short-lived, his blade entangled in meat and bone for only an extra second or two.

Time enough for Cyrille, his scream twisting from pure agony to seething rage, to sweep the tip of his blade through his enemy's throat.

Cyrille stood for a long moment, wavering on his feet. All he could think, with surprising clarity, was, *Without the pain and shock, I cannot help but think that the lifeblood of the first man I've ever killed spraying over my face and chest would probably upset me on some level.*

One step back toward the door, and the rapier slipped through the fingers of his unwounded arm. He glanced at it, wondered if he should pick it up, and couldn't remember why it might be worth the effort.

A second step and he fell hard to his knees, wounded arm clenched tight to his chest, pumping frightening quantities of blood, intermingling with Josce's own. The rest of his body seemed to grow cold, numb, as the wound throbbed and burned, growing worse with every breath.

His fingers fumbled at his sword belt. *Might serve as tourniquet, at least long enough to . . .* The plaster door, an arm's length away, began to blur, and then went dark, along with the rest of the hall.

❋

Widdershins felt herself yanked upright, clutched painfully hard by multiple fists around her forearms. Her stomach took a bit longer to pick itself up off the floor. She had to swallow hard, breathe deeply, focusing desperately to keep from dry heaving. The gasps served only to fill her lungs with more of the caustic fume, making her cough instead of vomit.

Beyond even that, though, she felt horribly sick. Her head pounded, her hands and her knees burned feverishly, and every muscle in her body felt limp as a dead snake.

"Olgun . . ."

She already felt him working, felt him soothing some of the worst of the discomfort, but it was slow. Sporadic. As had sometimes happened before, Olgun—who required his lone worshipper's deliberate intent to work most of his miniature miracles—was impeded by her own difficulty focusing.

Still, she was with it enough to know who she would see standing before her as she struggled to raise her head. She could tell from the ratty shoes, the corpse-thin legs, and the high-pitched, greasy tittering.

"Knew it was you, knew you'd come!" Fingerbone cackled. "Tricky, bouncing, dangerous little girl. If anyone troubled us, yes, you." His grin was awful; his breath was worse. "Searing concoction, my own formula. Just a smear atop the walls. Oh, yes, you would come over the walls, only way to avoid my friends, watching and waiting. . . ."

The expressions on the various Crows suggested that they weren't entirely sanguine with being identified as the mad alchemist's "friends," but none of them spoke up to contradict him.

Fingerbone's own smile abruptly fell and he lashed out, roughly snagging Widdershins's chin with long, grasping fingers. "Should be dead, though. More than enough contact to kill you dead, dead, even deader than that! Why aren't you still and stinking?"

Shins grinned through pale, chapped lips. "My god warned me about it and protected me from the worst of it. Hey, you asked."

The alchemist's eyes narrowed, and then he dropped a hand and walked back toward the cauldron. "Shoot her already."

The two Crows holding her released their grips and stepped away; apparently neither of them wanted to be standing beside her when someone shot at her, for some reason. She was, thankfully, strong enough now to stand on her own, possibly even to run—but sure as frying frogs *not* to try to fight them all.

One of the other thugs drew his flintlock.

"Olgun, can you . . . ?"

She was not entirely thrilled with an answer that amounted to *maybe*.

"Well, get ready to try."

The Crow raised his weapon.

"No, no, no! Stupid, stupid!" Fingerbone spun back, pointing irritably at the man. "Waste of a perfectly good corpse. Use *that*." His finger shifted to indicate the new ammunition, the balls formed from what had once been gold. "All of you load with that. Then *all* of you shoot! Dump her with the others, that much more to retrieve later."

"Oh, figs . . . Olgun, uh, do you think we're strong enough to pull that off with more than one gun?"

This time, she'd have been quite thrilled with a maybe. It wasn't what she got.

"I was afraid of that."

For an instant, she had some hope that the Crows would be foolish enough to all unload their weapons at once, giving her a chance to bolt. Alas, they weren't so stupid; the one who'd already been prepared to shoot her kept his weapon aimed as the others began to collect new ammunition.

But it was, at least, just the one.

"Time for something desperate, yes?" she whispered. "Be ready." Then, "Hey! Fingerbone!"

The alchemist cast an irritated glance back over his shoulder. "What, what? Busy!"

"I just . . . I've always been curious about alchemy. Answer me one question before I die?"

"Hmm?"

"Is it really, really dangerous to mix different alchemical mixtures without measuring or testing first?"

"What kind of stupid . . . ?! Everyone knows that, idiot girl!"

"Even just a tiny bit?" she asked innocently, followed by a whispered, "Olgun, going to need everything you can give me, and then some."

"Of course even just a—" Fingerbone's eyes abruptly widened.

"Now, Olgun!"

Shins hurled herself aside, clearing the Crow's line of fire, just as Olgun reached out. It took a heartbeat longer than usual, required a far stronger surge of power than it should, but the flintlock fired, the ball plowing harmlessly into the wall in a rain of dust. Widdershins's hand flew to one of the many pouches at her belt . . .

And came out with the wineskin, wadded into a lumpy leathery mass, that she'd brought at Reeve Veroche's request. In one smooth sweep, she popped the seal open with a thumb and, guided by her unseen companion, hurled it spinning into the open cauldron.

Gods, please work quickly, please be enough . . .

It worked quickly, and it was enough.

Shins didn't know whether the bubbling mess in the mechanism seeped through the wineskin's open neck or simply ate through the leather, but it washed over the lingering residue of the blighting agent almost instantly. The cauldron rang like a bell as something violently expanded or coalesced within, and the steam developed a sulfurous sheen. The smell, which Shins had expected to worsen, actually began to fade.

Fingerbone shrieked and began hopping madly about the device, twisting this knob, opening that valve, gibbering something about "pressures" and "temperatures" and "incompatible miscibilities." Where Shins was concerned, he couldn't have chosen any better response, as all the Crows who'd been in the process of reloading paused to gape.

The thief herself, of course, broke into a frantic sprint, feet pounding so hard on the stone that they hurt—or perhaps that was the lingering influence of Fingerbone's contact poison. Still, she might have made it out of sight before the newly inspired thugs could reload and fire, had not one of the *other* Crows—coming running from elsewhere in the subdivided chamber to see what the commotion was—collided with her as he came around the corner.

Shins recovered—untangling herself before driving a jab at his throat, a knee to his groin, and then an elbow to the back of his head as he doubled over—but not swiftly enough. The first of the flintlock balls whizzed past overhead, also embedding itself in a wall.

She dropped to her knees, using the groaning thug as partial cover, and yanked the flintlock from his belt.

"Olgun . . ."

The flicker of response was muted, exhausted—but hopeful.

Several of the Crows completed their efforts, all aiming their newly loaded weapons at the woman who'd caused them such trouble. Shins aimed back, fired first, squeezing the trigger with fingers that all but hummed with everything Olgun had left to give.

The ball flew true, past the Crows, over Fingerbone's shoulder, and into one of the device's many spigots.

Which promptly burst.

The screams of several nearby Crows as the spray spattered over them were horrific, soul shriveling. Fingerbone's shrill laughter as the flesh on portions of his body began to liquefy, slough off his bones, becoming some form of viscous, metallic sludge as it stretched and wobbled toward the floor, was far, *far* worse.

Widdershins—now forgotten by the remaining Crows, who had scattered in panic to avoid sharing their comrades' fates—allowed herself just enough time to vomit copiously before wiping her mouth clean and fleeing at a shaking, staggering run.

※

"Where the *hell* is he?!"

The surviving hostages, now gathered together in a single large group, cringed from Maline's outburst—though a few, including Calanthe Delacroix, rather less than the others. Some wept, some whimpered, some remained stoic and defiant, but not a one of them believed they would live to hear the clock chime again. Several whispered of a last desperate rush, an attempt to overwhelm their captors with sheer numbers and fury. So far, not enough of the nobles had agreed to try it, despite the impending—and very literal—deadline.

Except, thus far, their time *hadn't* run out; Maline hadn't begun marching them upstairs as he'd done the earlier groups.

"Rene!" He grabbed one of the Crows by the shoulder and hauled the man around to face him. "Go see what in the name of the gods' shithouse is keeping Josce!"

The thug nodded, took two steps across the room, then froze—as they all did—at the voice from above.

"Josce won't be joining you, Maline. He seems to have suffered a sudden fit of not being alive anymore."

Widdershins leaned over the second-floor balcony, elbows on the railing, chin in her hands, smiling prettily.

"Also," she continued, as Maline and the others stammered, growled, and pointed a variety of weapons her way, "you won't be getting any more of your special ammunition either. Fingerbone is, uh . . ." Even the memory of it made her face go vaguely green. "Well, his position in your gang is kind of fluid at the moment." Then, "Hush, Olgun. The funny is so I don't throw up again. Hey! Was *too* funny!"

"And you . . . What?" Maline had gone a furious red, the veins standing out on his neck. "Thought you'd come taunt me before I killed you? Maybe figured you'd watch me shoot a few of *them*, first?"

"Oh, no, no, no. Silly goose. I'm just distracting you. See?"

Nothing happened.

"Oh, figs." Shins pouted. "My count must've been off. It would've been so dramatic if—"

A barrage of shots sounded from beyond the main door, though what they might have been firing at was anyone's guess. It certainly wasn't the castle, or else they'd all have heard the impacts as well.

"You two!" Maline cried out, already moving, "Keep your guns on the prisoners!" Everyone else followed their leader, taking up a defensive position near the door. "What's going on out there?" Maline shouted up the stairs.

A distant, muffled answer drifted down from one of his sentries atop the wall. "No bloody clue! Bunch of soldiers just fired into the air!"

Widdershins, who'd been counting softly to herself since the fusillade—and far more carefully this time—piped in with, "Oh, right. That's a distraction, too."

Multiple flintlocks fired *inside* the castle, brutally cutting down the pair of Crows whose weapons were trained on the hostages. From multiple archways in multiple directions, house guards and constables flooded the banquet hall, led by Rosselin Veroche. Jourdain, captain of the Delacroix House guard, followed close behind her.

"Also," Widdershins called, louder now so she could be heard over the chaos, "we found your door."

"Please," Veroche said, not even bothering to aim her weapon at the master of the Thousand Crows. "By all means, resist."

For some reason, Ivon Maline declined.

❋

"Maline? Maline!"

The banquet hall was packed, mostly with aristocrats thanking their guards, hugging and laughing with friends and family, or standing stiffly while trying to convince everyone they'd been on top of things the whole time. Still, Shins had little trouble slipping, pushing, and occasionally elbowing her way through, intercepting the constables escorting the heavily manacled gang leader from Castle Pauvril.

"What?" He tried to step forward, jerked to a halt at the end of his chains, and settled for glaring. "The hell do you want?"

"Just a quick question." One she had almost, in fact, utterly forgotten about. "Why did you—or maybe it was the Carnots?— anyway, why were your spies waiting for me in Lourveaux? How did you know about my link to House Delacroix in the first place? I'd never have known about any of this if you hadn't pulled me in."

Maline hesitated a moment, then answered with a nasty grin. "Guess you'll never know, will you, bitch?"

The guards hustled him out, making no effort to be gentle as he stumbled again and again over the manacles. Shins didn't even watch him go; she was too busy staring off into space and reeling.

In that moment of hesitation, she'd seen the truth in his eyes, in his expression, the twitch of his lips and cheek.

He hadn't had the first idea what she was talking about!

The noises of the crowd fell away as her head once more decided to take a quick spin around the room without consulting her first. *He hadn't known.*

"That's the whole reason we're here," she breathed, utterly bewildered. "Olgun, what . . . How . . . ?"

Olgun, for all practical purposes, shrugged.

Something Lazare Carnot had done without Maline's knowledge? Possible—the patriarch was based out of Lourveaux, after all— but . . . Was the leader of the Thousand Crows the sort to accept a partnership in which he was kept in the dark? About *anything*? Not hopping likely.

She couldn't know for certain, Lazare having been shot and all, but it didn't feel right. Not with Maline's ignorance.

"So who the happy horses knows enough about me to watch for me at William's tomb?"

Olgun had no answers as to *who*, but he had a very strong suggestion as to *where*.

"Yeah," Shins agreed, sighing. "Would *have* to be someone in Davillon, wouldn't it?"

"Widdershins?"

She smiled, turning. "Hi, hero."

Cyrille, his arm tightly bandaged and strapped to his chest, blushed and actually scuffed his feet. "I'm not . . . I . . . Um . . . I . . ."

Shins clapped him on the shoulder—the other one, of course. "No, I mean it. I don't know if I could have gotten that door open and kept going with that wound."

"Yes, you could have."

"All right." Shins chuckled. "I could have. But most people couldn't. You did good, Cyrille. Got the guards here before I could have. You saved everyone as much as I did."

So deeply was the boy blushing, now, that it would only have taken a leaf-green outfit to disguise him as a giant rose. "Widdershins, I . . . Will you stay? For a while longer?"

Another chuckle. "Your mother might have something to say about that idea, yes?"

"Actually, it was Mother's invitation."

Widdershins very eloquently blinked at him.

"She wants to thank you. Properly. Feasts, rewards, all of it."

She almost said yes. Yes to it all: the comfort, the warmth, the chance to stop traveling for just a while. This time, when she sighed, it was full of genuine regret.

"Thank you, Cyrille. And please thank Lady Delacroix for me, too. But I can't."

He nodded as if he'd expected that reply, and perhaps he had. "Any chance I'll get an answer if I ask why?"

Widdershins hesitated, then lowered her voice so that, even standing beside her, Cyrille could barely hear her over the hum of the crowd. "I've been running from something for a long time now," she admitted to him. "I . . . lost someone. Thought I failed him, failed my friends. I hated myself for it.

"But . . . I left them behind, Cyrille. I was hurt, but they were, too, and I wasn't there. I've hated myself a lot *more* for that. Angry at myself, and taking it out on everyone else. I didn't even realize it until *you* made me. I'm grateful for that."

She stepped in, hugged him tight—gingerly, lest she hurt his injured arm—and moved back again. He watched her, his eyes glinting wetly.

"A lot of people died here today," she continued. "Some . . . because of me. But I look around, and . . . How many more *lived* because of me? Because of us?"

Cyrille nodded, smiling softly. "You didn't fail the friend you lost," he assured her.

"No. I understand that, now. I didn't fail Julien. I saved the others.

"And then I abandoned them. I have to—"

"I know. Go. Shins . . . Thank you."

Widdershins reached out, offering her hand. "Friends, Cyrille?"

His smile widened, and if it was a terribly sad smile, it was also a genuine one. "Always." He clasped her hand in his, and then faded back into the throng, leaving Widdershins to follow the path she'd chosen.

"Come on, Olgun." She pretended not to notice the tremor in her voice, and she knew her god and partner would do the same. "It's time to go home."

EPILOGUE: DAVILLON

"Good evening, my *lord*." The mocking condescension in the title was thicker even than the scented smoke that always swirled through the enclosed chamber.

From behind his desk, the Shrouded Lord, undisputed (mostly) master of the Finders' Guild, raised his head. The ragged hood and tattered garb blended, as they were designed, into the eddies of smoke, so that any observer might be hard pressed to say where one left off and the other began. It was, under most circumstances, an unsettling, even intimidating effect.

Tonight, he knew immediately that it wasn't going to count for much. In part, this was because the intruders had gotten this far, to the very heart of the guild's complex, and he hadn't heard a single sign of their approach. In part, because he hadn't even heard them opening his door, one of the most secure portals in the entire maze of winding corridors.

Mostly, though, because he recognized the voice.

"And to you, Lisette. Why aren't you dead? My people have very specific instructions regarding you."

The former taskmaster, as well as a handful of thugs—some of whom the Shrouded Lord recognized as members of his own Guild—poured into the room, slamming the door behind them. "You'd be astonished," she said, lowering her hood, "just how much most of the Finders really don't give a bloody damn about who's in charge, so long as the Guild runs smoothly. A few of them *did* try to kill me," she admitted, then shrugged philosophically. "They won't be trying again. Oh, don't give me that look. It wasn't that many of them. I avoided almost everyone on my way in. I always did know this place better than almost anyone else. Including you, Renard."

He felt the name as sharp and shocking as a physical slap. He tried to hold himself in check, hoped the combination of garb and smoke would hide any reaction he couldn't suppress, but he knew he'd flinched. And he knew, despite his hopes, that she'd seen it.

"I've no idea what you're talking about," he growled at her.

"Oh, please. Put some emotion into it. At least the little scab always seemed to take some pride in her lies."

"The little . . . Is *that* why you've come back, Lisette? Your grudge with Widdershins? She's not even *here*!" He leaned back, idly studying his former taskmaster, as well as the muscle she'd brought along. They hadn't even bothered to spread out or draw weapons; just clustered behind her, standing to heel like well-trained dogs. Two of them carried lanterns, presumably so they could make their way through some of the little-used and unlit corridors, but the rest stood empty-handed.

"I know that, idiot. I have people watching for her. She was just in Lourveaux not too long ago, actually. But she'll be back soon, I'm sure. In the meantime . . . there's so much else I want to do with my city. And my Guild."

"Your Guild, is it?"

"Mm-hm."

"And what of the Shrouded God? He's given us our methods and our rites for choosing who leads us. Nobody knows that better than you—"

"The Shrouded God can burn in hell," Lisette spat, "and kiss my arse on his way down."

The guildmaster recoiled, more shocked than when she'd spoken his true name. The woman had been one of the most zealous followers the Guild had ever seen, outside of its own priesthood. What could possibly—?

"He turned his back on me when I needed him," she continued, as if reading his thoughts, "when your pet bitch stabbed me in his own shrine! And again, when the rest of you turned on me!"

"*We* turned—"

"But that's all right." She sounded calm once more. "There are other—"

Enough of this. The Shrouded Lord—or Renard Lambert—raised a heavy flintlock from beneath his desk and fired.

Fired and hit nothing.

The former taskmaster moved fast, *so* damn fast, faster than Renard had ever seen a human being move. Faster, even, than Widdershins. Between the time his finger began to squeeze the trigger and the hammer fell, she had raised an arm as though catching an incoming punch.

And he felt the impact on his wrist, bruising flesh, shivering bone, knocking the weapon harmlessly aside. *But Lisette had never crossed the room.* Or rather, most of her hadn't. For the blink of an eye, just long enough to deflect his attack, her arm had *grown long enough to reach.*

It took him a moment of puzzlement and mounting fear to realize what had happened, and a moment more to force himself to believe it.

"As I was saying," Lisette continued as though nothing untoward had occurred at all, "I don't *need* the Shrouded God. There are powers in this world beyond cowardly, masked little deities—or forgotten, pagan ones, for that matter. More than a few, in fact. And *some* of them—some of them have as much reason to hate Davillon, and Widdershins, as I do."

A harsh, impossible wind ripped through the chamber, shoving the smoke aside and making the flames in the lanterns gutter.

And behind it, made faint by distance but growing louder with every passing instant, Renard could hear the squeals and titters of a chorus of laughing children.

ABOUT THE AUTHOR

Ari Marmell would love to tell you all about the various esoteric jobs he held and the wacky adventures he had on the way to becoming an author, since that's what other authors seem to do in these sections. Unfortunately, he doesn't actually have any, as the most exciting thing about his professional life, besides his novel writing, is the work he's done for *Dungeons & Dragons*® and other role-playing games. His published fiction includes the Widdershins Adventures YA fantasy series, along with *The Goblin Corps* and *In Thunder Forged: Iron Kingdoms Chronicles* (The Fall of Llael: Book One), from Pyr Books; as well as multiple books from other major publishers, including the Corvis Rebaine duology and the official computer-game tie-in novel *Darksiders: The Abomination Vault*.

Ari currently lives in an apartment that's almost as cluttered as his subconscious, which he shares (the apartment, not the subconscious, though sometimes it seems like it) with George—his wife—and a cat who is absolutely convinced that it's dinnertime. You can find Ari online at http://www.mouseferatu.com and on Twitter @mouseferatu.